CRIMEUCOPIA

Say What Now?

A Murderous Ink Press Anthology

****

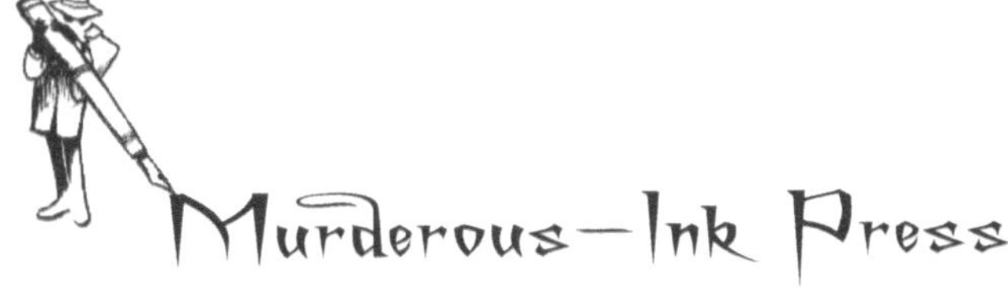

CRIMEUCOPIA

Say What Now?

First published by Murderous-Ink Press
Crowland
LINCOLNSHIRE
England
www.murderousinkpress.co.uk

Acknowledgements

To those writers and artists who helped make this anthology what it is, I can only say a heartfelt Thank You!

And to Den, as always.

Contents

Nude With Snow Geese was originally published in *Alfred Hitchcock's Mystery Magazine* in December, 2002

**The Jumper* was originally published in *CrimeStalker Casebook* Autumn 1999 issue

A Point in Every Direction....
(An Editorial of Sorts)

Sometimes editors are forced to reject submissions through no fault of the author. It could be a wonderfully written manuscript, but if the editor cannot place it, then what do they do?

MIP has been lucky in its flexibility and its "Can we start a new project with this?" attitude. That flexibility has led us to go from a proposed quarterly publication timetable, to publishing this, our 10th in the 12 months we have been fully active.

Some of the dozen authors contained within these pages are seasoned professionals, having been published in the likes of Alfred Hitchcock's, Ellery Queen's, or other notable publications, while some are making their publishing debuts as Crimeucopians. And while the quality throughout remains exceedingly high, the subject spectrum is the widest we've published so far. But that's only fitting when you consider that the theme of this Crimeucopia is that of *No Theme At All*.

So, kicking us off, **Peter Ullian** takes us back to 1933 and tells us that *The Sun Sets at the Hall of Justice*, before **Steve Bailey** takes us further back, into the Wild West, with his *Sureshot*.

Noreen Cedeño drops us into the 1960s and has us *Reaching for the Moon*, then **Edward St. Boniface** gets us up to 1973 and goes on to explain the dangers of *Portfolio Diversification*.

Cooking up a tale of just deserts, **Jan Glaz** lets us know that there's a slice of *Revenge on the Menu*, before **Eleanor Luke** explains the curious habits of the *Indicator indicator* – aka *Honeyguide*.

Momodou Bah makes his Crimeucopia debut and recounts his *Matters of Assurance*, before old hand – but young at heart – **Eve Fisher** reveals all, story-wise that is, in *Nude With Snow Geese*.

John M. Floyd's characters take time off to discuss the story of *The Jumper*, before **Joan Leotta** moves us into the murky world of people trafficking with a *Midnight Phone Call.*

Then it's back with the new, with a step back into the past, as **Glen Bush** recounts those *Dead Man's Blues,* and **DL Shirey** closes us out by offering us *A Slice on Secaucus Street.*

As with all of these anthologies, we hope you'll find something that you immediately like, as well as something that takes you out of your comfort zone – and puts you into a totally new one.

In other words, in the spirit of the *Murderous Ink Press* motto:

You never know what you like until you read it.

The Sun Sets at the Hall of Justice
Peter Ullian

I was in Jake's Joint on Broadway across from the north side of the Los Angeles County Hall of Justice, eating ham and eggs for breakfast and reading the *Los Angeles Informer,* when Daphne Drucker sat down next to me and slid a small, saddle-stitched notebook in front of me, the kind you pick up in a dime store for making grocery lists.

I looked at her. "Coffee?" I said.

"Read that," she said, and picked up a slice of ham off my plate with her fingers and began to nibble on it.

"You hungry?" I asked. I called out to the proprietor. "Hey Manny! Get the girl something to eat."

Manny, the proprietor, ambled over to us at the counter and refilled my coffee.

Manny was about twice as old as California and only half as sunny, but he kept your coffee cup filled. I had no idea who the "Jake" was for whom the coffee shop was presumably named. I had only ever known Manny to run the joint. Maybe he thought "Manny's Joint" didn't have the right ring to it.

"What're you having, Daffi?" he asked. Everyone called Daphne "Daffi," which was a laugh and a half because she was anything but. She was, if anything, kind of over-serious and a little dour at times, although she saved her playfulness and sense of humor for a select few, which, for some reason, included me, and, I won't lie to you, that made me feel pretty good.

"Just coffee for me, thanks Manny," she said.

Manny poured her a cup and moved down the counter to provide refills to the other customers. For an old guy, he moved fast, and he never spilled a drop, even if that was because he was too cheap to waste any.

"Hey, look at that," Daffi said, pointing at the front page of my paper. "They discovered radio waves emanating from the center of the Milky Way galaxy." She further perused the headlines. "And they say Prohibition might be over by the end of the year. And, let's see what else…FDR says the Tennessee Valley Authority is going to bring electricity to all the hillbillies over there. And Sally Rand did her fan dance at the Chicago World's Fair."

Daffi looked up at me and smiled. Daffi didn't smile often, but when she did, she lit things up…including me.

I pointed to another headline. "Also, Paraguay declared war on Bolivia," I said.

Daffi frowned. "Listen to you, Gloomy Gus."

I pointed to another. "And Hitler's burning books in Germany."

She looked at me, curiously. "I didn't know you read books, Rusty."

"Sure, I read books," I said. "Some of them don't even have pictures in them."

Daffi picked up the notebook and held it out to me. "Prove it."

I took the notebook from her and flipped through it.

The pages were filled with a cursive scrawl, a schoolgirl's scrawl, written in ink of a variety of colors, including, occasionally, pink. The pages were ragged, frayed at the edges, and in some places, the ink ran, from apparent droplets of either coffee, water, whiskey, or maybe tears.

"I've dog-eared the pages to which you need to pay close attention," Daffi said.

She had a crisp way of talking, like an actress, although there was nothing pretend about her. Daffi was a hard-blonde. I didn't know her age, but I knew at the age of fifteen (she'd told them she was seventeen) she'd driven an ambulance near the front during the War, so I'd have guessed her to be just to the North side of thirty. She wore bright lipstick and very little make up besides, and she worked as a secretary for the District Attorney's investigators, of which I was one. Our boss, Burton Fitzgerald, the LA County DA, liked the department secretaries to perform efficiently and to act dumb, to file paperwork, take dictation, and not ask any questions. Daffi could file with the best of them, but I guess she was so efficient, old Fitz hadn't cottoned on to how smart she really was.

Or maybe he had. Her smarts, after all, were hard to miss, and Fitz was anything but stupid, himself.

Daffi was pretty as hell, but she never played it up, never giving smiles out to her male coworkers, or flirting with them on coffee breaks. She was serious and uninviting, at least to most.

I guess I knew her a little better than most. I knew she could be whip-smart funny, and had that killer smile, if she had something to smile about.

I read one of the dog-eared pages.

I'm not so dumb myself, and pretty quick a sinking feeling settled in my gut over what those words described. I looked up at Daffi.

"Where'd you get this?" I asked.

"Prostie roust last night," she said. "Took it off a working girl cooling her heels in holding."

I held up the notebook. "Isn't that stealing evidence?"

"That's the thing, Rusty," she said. "No one's treating it as evidence. No one's treating it as anything at all. No one wants to read what's in it. No one cares."

I read another of the dog-eared pages. "But *you* do," I said. "You care."

"Rusty," she said. "The girl is only sixteen."

Oh boy oh boy, I thought. Daffi and this sixteen-year-old prostitute were going to get me into a world of hurt. I could see that already.

"Why'd you come to me with this?" I asked.

Daffi shrugged. "Who else am I going to go to?"

"Any one of a dozen other DA investigators?" I suggested.

"But you're my favorite DA investigator, Rusty." Daffi smirked at me. "Don't you want me to come to you?"

"With this?" I said, holding up the notebook. "Not so much."

"And yet," Daffi said. "Here we are."

Here we were, indeed.

I finished my coffee and threw some cash on the table.

"Let's go see old Fitz," I said.

Daffi stood up, stifling a pleased smile. "Yes," she said. "Let's."

District Attorney Burton Fitzgerald sat behind his wide, mahogany desk in his dark-wood paneled office in the downtown Hall of Justice building on Temple between Broadway and Spring and glared at us after we brought him the notebook and explained the story it contained. Bright California sunshine streamed in through the blinds, but that didn't do anything to improve my boss' mood.

"This is your doing, isn't it, Drucker?" he said, looking at Daffi.

"Guilty," Daffi admitted.

Old Fitz pointed an accusatory and thick thumb at me. When he was really serious about something, he pointed with his thumbs.

Fitz was a middle-aged, balding, and fleshy man, but he was tough. Like me, he'd fought in the Great War, and like me, he'd come home with more than a few injuries and scars, the kind he carried on both the inside and the out. On the outside, he walked with a limp because his right knee was shot up all to hell going over the trenches in France. Inside, well, that wasn't my territory. You'd have to ask the man himself, and truth be told, he probably wouldn't tell you.

"Why can't you rein in your girlfriend, Rayner?" he said, grumpily.

"I'm not Rusty's girlfriend," Daffi said, pleasantly but firmly. She was a girl who valued her independence.

Fitz held up the notebook. "Do you know what you've brought me, here?"

"Yes, sir," Daffi said. "We've brought you evidence that children are being pimped out to Prescott Sterling Mills, sir. Probably others, too."

"You know who Mills is, right?" he said.

"He's a real estate developer," I said.

"He's a filthy rich real estate developer," Fitz clarified. "He's worth at least twenty million dollars. You know what you can buy in this town with twenty million dollars?"

"A lot of children, for one thing, boss," I said.

"A lot of cops and politicians, too," Fitz said.

"Isn't that not supposed to make any difference?" Daffi asked.

Fitz glared at her some more as he tossed me the notebook and said "proceed carefully, Rayner. See what you can find. Keep me informed. Drucker, you tag along with Rusty as his, I don't know, mobile secretary, interview stenographer, note-taker, what-have-you. We don't dare put anyone else on this until we know what we've got. Do not make a move against Mills without running it by me first." He reached into a desk drawer and came up with a huge, ripe grapefruit. "Here," he said, tossing it to me. I caught it, but dropped the notebook, which Daffi swiftly picked up.

The grapefruit was heavy and looked about the size of a cannonball, the big kind. "It's from my sister's citrus grove in Claremont," Fitz said. "She sends me crates of the stuff. I've got more grapefruit than I know what to do with. I don't even like the things. Taste like bile, as far as I'm concerned."

*****

"Oh, I don't like that stuff," Olivia Daye said, sitting across the table from Daffi and me in the interrogation room on the tenth floor of the Hall of Justice as I offered her the grapefruit. "Tastes like vomit."

I put the grapefruit aside and offered her a cigarette. This, she accepted. I lit a match and held it out for her. She leaned into the flame and lit her cigarette. She took a deep drag and tilted her head upwards and let out the smoke in a long, provocative stream.

She may have been a teenager, but she didn't smoke like one. She smoked like a dame. That didn't mean much, though. A lot of girls smoked like dames, even if they were just girls. They learned how to do it from watching movies.

I pivoted toward Daffi, my match still aflame. She tapped my pack of Luckies until the end of a cigarette appeared. She brought the pack to her mouth and when she put it down on the desk again, she held a Lucky between her lips. I put the flame to the end of her cigarette, and she puffed. I decided to live dangerously and conserve matches. I kept the match burning and lit a Lucky for myself, blowing out the flame just before it reached my fingers.

I took a drag, and Olivia surprised me with a shy giggle.

"You must have been in the War," Olivia said. "The way you cup your cigarette so no one can see the burning tip. Like you're still in the foxhole."

"You're a very observant girl," Daffi said.

"My daddy fought in the war," Olivia explained.

"Where's your daddy now?" Daffi asked.

5

Olivia shrugged. "We didn't get along so good," she said.

"Is that why you left home?" Daffi asked.

Olivia nodded.

"Where is home?"

"East," Olivia said, vaguely.

I let that pass. "You're sixteen, is that right?" I said. She nodded. "And you work as a prostitute?"

She looked down at the table between us. "I guess," she said.

"You have a madam? Or a pimp?" I asked.

"I just walk the streets, mister," Olivia said. "At least, that's what I do now."

She looked sixteen, despite the hard, haunted expression on her face and in her eyes, and the way she tilted her head to let the smoke out of her lungs. Her hair was auburn, and her nose was lightly freckled. She had a small gap between her front teeth.

I held up her notebook. "This yours?"

She looked up again. "Hey," she said. "That's my diary."

"Now it's evidence," I explained. "You want to explain it to me?"

"You read it?" Olivia asked. She looked horrorstruck.

"*I* read it," Daffi said, I suppose on the assumption that Olivia would be less mortified knowing a woman had excavated her secrets instead of a mug like me. "I'm Daphne Drucker. You can call me Daffi."

Olivia laughed, nervously. "Like the duck?"

Daffi smiled, indulgently, "Sure," she said. "If you like. This is DA Investigator Reuben Rayner. He's a good egg, don't worry. You can call him 'Rusty.'"

Olivia looked at me, big-eyed. "On account of the red in his hair?" she asked.

Daffi smirked at me. For some reason, she thought that was funny.

My hair isn't really that red – more of a ruddy brown, with red highlights when I spend time in the sun…and there's a lot of sun in Los Angeles. Even so, everyone calls me 'Rusty.' I guess I'm a little sensitive about it. I don't really know why.

Which is probably why Daffi, knowing as ever, was smirking at me.

"Olivia," I said, "what do you mean in your diary that you were 'sold' to Mr. Mills?" I asked.

Olivia looked at me like I was stupid. "That's what Mr. Mills does," she said. "He buys girls."

"Underage girls?" I asked.

"I think the word you're searching for is 'children,'" Daffi told me, sternly.

"What does it mean," I continued, "to 'buy' a girl as far as Mr. Mills is concerned?"

"He pays a lady named Francine Taylor to deliver him girls," Olivia said. "She mostly finds runaways, like me, because no one knows us and no one cares. She cleans us up and drops us off. He does what he likes with us. For as long as he likes."

"Where does Taylor deliver the girls?" I asked.

"Mr. Mills' place," she said. "In Beverly Hills. When he's done with us, Lucien, his driver, drops us off on the corner of Sunset and Sepulveda. Or at least, that's where he dropped me off. I don't know what Mr. Mills paid Miss Taylor, but he left me standing there with one dollar twenty-five cents and the clothes on my back."

"How long did he—". I hesitated for a second. I had a hard time forming the words in my mouth, they sounded so heartless.

Sensing my hesitation, Daffi broke in. "How long did Mr. Mills keep you at his place in Beverly Hills?"

"For about six months," Olivia said. "He cut me loose when I turned sixteen."

I felt a lump in my throat. "You were fifteen when he—". And again, I hesitated.

"When he 'bought' you?" Daffi interjected.

Olivia nodded.

"What did you do when they dropped you at Sunset and Sepulveda?" Daffi asked.

"I walked to the Hacienda Arms and asked Miss Taylor if she would hire me as one of her girls."

The Hacienda Arms was a former apartment building on Sunset that now housed one of the busiest brothels in LA County, serving an exclusive Hollywood clientele.

"What did Miss Taylor say to you?" I asked.

"She told me I looked like a filthy street urchin and to get out of her sight before I scared off the movie stars," she said. She looked sad. "I don't know why she said that. I was clean enough."

Daffi took a deep breath. "We're going to have you write a statement and sign it," she said. "Write down everything. Don't leave anything out."

*****

Olivia did not leave anything out.

Daffi and I sat on a park bench in Echo Park, looking at a guy rowing his girl in a boat, and at the foot traffic on the footbridge, and at the palm trees that lined the water, and took turns reading and re-reading her statement, while sharing segments of Fitz's sister's grapefruit.

"I don't know why people don't like grapefruit," Daffi said.

"It's bitter," I said, my eyes on the pages.

"I like it because it is bitter," Daffi said.

"'And because it is my heart,'" I muttered.

Daffi smiled a little in the corner of her mouth. "You do read books, after all, Investigator Rayner," she said. "You know Stephen Crane."

"I don't know him personally," I said. I held up Olivia's statement. "I do know this statement is going to give us no end of trouble. *That*, I know personally."

Daffi scowled. "Did you read the things he did to her?" she said. "In her statement and in her diary, both? It's like the ever-loving Marquis de Sade, Rusty. A girl of fifteen."

"When you were fifteen you were driving an ambulance on the front lines."

"Not the same thing, Rusty. Not the same thing at all. Think on that for a second. A girl of fifteen."

I didn't like to think on it much, but I guess I had no choice. "Do you know who Francine Taylor is?"

"I've worked in the DA's office longer than you have, Detective," she said.

"I think I know the madam who runs the 'House of Francine'."

The "House of Francine" was what they called the whore house in the Hacienda Arms. It was popularly referred to as "the Sunset Strip's classiest brothel," and it catered to Hollywood's biggest stars, producers, directors, and moguls. It also paid forty percent of its profits to politicians and police. Off-duty cops served as bouncers and security. It was all run by Guy MacAfee, a former vice cop who now ran half the vice in LA, and had most of the police department, including Chief James E. Davies, in his pocket.

"Then I guess you also know who Lucien the Driver is?" I said.

Daffi nodded, seriously.

Lucien was undoubtedly Lucien "Lucky" Wheeler, a former G-Man turned private muscle, fixer, and bodyguard. Now, it would seem, employed by Prescott Sterling Mills.

"So?" I said. "What do you think we should do about it?"

Daffi frowned, deep in thought. "Go to old man Fritz, I guess," she said. "He said not to make a move without him."

*****

Burton Fitzgerald wasn't any happier about Olivia's statement than I was.

"I'd pull my hair out if I had any left," he said. He sat slumped behind his desk, his hands laid flat upon it, his fingers spread open, like he was ready to spring, but didn't have the heart for it.

"You've still got some hair on the sides, Boss," Daffi said, pointing helpfully in case he'd forgotten where the last of his hair resided. "You might be able to grab a fistful from just above your ear."

"I think it's too short above his ears, Miss Drucker," I said.

Fitz opened his desk and took out a grapefruit even bigger than the last one and hurled it at me. For an older guy, he had a hell of an arm. That toss meant business.

Even so, I caught the grapefruit and held it at my side.

"Are we playing catch?" I asked.

"You two having a good laugh at my expense?" Fitz said.

"No sir," I said. I could see he was in no mood for our roasting.

"We're having a laugh, but it's not so good," Daffi said.

"You're fired," Fitz told Daffi.

"No, I'm not," Daffi said. "You'll never find a girl who can type half as fast as I can."

"You're right," Fitz said. He turned to me. "You're fired."

"No, he's not," Daffi said. "He's your best investigator."

Fitz stood up from his chair suddenly and limped to the window behind his desk, looking out on Temple Street. He stood there for a while. Daffi and I both knew better than to continue to roast him while he tried to figure out the angles.

In LA, there's always angles that must be figured out, and if you don't figure them right, they can turn out to be sharp angles and they will cut you but good, and I'm not necessarily speaking in metaphors.

"We can't raid the House of Francine," Fitz muttered. "MacAfee's got the PD and the Sheriff's office in his pocket, not to mention guarding the front door. I don't want my investigators getting into a gunfight with the boys in blue."

Daffi took a step towards him. "Here's the thing, boss," she said softly. "This appears to be an ongoing operation. Somewhere, there's a room full of young girls – or maybe several rooms, I don't know, and I don't know how many girls – waiting to be pimped out to LA millionaires."

"Jesus Christ on a cracker, you two," Fitz said. "You've got me in a spot."

I waited a moment, then said, "what do you want us to do, Boss?"

Fitz took a deep breath. "You take in Mills, Rusty," he said. "Can you do it on your own? Because I trust my investigators, but only so much. They're not bent the way Chief Davies' cops are bent, but this is Los Angeles. They aren't angels, either. Most of them are on someone's payroll, if not the same payrolls as the cops."

"I can do it," I said, without knowing if I was lying or not. I was pretty sure I could take in Mills, no trouble. It was Lucky Wheeler I wasn't so sure about.

"I can help," Daffi said, not for the first time reading my mind.

"Out of the question," Fitz said. "I won't have it said the DA's office has to rely on secretaries to do strong-arm work. It's bad enough I have you investigating."

"She's done better investigative work in the last three hours than any of your guys have in the last three months," I said. "Except for me, of course. There's no reason to think she won't be just as good at the strong-arm stuff."

Fitz spun towards me. For a second, I braced myself for another grapefruit flying in my direction. He pointed at me with his thick thumb, the tell that meant he meant business.

"You get Daffi hurt or killed, and you are finished in LA County, Rayner, am I clear?" he said.

"As the day is long, Boss," I replied.

I knew I needed Daffi's help to do this thing.

I just wasn't so sure I could keep her from getting hurt or killed.

*****

There was no way we were going to take Mills in his Beverly Hills home without backup. So, early the next morning, we waited outside his downtown office until we saw his V16 Cadillac Series 452B arrive and pull into his designated parking spot.

I was hoping Mills himself was at the wheel rather than Lucien Wheeler, but of course, no such luck. I could see Wheeler at the wheel, all right, looking fit and big and strong and coiled for action. I knew we'd have to make our move fast.

I nodded to Daffi and stepped out of my Packard, approaching the Caddy from the driver's side, my gun drawn and held down at my side. Lucien must have seen me in the side mirror, which I had anticipated, but he saw me sooner than I'd have liked.

He had the door half open and one foot on the pavement when Daffi drove my Packard behind the Caddy and stopped short, the brakes squealing, blocking in the Caddy.

Wheeler was half-in and half out of the car.

I ran to the driver's side door and slammed it into him.

The window made contact with his head and shattered. Wheeler fell back into the driver's seat, stunned, groping for his pistol in his shoulder holster. I reached into his jacket before he did and disarmed him.

Daffi was on the other side of the car, holding her .22 two-handed, pointing it at Mills, who sat calmly in the back seat.

Mills was a dapper man of average height and build. I'd have put him at about forty-five, his hair mostly black and thinning a little on the top. He smiled back at Daffi and her .22.

"Are you going to kill me with a that peashooter, dear?" Mills asked through his open rear window.

By way of reply, Daffi pivoted, and fired.

The .22 isn't loud like a .38 or a .44, more of a crack than a bang, but it's loud enough, and when the bullet Daffi fired blew out the Caddy's rear window, she'd made her point pretty well. Mills put his hands to his ears and crouched low, hoping to avoid a second bullet. Daffi pivoted back and held him at gunpoint.

That girl had ice water in her veins, I'm telling you.

"Rusty, what the hell?" Wheeler said, holding a handkerchief to his forehead, from which a small stream of blood trickled, from the force of the door or the broken glass, I couldn't say.

"Did I hurt you, Lucien?" I asked, innocently.

"You slammed the damn door on my head, you whacky-jack," he said. "What gives?"

"You're both under arrest," I explained.

"Ah, no, Rusty, don't tell me that," Wheeler said, unhappily. "Don't do this to yourself. This is not the way things are done."

"If you cooperate," I said. "I'll give you a grapefruit."

Wheeler looked at me like I was nuts. "And what if I don't cooperate?" he said.

"Then I'll give you two grapefruits," I said, and I took out a pair of handcuffs.

*****

Mills and Wheeler were out on bail in a few hours, which didn't surprise me, and didn't really even worry me all that much. The prosecution was going to be the real test. Mills obviously hadn't been able to buy Burton Fitzgerald. The question was if the same could be said of a judge and jury.

It took all of the day and part of the evening to bring Mills and Wheeler in and to process the paperwork.

Daffi and I sat side by side at the counter in Jake's Joint, looking at the sun setting on North Broadway and the Hall of Justice looming above it. I ate a hamburger and drank a cup of coffee. Daffi ate chicken salad on rye and also drank a cup of coffee. She took hers black.

Daffi took out a flask and poured from it into her coffee cup. She held it up and looked at me, in invitation. I accepted. She poured some into my coffee as well.

Prohibition hadn't ended yet, but Prohibition had never stopped a single person I knew from taking a drink when they wanted to, as far as I could tell. Certainly not Daffi.

Certainly not me, for that matter.

I drank, swishing the coffee and brandy in my mouth before swallowing and asking Daffi, "why did you shoot out the Caddy's back window?"

Daffi shrugged. "It seemed like a good idea at the time. Why did you slam the door on Wheeler's head?"

Now it was my turn to shrug. "It seemed like a good idea at the time," I admitted.

She clicked her coffee cup against mine, and we drank a silent toast.

"You're pretty handy with a pistol," I said. "For a girl."

Daffi chuckled. "My daddy taught me how to shoot."

"That so? I'd like to meet your daddy."

"You will," Daffi said, and took another swig of spiked coffee.

What did she mean by that? Was she planning on introducing me to her parents? What did that mean? Did she think we were courting?

The truth was, if she'd asked me to marry her right then, I probably would have. The more I saw her in action, the more remarkable she became to me.

Before I could press the matter, Guy MacAfee had slid into the seat next to me.

"Rusty," he said. "How do you eat in a dump like this?"

I saw Manny, further down the counter, look up and give MacAfee the evil eye.

I looked up at Guy MacAfee. He was well over six feet tall, thin but powerful, and towered over almost everyone. He was about forty-five, and he was one of the most fearsome men in LA.

And he was sitting right next to me at the counter.

"Mr. MacAfee," Daffi said. "What brings you all the way from your home in the Biltmore Hotel?"

"I'm glad you asked me that question, Miss Drucker," MacAfee said. "And the answer is: your boss summoned me from the Biltmore this very afternoon."

"I never took you for a guy who gets summoned anywhere, Guy," I said.

"I like what you did there, with my name," MacAfee said. "Guy' and 'guy.' Cute. Be that as it may, old Fitz had a very earnest proposition for me, which involved retrieving about a dozen women from various locations, including from the arms of some very unhappy, and very rich, men."

"You said 'women,' Guy," Daffi said. "I think you meant 'children.'"

MacAfee frowned at her. "I always liked you, Daffi," he said. "You got sass." He turned to me. "Daffi thinks she can say what she likes because she's a broad, and she thinks that means no one is going to punch her in the mouth."

"You throw a punch at her, and she'll probably shoot you in the testicles, Guy," I said.

MacAfee furrowed his brow and regarded Daffi. "You heeled, Miss Drucker?"

"A girl has to know how to dress right for the occasion, Mr. MacAfee," she said.

MacAfee shrugged. "Good thing I'm a gentleman, then," he said, as he took an envelope out of his jacket pocket and slid it across the counter towards Daffi and me.

I looked at the envelope. I looked at Daffi. I looked back at the envelope.

"That's incentive for the two of you to stay out of my business," MacAfee said.

I slid the envelope back to MacAfee.

MacAfee looked puzzled. "Aren't you even going to count it?"

"I don't need to count it, Guy," I said.

"Ah, jeeze, Rusty, come on," he said. "You've been a cop of one kind or another since almost the end of the war. You know as well as anyone that no one trusts a guy who won't take a pay-off."

"I guess that's why I have so few friends," I said.

"Come on," he said. "Don't you want to eat steak instead of hamburger?"

"I like hamburger," I said, and took a bite of my hamburger.

"See here," MacAfee said, looking pained. "I've either got to pay you off or kill you. That's how things work in LA. The thing of it is, I hardly ever need to kill a guy. Everybody knows the smart move is to take the lettuce."

I held up my hamburger. "I take my hamburgers without the lettuce, Guy," I said.

"Are all of those girls safe?" Daffi asked.

MacAfee made a big show of crossing his heart. "With God as my witness," he said. "PD Juvenile Division is reuniting them with their parents as we speak."

"Promise us there'll be no more underage flesh trade in LA County, Guy," I said.

"Ever," Daffi said.

"If I give you my word, will you take the pay-off?" MacAfee asked.

"Your word will *be* the pay-off," I said.

"For Pete's sake, just take the dough, Rusty," MacAfee said. "Daffi, talk some sense into this mug."

"He's making perfect sense from where I'm sitting," Daffi said. "You stay away from kids, we stay away from your affairs."

MacAfee lowered his head and rubbed his temples. "You're as daffy as your name, Daffi," he said. Then he lifted his head. "Ok. You have my word, kids. No flesh peddling with anyone under sixteen."

"Twenty-one," Daffi said.

"I'll shoot you both right here," MacAfee said. He sounded angry.

"Eighteen," I said, quickly, sensing we were on thin ice. "We'll settle for eighteen."

"You think you can dictate terms to me?" MacAfee said. He was still angry. His thin, long face was red.

I turned to him. "Guy," I said, "today, Daffi and I arrested twenty million dollars and rolled up your child flesh peddling operation. You're Goddamn right we're dictating terms. You can kill us, sure, and you'll have to, because otherwise we will go after every level of your operation one piece at a time. Want to see what kind of trouble we can cause before one of your goons manages to gun us down? And don't forget, we're both pretty good with gunplay, so that could be a while."

The red faded from his face and MacAfee stared at us, blinking like someone had slapped him. "I don't know if you got sand or if you're just plain bedbug crazy, Rusty. Or daffy, like your girlfriend, here."

"The only question you should be asking," Daffi said, "is why haven't you accepted the terms and declared victory, already?"

MacAfee glared at us. You could almost see the steam rising from his ears.

Then, he shrugged, picked up his envelope, stuck it into his inside jacket pocket, and said, "eighteen it is."

"Really?" I said. "I thought we were going to get into a gunfight right here on North Broadway."

MacAfee smiled. "It's easier to go along with you than to kill you," he admitted. "Dead DA investigators makes for bad press. We'll lose some money on the young girls, but we'll make it up. We'd lose more if we offed you and had to deal with the aftermath, the reformers and the newspapers screaming for investigations and the like. This way, it'll be easier all around. I didn't like the flesh trade in the younger set, anyway. That kind of thing makes my skin crawl. So, we're done here. Deal."

He extended his hand, and I took it. His grip was like a vise. I felt my knuckle bones rub against each other.

"I better shake the broad's hand as well," MacAfee said, and shook Daffi's hand.

Daffi looked him hard in the eye and squeezed back.

"Rusty, your broad's got a hell of a grip," MacAfee said. He put his hat back on his head. "Either of you cross me again, they'll find your heads in Laurel Canyon, your torsos in Echo Park, and your limbs on the Municipal Pier. I hope that's not too subtle a hint for you."

"Yeah, that makes it pretty plain, Guy," I said.

"You two make a lovely couple," MacAfee said, and tipped his hat, jauntily.

"Make sure I never hear from you again unless it's a wedding invitation."

Then Guy MacAfee, one of the most powerful criminals in LA, was out the door.

Daffi poured additional brandy in our coffee cups. A lot of it.

"We were lucky to get out of that alive," I said, letting out the breath in my lungs. I felt like I'd been holding it in forever.

"It's a hell of a thing when you have to negotiate the age of the girls the hoods peddle in this town," Daffi said, "because you know there's nothing you can do to put an end to the flesh trade altogether. All you can do is try to limit the damage they do." She looked sad.

"Welcome to LA," I said.

"You're the out-of-towner, Brooklyn," she said. "I was born in Glendale."

"Drink up," I said. "I'll drive you home."

*****

I was in a sound sleep, dreaming of grapefruit trees growing in the California sunshine, when I was jolted awake by the jangling of my bedside phone.

I reached for the phone and knocked it off the side table. It fell hard to the floor. The receiver fell from the cradle, and as I groped for it in the dark, I could hear Daffi's voice, distantly, coming through it.

When I finally got the phone to my ear, Daffi said, "get down to the Hall of Justice, now."

"What's going on?" I rasped, my throat dry.

"Someone paid Olivia Daye's bail."

"In the middle of the night?" I said. I blinked my eyes, trying to force them to wake up.

"It's a set-up as sure as your hair is red, Rusty."

"Where is she, now?"

"She broke into the custodian's office and called me from his phone. She's hiding in a utility closet. At least I hope she is. I hope they haven't found her."

"Who is this 'they?'" I asked.

"Your guess is as good as mine," she said. "I'm leaving now. Get over there, Rusty. Fast."

I got to the Hall of Justice in double time, but Daffi beat me to it. I found her with Olivia in the lobby.

"Let's get out of here," I said, as I drew my Colt Detective Special.

Taking my cue, Daffi drew her .22.

We walked out of the building and down the steps to the street. As we turned towards our automobiles, I heard a man's voice from behind us.

"Are you Olivia Daye?" the man said.

I turned, my pistol trained on the man, and cocked back the hammer.

The man stopped short and put up his hands.

"Cover my flank, Daffi," I said. "Sweep the perimeter to make sure no one's sneaking up on us."

She may have been behind a wheel in the war, but Daffi knew what combat looked like. She squared off and swept the perimeter, her .22 at the ready, Olivia sandwiched between us.

"Take it easy, pally," the man said. He was about my height and age, but his hair was dark, and he wore a thin mustache on a boney face.

"I'm not your pally," I said. "Who sent you?"

"I work for Mr. Mills' lawyer," he said. "I have a legal document I need to serve."

He reached inside his jacket.

I brought my pistol down on his head and raked his skull with the butt, opening up his scalp. His eyes went glassy, and he wobbled. I reached into his jacket and found a Smith and Wesson in a shoulder holster. I removed it with my left hand and struck him again across the head with his own weapon, for good measure.

The man dropped to the pavement, his hands to his head, his hair damp with blood. He was conscious, but barely. I rifled through his pockets and found another cash-stuffed envelope, not unlike the one Gus had tried to fob off on us.

"That was what I was reaching for, not the iron," he protested, weakly.

"You were going to pay her to recant her accusations against Mills?" I said. "What if she refused?"

The man didn't answer.

"That was what the Smith and Wesson was for," I answered for him.

I threw the envelope at him, and the cash scattered, fluttering around in the light breeze like autumn leaves.

"You sure do have an antagonistic relationship with money," Daffi said.

"Let's blow," I said. "*Rapido.*"

"*Rapida*," Daffi said. "I'm a broad, in case you forgot."

I had not forgotten.

How could I?

*****

Olivia rode in Daffi's DeSoto and I followed Daffi in my Packard to her sister's place in Roscoe.

Her sister was vacationing with her husband and kids at a nearby campground in La Tuna Canyon for a few weeks, but Daffi had a spare key to their bungalow in Roscoe. She let us in, and I cased the joint, locking all the doors and windows.

"I'm scared," Olivia said. She was shaking.

Daffi sat her down at the kitchen table, retrieved the secret stash of booze from behind the bookcase, and poured Olivia a shot of brandy.

"Drink that," Daffi commanded. "Drink it all and drink it fast."

Olivia did as commanded. The brandy went down without too much trouble but left her coughing and sputtering in her chair.

"Oh cripes!" she cried. "That's worse than grapefruit."

Daffi made her down another. She coughed and sputtered some more, but the brandy had the desired soothing effect.

"Better?' Daffi said.

Olivia nodded. "Better," she said.

"Don't worry," I said. "We'll get you through this."

"I can't go back to my father," Olivia blurted out, suddenly.

Daffi and I exchanged a glance.

"You don't have to go back to him," Daffi said. "Do you want to tell me why?"

"I can't, that's all," Olivia said. The booze made her cheeks rosy, but she had a blanched look on her face when it came the subject of her father.

"Is it because you're ashamed of what happened to you?' Daffi said. "If it is, don't be. You didn't do anything wrong."

"That's not it," Daffi said. "My dad…he's no good."

"No good in what way?" Daffi asked.

"I mean…he's no better than Mr. Mills, even if he don't got the same kinda scratch."

That was a lot to take in, and neither Daffi nor I pressed the matter.

Olivia said she was feeling tired, and who could blame her? It had been a hell of a night, and now it was almost morning. Olivia went to bed in the kids' room, and Daffi and I opened a bottle of Scotch and sat in the living room making a large dent in it.

"That girl's been through a hell of a lot," I said.

"What are we going to do with her?" Daffi asked. "Where's she going to go when all this is done?"

"One step at a time," I said. "Let's get her through the trial, then figure out the rest of it."

"Can you stay the night?" Daffi asked. "What's left of it?"

I almost choked on the Scotch.

"Not in that way," Daffi said, sternly. "For protection."

I coughed and sputtered and cleared my throat, which burned from the whisky.

"Of course," I said. "That's what I thought you meant."

*****

I stayed the rest of the night, what few hours of it remained, dozing on the couch, my pistol in my hand, and the Smith and Wesson I'd confiscated from the man on Temple Street lying within reach on the armrest beside me.

*****

At a pre-trial hearing in the morning, Burton Fitzgerald dropped all charges against Prescott Sterling Mills and Lucien Wheeler.

The court room exploded into uproar. The morning papers had gone to town on the Mills story and the room was packed with reporters and onlookers eager to see a rich man get his comeuppance in the middle of an economic depression.

No such luck. The court watchers jumped to their feet. Reporters dashed for the doors to call in their stories. Citizens shouted their disbelief and disapproval of the proceedings. The judge, a lean, bald, bespectacled man, banged his gavel with increasing force, ineffectually.

I tried to make my way through the crowd to confront Fitz, but the throng of people was too thick and by the time I made it to the prosecutor's table, my boss had limped out a side door, and the bailiff blocked my way.

I turned on my heel to follow the reporters out the door and fight my way to Fitz's office, but standing there in front of me was Lucien Wheeler, a bandage on his forehead, and a mean expression on his face.

Before I had a chance to say something clever, he punched me in the gut.

Wheeler was a strong man. The air fled my lungs and I doubled over.

He didn't say a word, just walked away, leaving me gasping for breath and trying not to throw up.

I guess I was lucky the room was so crowded, and he didn't have space to properly wind up for the gut-punch he'd delivered. I'm a pretty big guy, six feet tall and I've maintained my fighting weight since the end of the War, but Lucky Wheeler threw a hell of a punch.

*****

After having my guts punched out, I needed some air, so I postponed going to the DA's office to confront Fitz, and I went outside to the street.

I found Daffi standing on the sidewalk in front of the Hall of Justice. She was staring off into the distance, above the buildings and into the blue California sky, as if she could make sense of all this if she kept looking long enough.

She turned to me. "What happened?"

I shrugged. My breath was back and I wasn't in danger of losing my breakfast anymore, but my belly hurt like hell, and even the gesture of shrugging made it hurt worse.

"Let's find out," I said.

*****

Rosie, Fitz's stern and terrifying receptionist and gatekeeper, told us he was not available, but we brushed by her and barged into his office, anyway, Rosie on our heels. Fitz looked up at us from his desk in surprise. People did not normally defy Rosie.

Fitz nodded and continued to peel yet another gigantic grapefruit that sat on his desk. Rosie quietly withdrew and shut the door behind her.

"I don't want to hear it," Fitz said. He popped a segment of grapefruit into his mouth and chewed. His face screwed up momentarily at the bitterness.

"We had him dead-to-rights, Boss," I said.

"How old are you, Rusty?" Fitz said, chewing.

"What has that got to do with it?" I asked.

"How old are you? I can look it up in my files, but I'd rather you told me. I'm eating right now, and I don't want to get grapefruit juice all over the paperwork." He popped another segment into his mouth.

"I was born with the century, Boss," I said. "I'm the same age as the year. Thirty-three."

"Thirty-three, huh?" Fitz said. He peeled another grapefruit segment, but this time, instead of eating it, he used it like a pointer to gesture towards Daffi. "How about you?"

"I tell everyone I'm twenty-eight," Daffi said. "Which means I'm really thirty-one."

"So?" Fitz said. "When are the two if you going to grow up?"

"I don't get your meaning, Boss," I said.

"You two both know the score," he replied. "Why pretend you don't? Don't try so hard to live up to your name, Daphne. You and I and your boy Rusty here all know one thing you ain't is daffy. You know how things work. So does Rusty. Why are you trying to change it?"

"Because it needs to change," Daffi said, quietly but firmly.

"Ok," Fitz said. "But what made you think you could make me the centerpiece of your reform campaign?"

"Because that's your job," Daffi said.

Fitz jumped to his feet and slammed his fists down upon his desk so hard the segments of his grapefruit jumped into the air. "I know my job!" he snarled. His face turned red and a vein throbbed on his forehead.

Slowly, the color faded from his face and he sat back down. "Look at the scorecard, for Pete's sake, you two," he said. "We got those girls out of the hands of the rackets and put a stop to the underage flesh trade. What did we lose in return? A chance to put twenty million dollars behind bars. I can live with that. So should you. Here." He reached into his drawer and tossed us another grapefruit. This time, Daffi caught it. "That's the last of them. My sister sold the citrus grove. No more free lunch."

"I thought you knew, boss," Daffi said. "There's no such thing as a free lunch."

*****

Daffi and I sat on a bench in Echo Park, peeling our grapefruit, and eating our last free lunch. There were no rowboats out today, but there were still plenty of palms swaying gently in the breeze, like they had not a care in the world.

"What was it you said to MacAfee?" I said, as we sat there, glumly. "Why haven't we accepted the terms and declared victory, already?"

"Because the terms are garbage," Daffi said.

"That's LA all over," I said. "Every ocean breeze carries with it the scent of oranges and corruption."

She looked at me. "Do you think Olivia's safe? Do you think they're still going to come after her?"

I shook my head. "I have no idea," I said.

"Will you stay over again at my sister's tonight?"

"Sure," I said. "Let me run home for a fresh change of clothes and I'll be right there."

*****

I went home to my modest bungalow on Orme Avenue in Boyle Heights, showered, changed, and as I was almost out the door, my phone rang.

I picked it up.

"Guess where I am?" Burton Fitzgerald said.

"Spending a last nostalgic evening at your sister's orchard eating grapefruit?" I said.

"I'm at Daffi's bungalow in Lincoln Heights."

23

That didn't sound good. "What are you doing there?" I said.

"Where's the girl, Rusty?"

"What girl?"

"You know which one," Burton said, irritably. "We're going to take her back into custody."

"Olivia?" I said, incredulous. "You can't be serious."

"She's still got street walking charges against her."

"Mills goes free, and Olivia gets shafted?"

"I don't see it that way," he said.

"What other way is there to see it, Boss?"

"Where's Daffi?"

"How do you know the girl's with Daffi?" I said.

"Where else would she be?"

"Street walking?" I suggested.

"Last chance, Rusty."

"I'm beginning to think you're not the guy I took you for, Fitz."

"Sorry to disappoint you," he said. "Since the girl's not here, I'm assuming they're both at your place. I'm sending a patrol car over to collect her now. Don't try anything funny, Rusty, or I'll hit you with a harboring a fugitive charge so fast your head will spin."

I gently replaced the receiver in the cradle, so Fitz wouldn't know I hung up on him. I hoped that might buy me a few seconds. Then I went out to my car and headed for Roscoe as quickly as I could.

*****

I took a circuitous route to Daffi's sister's house, in case I was being followed. Finally, convinced I hadn't been tailed, I pulled into the driveway, went inside, and told Daffi what had happened.

She looked at me like she was not at all surprised.

"They're protecting Mills, trying to take Olivia off the boards," she said.

"How you want to play this?" I asked.

She looked thoughtful. "I think it's time we did a little fishing, Rusty."

"Fishing?" I said. "On the Municipal Pier?"

"In the Hall of Records, dummy."

*****

The sun was setting on the Hall of Justice by the time Daffi and I stood in front of Burton Fitzgerald with the fish we'd hooked on our expedition to the House of Records.

"So, Fitz," Daffi said, "it turns out your sister did pretty well when she sold the citrus grove."

Fitz screwed up his face. "What are you getting at, Daffi?"

"The property was valued at nine thousand and she sold it for eighteen," she said.

"The buyer must really like grapefruit," I said.

"Who doesn't?" Daffi said. "Everybody likes grapefruit. Just ask Lucky Wheeler. Since he's the guy who bought the property. For twice what it's worth."

"Lucky must really like grapefruit," I said.

"I wonder where he got the cash, though?" Daffi said.

"How the hell should I know?" Fitz growled, but without conviction.

"Yeah, I think you know, Burton," I said. "I think you know Wheeler got that dough from Mills. And I think you know why. They say no one trusts a guy in Los Angeles unless he's willing to take a pay-off. I guess by now you must be trusted by all the right people."

Fitz looked down at his desk and rubbed the bridge of his nose. He looked somehow deflated, like his bulk had sunk into itself.

"What do you kids want?" he said, without looking up. "Money?"

"If we wanted money, Fitz, we'd have it by now," I said.

"Rusty's turned down more pay-offs in the last few days than, it would appear, you have your whole life long, Burton," Daffi said.

"This is why no one likes you, Rusty," Fitz said. He looked up. "Either of you."

"I guess we didn't join your department to be liked, Fitz," Daffi said. "Too bad you did."

Fitz made a fist and brought it down on the desk, but without the force he'd had before. He looked tired.

"What the hell do you clowns want from me?" he croaked.

"Drop the charges against the girl, Fitz," I said.

"Done," Fitz said, wearily. "What else?"

"Hire me as an investigator," Daffi said. "I'm tired of taking dictation."

"I don't employ women investigators," Fitz said.

"You do now," Daffi said.

Fitz sighed. "Done. Anything else?"

I looked at Daffi. She looked at me. We both shrugged. We looked back at Fitz.

"We'll let you know, Boss," Daffi said.

*****

We stood on Temple Street as the sun set on the Hall of Justice. I tapped out a Lucky for Daffi and one for myself, struck a match, and lit them both.

"So," Daffi said. "The girls walk. And so do the crooks."

"Everyone walks," I said. "Everybody wins."

"The crooks win," Daffi grumbled. "The girls survive."

"That's better than it was before," I said.

"I guess."

"No sacrifice, no victory," I said. "That's what the Greeks say."

"That's all Greek to me," Daffi said. "How come the same people keep doing all the sacrificing and the same people keep walking away with all the victories?"

I took a deep drag on my cigarette and felt the smoke fill my lungs. I breathed it out slowly into the gloaming.

"That's just how it goes, I guess," I said, finally.

"That's how the men who win designed it to go," Daffi said.

"You're sounding like a Marxist."

"I am a Marxist," she said. "A Groucho Marxist."

"Me too," I said. "But I'm more of a Chico Marxist myself."

She smiled, but just a little.

"We made some progress tonight," I said.

"Around the edges," she said.

"For those girls, that's everything."

Daffi took a long pull on her own cigarette. "I guess you're right about that, Rusty."

"Let's eat," I suggested. "I'll buy you a steak."

"We better get back to Olivia, and tell her the news," she said. She sighed. "We've got to figure out what to do with that girl, Rusty. She doesn't want to go back to her father, and I'm not going to turn her loose to walk the streets. You looking to adopt a teenage girl by any chance?"

"I wasn't," I admitted. "But I'd consider it if you'd adopt her with me."

Daffi chuckled. "Are you asking me to marry you, Rusty?"

"What would you say if I did?" I said. I didn't really think that was in the cards, but God hates a coward.

"I'd say you were just about as crazy as a bedbug and daffy as a duck," she said.

"You'd be right about that, Daffi," I said.

Daffi dropped her cigarette on the sidewalk and ground it out with the toe of her shoe. "Let's get back to Olivia and figure this all out later."

"Ok," I said, dropping my own cigarette and crushing it out.

"Let's pick up a couple of steaks on the way and I'll cook 'em."

"You know how to cook?" I said.

"Sure, I know how to cook," she said. "Why shouldn't I know how to cook?"

I shook my head and grinned. "No reason," I said. "Just as long as there isn't any grapefruit involved."

"No grapefruit, but if you play your cards right, after we eat and put the kid to bed, we can finish off that bottle of Scotch."

"Is that the only thing that'll happen if I play my cards right?" I asked.

Daffi regarded me with amusement. "I don't think you're a good enough cardsharp to make *that* happen, Rusty," she said.

"You never know," I said. "I have a hell of a poker a face."

Daffi put her hands on her hips and squared off, facing me. "That all you got?" she said. "A poker face?"

"Cook us those steaks and we'll find out," I said.

"You haven't got a poker face, anyway," Daffi said. "I can read you like yesterday's funny papers."

"What is my face telling you now, if that's the case?"

"That you want to eat a steak and polish off a bottle of Scotch. And get a little daffy, afterwards. Double entendre intended."

"Shows what you know," I said.

"That's not what you want?"

"Sure, it is," I said. "As long as we do it together."

"Double entendre intended?"

"That depends," I said.

"On?"

"On whether or not you want it, too."

Daffi scrutinized me for several moments.

"Well," she said. "There's only one way to find out, I guess. Let's go home and eat those steaks and put the kid to bed and drink that Scotch and see what happens."

And wouldn't you know it?

That's exactly what we did.

Sureshot
S.E. Bailey

Staggering in pitch darkness on splintered wood and twisted metal, hot steam and the stench of cordite rising. Men's curses and cries of dying horses fill her ears.

She walks in Hell wearing a torn nightgown—her shooting arm hanging limp, agony coursing down her spine.

Where's Frank? She blacks out as she hears him. Strong arms encircle her,

'For God's sake someone get a doctor.'

*****

Annie sat up; breathless, sweat-drenched.

Another vile dream.

Frank lay beside her. Her cries hadn't woken him this time.

*****

The crash happened November 1901—six months gone.

Bill Cody's Wild West show's overnight train to Danville had never made it. Annie and Frank had slumbered in their Pullman as the train had crashed. Her whole life since that night had been one long train wreck.

These days a full night's sleep was a distant memory. Recollections her waking mind kept hidden returned, stronger and uglier, each night.

She lay exhausted as Frank slumbered.

The two of them in a hotel room, the way it'd been for years. Although the Ohio Grand was a place they could never have afforded once.

Money and their hotel rooms had got better down the years but things hadn't altered between them—she'd always been his Annie, his girl. Even when, to the rest of the world, she'd been Annie Oakley—Little Miss

Sureshot—the world-famous trick-shot shootist.

Not that she looked like 'Little Miss' anybody these days. At forty-one she'd still looked good until, days after the crash, her chestnut hair turned ice-white. Her face, once open and warm, now only showed frustration and pain.

She decided finally, as she lay there, to end the nightmare of the last six months.

She'd do it today.

After the train wreck they'd quit Cody's show and returned to Greenville, her hometown in childhood. All those fancy doctors had told her she'd never shoot again; said it like an afterthought, as if she should share their delight. She'd survived, albeit with white hair.

Even Frank didn't understand.

Shooting wasn't something Annie was good at—shooting *was* her. The game she'd killed in those Darke County backwoods as a child had kept her folks from starving. Shooting had raised her from dirt poverty to wealth and worldwide fame.

But shooting was more than that and always had been.

Annie found her true self in the thoughtless arc of movement when she made a shot. Her very soul lay somewhere in the gunmetal and the rosewood of her rifles.

*****

She got out of bed, careful not to waken Frank.

The mantel clock said almost five. Annie could see glimpses of April dawn through window shutters.

Today she'd bury the hell of these past six months in the same Ohio woods where she'd started out. She opened the rifle chest's drawer and chose the Remington, slim and single barreled—almost feminine. Then she dressed quick and quiet in breeches, boots and hounds-tooth coat—all of the time watching Frank.

*****

Broadway was changed. She'd been back a few times down the years. Always so different.

Telegraph wires above the street, half-completed tram track down its middle. It'd been dirt road when she was a kid.

Everywhere changing. April 1902—didn't even sound right, the 1800s gone. She was living in the far future—but as what? A relic from a Wild West audiences knew only from dime novels?

Now; even that in doubt.

Invitations still arrived daily—offers to go on stage, write memoirs or join rival Wild West shows. None of them knew that she now shuddered like an old woman every time she tried to fire a gun.

She turned onto West Main, heading out of town. Clerks and delivery men worked early at storefronts—the business of making money same as ever. A gun-toting hunter must be a rarer sight than in her girlhood. But she'd been rare even back then. Because she'd been a girl. A girl who handled guns better than any man who'd ever lived.

A train crash, white hair and bad dreams wouldn't change that.

But one thing troubled her—Frank.

He'd been quiet this last week in a way she'd never known. Was she still his Annie, even if she couldn't shoot? He'd told her it didn't matter—had been so happy they'd survived the train. Told her they had each other and money enough—said all she needed to hear.

But was it really true?

When she'd shot ash from the Kaiser's cigar (whilst it was still in his trembling mouth) on the '89 European tour Frank had said her shooting was *surer than death, taxation or the Good Lord's judgment.*

It'd become his favorite saying ever since.

He'd told her she worked miracles with her guns. Miracles were her currency … back then.

She'd turned lead bullets to gold, for them both.

But something had changed. His silences, the black moods over this last week, made her doubt him.

Was Frank really no different from the rest, be they crowned heads or slum dwellers, who they'd played to the world over?

Maybe it was Little Miss Sureshot, not plain Annie Oakley, that he loved.

Frank had feigned sleep—her bad dream had woken him.

She'd headed out and taken the Remington. He couldn't help but smile, even now.

Going to the woods. Part of him had known it'd been her plan in returning. She was going to shoot—or try to. Years spent watching her from backstage as she made her shots and bathed in the crowd's roar came back to him.

But memories couldn't conquer his present fears.

He crossed to their suite's bureau, unlocking the draw.

Three cards in the space of a week. Frank took them out, laid them on the writing shelf. He found that his hands trembled.

He took each one from its envelope, putting them side by side. Each card was jet black. A design, a staring human eye, looked at him from the middle of each one. Each eye had the heading 'MESMER' in snake-like white serif above it.

He felt faint; the gaze of a three-eyed monster searing his soul.

He shuddered.

It was the truth; he was in the gaze of a monster.

He was … Annie was … everything he'd become and all they'd achieved lay in the balance.

He flipped the cards over, looked at the writing on the other side. It took all his strength to do it.

Familiar writing, spiky and crazed looking. The demands of somebody insane—or plain evil.

Frank felt like he had long ago—a frightened boy again; all his hard-won strength and self-belief destroyed by three post-cards. And it'd happened when Annie needed him most. He picked up the third card. The one with the summons.

Frank was shamed to find tears in his eyes.

*****

Annie crossed to the woods at Mud Creek. Greenville's outskirts were as she remembered; a few lumber yards and warehouses were the only business.

She paused at the rail track skirting the woods, sudden panic stealing her breath. After a pause she crossed, then followed a lumberman's trail into the backwoods.

Old feelings; same as always before shooting. Her body in motion but the real her—her mind—somewhere else; in a moment yet to come.

Another feeling … the old fear; the gnawing fear that had once lived alongside her ability. The knowledge that *everything*—Ma and the younger kids being able to eat—depended on her making the shot.

She'd thought wealth had killed that fear long since—yet here it was.

A fox squirrel sat on a white pine. Annie's body and mind attuned. She raised the Remington; thoughts and sinews connecting to the wood's stillness.

Then a noise roared through the clearing, an engine and the scream of a horn. The trees shook.

Now she was on the ground, shudders and sobs wracking her body. A freight train must've passed on that track bordering the woods—unless she'd imagined … She pushed that thought aside—she'd never been fanciful. She wasn't insane.

She'd always been just who she was. And was still … who?

✶✶✶✶✶

West Main, bare an hour after starting and already more busy.

Crossing Broadway she saw an advertising hoarding. Among adverts for animal feed and patent medicine sat a larger, jet black poster. A staring eye gazed on her, like a malicious god. As if it could see the failure she felt inside—though all anyone else would see was a determined woman striding towards The Grand.

The legend 'MESMER' was emblazoned ornately above the eye and smaller, plainer type below read 'Communion of the Dead'.

A medium show—his final date a few nights ago. 'Mesmer' had played the Opera House. He must be successful.

She trembled; feeling anger for her inexplicable moment of fear.

✶✶✶✶✶

The Grand was busier now. In the foyer other guests gawped. Annie met no-one's eye. Once poverty had separated her from folks like these, these days it was her fame.

She felt empty.

Back in the suite she thought for a moment how bone-weary Frank looked as he rose now from the bureau.

He must've deduced from her clothes and the Remington where she'd gone. Her face must've told him that she'd failed.

He held his arms out.

'Come here girl,' he said softly.

*****

Frank had called her 'girl' the first time they'd met ... and ever since.

She'd been fifteen, he ten years older and already a renowned shootist nationwide.

She'd entered a contest he'd been expected to win easy—the two hundred dollar prize could feed her, Ma and the kids all winter.

The State Fair crowd, after a moment's dumb-struck silence, had roared with laughter as she'd approached the stoop—a girl with a crude muzzle-loader standing almost half her size.

Frank alone hadn't laughed—a moment of confusion in his blue eyes, slowly changing into admiration. The crowd's laughter silenced him to everyone but her.

'Well done, Girl,' he'd said quietly. 'Well done for coming here today and trying.'

Back in the now—the suite in 1902—she sobbed on his shoulder, his arms around her.

Annie didn't need soft words—she needed to win again.

Like she had at The State Fair on the day they'd first met.

*****

Annie broke Frank's embrace, ready to tell him she'd go to the woods 'til it all came right—if it took the rest of her life.

The words caught in her throat. She made a small sound of fear and surprise. She'd seen the cards. Three facsimile designs, the piercing eye underneath the snaky 'MESMER' heading.

She crossed and turned a card. Frank flinched as she read the spiky handwriting.

'Frank ... my best-trained dog. Private Séance at McGill mansion—8 sharp tonight.

Heed my whistle.'

Frank's face showed shame but anger too that she'd read his mail.

'My best …? Who's writing to you that way?'

His voice quavered like she'd never heard before.

'He's called Baughman—that's one of his names. He's from my past, way before we met. Someone I'd thought…hoped… was dead.'

Annie spoke softly,

'His billboard's on Broadway. Who is he? Some medium … magician … what?'

Frank fought for breath, 'He's the worst demon from Hell's darkest pit.' He continued, more to himself than her. 'When shooting came good for me he got in touch, second hand messages from other acts on the road, a telegram one time. I ignored him. Last time was when we joined Buffalo Bill's. He'd heard of you … your success. He wanted some … thought he had something on me. I ignored him and … he never got in touch any more. I'd thought … hoped … he'd died.'

'And who is he, this Baughman or Mesmer? Why's he addressing you like a dog?'

She'd tried to speak gentle but Frank winced; though he carried on telling what she needed to know.

'There's things you don't know, things from when I was young. I was like you—had it real tough starting out but it was worse for me, I had no folks. I made a life on the road in vaudeville shows. It's where Baughman met me. He saw I had quick hands, that I learned real fast. I helped him in his show, his first act was a pack of trained dogs he'd have do tricks.'

Frank's voice shook.

'Baughman's act was a fraud even then. He scammed anyone we came across. I did everything he told me. I was his shill in sidewalk dice games, his card counter in poker hands, his stooge on stage.'

His voice dropped to a whisper. 'That's not the worst he made me do. I was just a kid … stuff I'll never tell nobody …'

Then he didn't need say more because Annie had him, pulling him close and tight towards her.

Seven thirty found Frank and Annie in their finest clothes. Frank looking strong again, how she'd always known him.

Any ideas Frank had, of going alone to face 'Mesmer' or of not going at all, were shot down quicker than wood pigeon by Annie.

She'd learned young that troubles couldn't be outrun.

She'd told Frank they'd hear whatever threats or demands this 'Mesmer' had to make.

Then they'd look him in the eye together and tell him to go to hell.

*****

The McGill mansion was downtown in Greenville's old money district, among the homes of lumberyard millionaires, railroad speculators and one-time cattle barons.

The mansion was the grandest.

The original McGill, founder of the wealth, was long dead even in Annie's girlhood. His house and family remained a big deal in Greenville.

Even her own wealth and fame couldn't quell nervous jitters as she and Frank arrived—though nobody looking would think her anything but resolute.

The McGill who'd owned the house when she was young died last year, a fierce looking man who'd augmented the family money with ruthless expansion of Greenville's lumber trade.

Annie knew that Randolph McGill, the old man's only heir, now owned the mansion and family fortune.

Randolph had been, by all accounts, a disappointment to his father.

He'd spent his childhood at an austere military school out east but young McGill's interests lay in the creative arts; painting, theatre and, more recently, spiritualism.

His interests but not his talents. Local stories maintained that Randolph was freely squandering the family money on the lavish patronage of any charlatan able to flatter him convincingly.

Annie knew that was why Baughman was holding his 'seance' here tonight.

She glanced at Frank. He looked strong—almost fierce—as the door opened.

A dark-skinned young man wearing a golden turban and a richly decorated frock coat stood before them.

He spoke with the musical cadence of the Indian sub-continent.

His voice was humble and eyes meekly directed downwards.

'Sahib and Madam—you are arrived. The party is complete. I am instructed, please, to escort you to the parlour.'

They crossed a huge entrance hall into an even larger room; oak panelled and expensively furnished, with huge paintings covering the walls.

In the centre lay a table set for a séance. Three people waited; an extremely elderly but clearly wealthy lady on the left, a slender young man with a weak chin on the right—she knew this to be Randolph McGill. Mesmer sat in the middle of them. She met his dark eyes but didn't find it easy.

He was in late middle age but powerfully built and dressed as exotically as his man-servant, in a gold and crimson frock-coat. His wore a cold, sardonic sneer.

'He's here,' he roared, with what sounded like triumph.

Frank spoke quietly. Even Annie detected no tremor.

'We came here for one reason only, to tell you never to contact me again. The hold you had on me back then ... it's gone.'

Frank glared at the table's laid out paraphernalia.

'That boy under your control—that's the only ghost laid to rest tonight.'

Baughman and Frank locked eyes. The elderly lady to Baughman's left looked awoken by the hostility.

The Indian manservant stationed himself in a corner the gaslight didn't reach and watched; unnoticed, impassive.

Randolph McGill broke the tension.

'I ... th ... think we're all getting off on the wrong foot,' he said.

Annie could see his discomfort. She'd heard tell about old McGill's viciousness around his son's 'unmanly' stammer.

He breathed slowly, negotiating his next words with care,

'I invited you and Ms.Oakley here, Mr Butler ... I heard you were back in Gr...Greenville and I ... I have fond memories of seeing you shoot wh...when

I was young.'

Annie almost smiled, Randolph was no more than twenty. His awkwardness made her like him; a rich boy playing ghost catcher or theatre producer but he was trying to be hospitable.

She took Frank's arm. There was more to their invite than what Randolph said. Baughman was in control and had something in mind.

She needed to find out what.

'We'll stay Mr McGill,' she said, 'although we won't make it a long evening.'

She met Baughman's eyes and carefully said, 'What's dead and gone is finished. Attempting to resurrect the past ends badly for anyone fool enough to try.'

Baughman's dark eyes didn't leave her.

A child-like smile covered Randolph's face. He seemed oblivious to any undercurrents in the séance room—real or supernatural.

'H... how wonderful!'

He indicated the elderly lady to Baughman's left.

'Y...you clearly know M ... Mr Baughman. This lady here is Mrs Borman.'

'Mrs Edith Borman?'

The lady smiled dimly and nodded.

Edith Borman had been an elderly widow even in Annie's girlhood. She must easily now be one hundred years old.

Her late husband Nathaniel had owned vast tracts of Ohio land and had spent his life building his varied business interests.

Mrs Borman had never remarried and must be amongst the nation's wealthiest women but looked placid and vacant—vulnerable, not powerful.

That was why Baughman had her here.

Disgust and anger rose in Annie. Baughman had made one error.

She'd been invited alongside Frank.

She hadn't got to be who she was without knowing predators.

Wolves of Baughman's kind try to pass as good men. But he was just a wolf all the same, not some demon from the pit.

She felt cold certainty that Randolph McGill and Mrs Borman were now in real danger, as were she and Frank.

She wasn't afraid. She was tense, senses heightened, like before shooting.

One way or another she'd finish this Baughman. He'd been in her cross-hairs the moment he'd threatened Frank.

He was still staring. He'd gazed at her throughout Randolph's introductions.

'Be seated,' he murmured.

His voice was low and powerful.

She sat at the table, leading Frank to the seat beside her, without breaking Baughman's gaze.

Randolph McGill beamed, Mrs Borman gazed vacantly. Annie could feel Frank's tension without looking at him.

'The dead will have their due,' sighed Baughman. He threw a quick glance at Frank, who shuddered like he'd been struck.

'We've spent our lives in vaudeville,' said Annie. 'Save the theatrics for fools who give them credence.'

Baughman smiled. Randolph McGill looked hurt. Annie felt instant regret—like she'd scolded a child for believing in Saint Nick.

'B...but weren't you a f...friend of the Indian S...Sitting Bull? I ... I've h...heard tales of h...his dreams, they ... they s...say he could see the future and r...read peoples' souls.'

Baughman sneered, 'What I offer here tonight is the real thing Mr McGill. After tonight's communion stories of a fraudulent shaman in a travelling fairground won't impress you ... A dress-up redskin to go with the costumed cowboys.'

Annie clasped Frank's arm, halting his rising from his chair and spoke quietly.

'Mister, listen and listen well. Whatever the truth of his beliefs Sitting Bull had no pretend about him. There's no fakery about me, nor Frank neither.'

She said the next words so quiet that only Baughman heard,

'There's only one fraud here, mister. I'm looking right at him.'

Annie saw real anger rise in his dark eyes but he kept quiet—he had to remain serene and godlike in front of Randolph and Mrs Borman.

When he broke the cold silence he sounded calm,

'Come now Miss Oakley ... or is it Mrs Butler? I know how double acts work.'

He looked pointedly at Frank, who sat pale, furious and silent.

'You're the one the audience looks at ... but do you really claim Butler here's never shot down a target from stage-side?'

He chuckled,

'That's where it all happens ... the place no-one's looking. Misdirection. You think you see what you're seeing but you're not—or if you are, then it's not in the form you think.'

He looked round the table, 'That's show-business folks.' Then he looked suddenly wary, like he'd said too much.

He glanced round the room announcing grandly, '... Which is why I left that tawdry world behind ... when I discovered my real power—communing with The Dead.'

Randolph looked fascinated, Mrs Borman still stared blankly and Frank seethed.

Annie felt his fist tighten in her hand—knew he would rise and strike Baughman's sneering, lying face. She'd no longer be able to prevent him. She didn't, in fact, want to prevent him.

Before it could happen Baughman's man-servant suddenly spoke.

He sounded distant, like he'd not even been aware of the argument.

'Sahib. What, please, is this?'

Everyone except Baughman jumped slightly, they'd forgotten the manservant standing silently in darkness. Everyone turned towards him now.

He indicated a huge painting on the wall to their left.

The canvas dwarfed the gaslights on each side, most of the image lay in darkness.

Baughman's servant, who from his accent's sharpness must be a recent arrival, clearly knew little of America or its native tribes.

The talk of Sitting Bull must have given him the confidence to ask about the picture's meaning.

It showed a corpulent man in Colonial era clothes sitting at a table, flanked by uniformed officers and white frontiersmen.

To the central figure's left there stood an Indian chief with an entourage of tribal warriors. The tribe's looks were cleverly conveyed by the artist—appearing both noble and impressive but also defeated and submissive.

Randolph McGill spoke excitedly. 'The picture's been in the family for g-generations. It's called *The Treaty of Fallen Timbers*. At the c-centre is 'Mad' Anthony Wayne—g-general of the whites and f-founder of Greenville. The of-of-officer on his l-left is C-Curtis McGill ... my own gr-great grandfather.'

Annie noticed, as everyone looked towards the servant and the painting, how Baughman was the only one looking away.

She caught Baughman's expression. His eyes were bitter, his face set hard.

A shudder played down her aching spine.

'And what please Sahib is this most excellent picture showing?' said Baughman's man-servant.

His eyes drank in every detail.

Randolph giggled like a young girl.

'I-it sh-shows the wh-white man st-stealing Ohio,' he said. 'W-when General Wayne won the final b-battle the treaty th-that allowed pioneers free passage through Ohio.'

Randolph paused and breathed carefully. He seemed to enjoy telling this tale.

'Th-the native in the picture is Tecumseh ... chief of the Shawnee. D-dealing with the w-whites was s-supposed to g-guarantee their lands but the w-whites lied. The Indians ended up with nothing.'

Randolph laughed and ostentatiously looked round the ornate drawing room,

'I ... I can hardly f-feel sorry. M-my own family wealth st-started growing the day we stole Ohio f-from the tribes.'

'Oh Sahib!' cried the man-servant, 'This is indeed a wonderful story. Look at the marvellous achievements in this region ... reminding me so strongly of the British interventions in my own dear homeland.'

Randolph smiled.

Baughman reacted differently. He stood commandingly. Annie saw how his servant recoiled from his gaze. He looked downwards and shrank humbly from sight back into the room's darker recess.

Baughman barked out one harsh and bitter word in a language known only to himself and his servant. His meaning, however, was clear. He was ordering the man to be silent—and threatening him.

A memory crosses Annie's mind...a fleeting glimpse she can't retrieve, just below the surface. She knows that something doesn't fit. She feels an urgent fear she can't name—Deceit is here...and danger.

Baughman turned back to them, calm and genial again, as if the incident hadn't happened.

Then his eyes swept the room; looking upwards, within seconds, only the whites of his eyeballs showed.

A low, guttural sound rose from him until it was unbearable. He spread his arms wide—encompassing all present.

A fixed, other-worldly grin covered his face. Everyone now was focused on Baughman.

Annie felt her breath unwillingly held in, her heart racing.

His moans formed into hissed and urgent words.

'Make haste ... the gateway aligns ... Communion of the Dead is come.'

He came out of his trance and stood unsteadily, looking pale. He spoke normally, 'Ladies and gentlemen—excuse me. Communion is near. Place any metal objects about your person on the silk cloth located on the séance table.' He indicated the red silk lying amongst other paraphernalia on the table. 'Metal can be hurled by malign spirits—for our safety ... if you please.'

Randolph removed a pocket watch, a tie pin and a chain with keys, then even his silver cufflinks onto the waiting silk. Mrs Borman put in an old and surprisingly cheap-looking charm bracelet which she stroked affectionately, along with some hat pins. Frank's gaze met Annie's, he rolled his eyes and shrugged before throwing in his own cufflinks and a few dollars in coin.

Annie placed a shiny, nickel-plated handgun onto the pile.

She saw everyone's surprise and the deep annoyance in Baughman's eyes—anger at being upstaged. Their interest wasn't just because she'd brought a gun, it was also due to the gun's fame.

Annie's Smith and Wesson Model One was known world-wide. The polished silver glinted—even with only dim gaslight to reflect it. There was light enough to see the inscription engraved in the round ribbed barrel,

'*Sureshot*'

Baughman spoke first, failing to keep a touch of wonder from his voice,

'It's Sureshot—the gun Buffalo Bill gave you.'

Annie answered coldly.

'Cody said I always make the shot at the moment it's needed—like destiny. That's why he named it Sureshot.'

She realized, at Baughman's sneer, she'd given herself away—had sounded boastful, the way needful folk do.

He spoke with quiet malice, 'And was Cody correct? Have you made a shot recently? I hear you haven't fired a gun this last half year—since your misadventure on that train.'

She met his eyes, 'I'll make the right shot—at the right time.' She spoke with confidence she didn't feel.

The scolded manservant shuffled quietly towards the table, carefully enfolding and removing the metal objects.

Annie heard him mutter, as if for her benefit alone, 'I am never travelling by the train ... oh dear, no. They do not allow my kind to travel in first class ... oh no madam, not even in my own land.'

Then he was gone, swallowed into the darkness of the room's far corner.

Baughman ushered everyone to the séance table, 'If you please, Communion of the Dead is about to begin.'

They sat, palms on the table, as Baughman chanted.

Annie scanned their faces—Randolph wide-eyed and open- mouthed, like countless children she'd seen at Cody's Wild West. Mrs Borman suddenly less vacant—like she was aware of what was happening; an excited and almost girl-like smile on her ancient features. A sheen of perspiration glistened over Baughman's enraptured, ugly face and the noises he made sounded like a real language.

Frank's face disturbed her. He was afraid, although no-one but she would know.

Baughman's eyeballs rolled back so his eyes showed white again. He spoke but his lips didn't move and the voice that issued forth was not his own.

'Edith.' He cried the name out in an accent that could have been carved from Ohio timber. Mrs Borman sat up—animated by intense emotion—terror, sadness and joy in equal parts.

'Nathaniel,' she gasped. Her voice sounded enraptured and uncontrolled—like a young girl finding love for the first time. 'Nathaniel ... you found your way back to me!'

The voice continued,

'Edith ... this ain't easy ... give Mesmer all he needs ... he's the trail scout of these lands beyond ... he can find the true path home. Edith, remember when ...'

Then Baughman stopped—his eyes now returned to normal as he sat pale and shaking.

His exhaustion looked real.

'What happened?' he asked. 'Was there a manifestation?'

A single tear rolled down Mrs Borman's shrivelled cheek.

'Nathaniel,' she sighed. The grief in her voice was the saddest thing Annie had heard in an age. Her hand sought out Frank's under the table.

Randolph McGill looked awe-struck. Annie sensed bitter anger behind Frank's empty looking face.

'Charlatan,' he hissed—although Annie thought only she and Baughman heard. 'You're still a heartless charlatan.'

Baughman glanced at Frank and almost seemed to smile.

'The presence of a non-believer is of no account to the spirits,' he said loudly. 'The gateway is open, Communion is in progress.'

He added quietly, 'Nothing will halt it ... The Dead will have their due.'

Annie saw Frank wince—though he held the medium's stare.

Baughman resumed chanting and his eyes rolled back to whiteness. After long minutes he spoke—again his lips didn't move and the voice wasn't his own.

Now it was old and harsh.

'Randolph ... Randolph ...'

Randolph's chin quivered, his eyes tearful. He put Annie in mind of a child more than ever.

'F-father!' he gasped out loud, 'I-it's me, your R-Randolph.'

'My boy,' said the voice—its tone almost paternal, 'You found me ... well done boy ... now bring me home. Pay the ferryman, boy. Help Mesmer to help me ... give all he needs ... promise me boy.'

Tears ran freely down Randolph's face, though he smiled proudly at his dead father's praise. He sobbed loudly and openly. 'Oh F-f-father. I ... I knew you l-l-loved me really.'

Annie looked downwards—caught half between shame at the show of himself he was making and sorrow for his sadness.

The voice continued then faded. 'Randolph, remember the time I sent you back East. I know now I was wrong. I need to tell you that...'

The voice stopped

Baughman appeared to come round to himself again, making a big show of exhaustion.

The only sounds now were hard breathing and sobbing.

'Seems surprisin',' said Annie. 'The first messages these dead folk send is tellin' their kin to give you money.'

'Wait!' Baughman gasped. 'Communion resumes ... another spirit demands a hearing.'

He returned into trance—eyes white, chanting. The next voice spat from his unmoving lips was harsh and clearly female.

'Frank Butler—you done this. You said it was him but he's givin' me voice in this world. It was you Frank Butler ... all and only you. You got to make this right Butler, you need ta ...'

The voice never finished because Frank leapt up; upending his chair and swinging his fist hard across Baughman's face in one quick and fluent motion.

Baughman fell backwards landing heavily; Mrs Borman and Randolph McGill stood—shocked from their own thoughts by Frank's speed and raw hatred.

Annie looked momentarily to the old lady but her worries quickly centred on Frank—he was white and shaking, eyes wild.

She put her arms round him. He didn't even notice.

'You damn fraud,' he snarled. 'You dare masquerade as her ... after all you did.'

Baughman was helped to his feet by the Indian man-servant.

'You know who it was Butler,' he snarled. 'Iris Matheson ... she paid with her life believing your lies ...'

He stopped talking as Frank reached for the table where the metal objects lay. He pocketed his own things. Then he picked up Sureshot.

He held the gun as he turned back to Baughman. For a moment they all stood silent.

Then Frank handed Annie the gun and spoke with certainty, not anger. 'My wife and I are leaving. If you ever contact us again—I'll kill you.'

They left the mansion with Baughman's shouted threats, and the high-pitched pleas of his man-servant to calm himself, ringing in their ears.

*****

At the hotel Annie demanded answers.

'Lay it out straight Frank—who's Iris Matheson? Why did her name get you so riled?

Frank avoided Annie's hard gaze.

He was hurting but Annie had to know.

'I'm waitin'.'

'She ... was someone dear to me back then. She helped me startin' out. I ... I'm sorry Annie ... I loved Iris'

Annie felt the breath leave her—like she'd been hit.

An idea—rather than an image—of a beautiful girl whose hair wasn't white flitted painfully through Annie's mind.

She wanted to holler but spoke quiet,

'Go on.'

Frank talked like he was alone, staring ahead; as if watching scenes from the lost days of Baughman, Iris and himself.

'Iris was a little older than me. She'd had a tough start too. She joined up with me and Baughman ... helped us with our scams. She was a natural at making folk believe ... and also so ... so wild, so free.'

He looked up at Annie, seeming to see her for the first time.

'Oh ... it wasn't like what we ha...'

'I don't want to hear. Just tell it.'

'Me and Iris were like brother and sister in the early years then as we got older we got to be ... real close. I started seein' what Baughman did was just plain wrong. I persuaded Iris we should up and leave. I wanted out of that life—for us to be honest folk. Also Iris saw I was a natural shot, one of the other acts had let me try out his guns. Iris said I could learn it real well if I practised.'

He looked at Annie but she said nothing. Frank continued,

'Iris knew where Baughman kept the money—we knew it was bad money but thought it could start us a good life. We stole it and ran. He almost caught us boarding the San Antonio stage ... screaming after us ... tellin' Iris she'd die and be cursed to Hell. He always claimed some kind of powers—even then.'

Frank put his face into his hands—he looked small and his next words sounded weary.

'And the worst of it was it came to pass. Iris had always given some credence to Baughman. After a few days in San Antonio she fell sick—real sick.'

He looked up at Annie.

'She died. Her dyin' words were telling me to use the money to set up as a trick-shot shootist. Buy some guns and learn the skills. But she was frightened of the Hell he'd promised, scared it was all true.'

They stayed silent a long moment after Frank finished.

Finally she reached towards him, ran her fingers through his hair—part angry, part sad and all of her loving him ... different than before but maybe even more.

'It wasn't your fault,' she said. 'None of it Frank.'

She shuddered as a sob came from him.

'Now listen,' she said, her voice harder. 'Get yourself in hand. That man ain't going away ... not unless we make him. He's finding a place among the rich and powerful. He'll attack our name Frank, our good name.'

Frank looked up and wiped his eyes, no more tears fell.

'What will we do?'

'We find him tomorrow, before he skips town. We tell him we've hired the top law firm in the U.S … one that senators, railroad owners and the like retain. We tell him if he dares breathe or scribble one word against us that we'll ruin him—he'll end his days eatin' scraps in the county poor house.'

'He knows things about me, things I did …'

'You were a boy. He was a grown man. Can he tell a thing where his guilt wasn't greater than …than yours.'

Frank flinched. Their eyes met—they were changed but she wasn't sure how. Not yet.

'You're a man now Frank … my man. And I'll fight a thousand Baughmans for what's mine.'

*****

They rose at daybreak. He told her all the aliases Baughman had used. His habit back then had been to register under a false name at a flophouse in the poorest area of whichever town they were in.

'Wherever he is in Greenville it won't be plush and he won't be calling himself Baughman, or Mesmer.'

He completed the list. Annie counted sixteen possible aliases.

'What about the Indian servant? A man in a golden turban won't be hard to find in Greenville.'

'Baughman's clever—he'll dress his servant plain and house him someplace else, along with all his props and tricks. They'll leave town at different times and arrive at the next place separately. Baughman will also dress plainly and behave quietly—so no-one pays him any notice. He travels light and incognito, so when he needs to get away he can do it quick.'

'We'll try Meeker's. It'll be quicker if we split—you try Dayton, I'll do Shore Street.'

Frank's protests about not wanting his wife on the streets of Meeker's Ward alone were shot down by Annie's hard look.

Mid-morning she trawled the low rent rooming houses on Dayton. Filthy timber framed tenements, unpaved roads like the dirt tracks of her youth and the succession of hollow-eyed, thin- faced reception clerks—the grim familiarity of poverty. She hated Baughman for forcing her here again, even for a few hours.

Worse still—no-one had an answer. All the aliases drew blank stares and suspicious denials. Baughman wasn't anywhere on Dayton.

She stood outside her fifth rooming house. Glaring sunlight and the street's ugliness discomforted her. Factory workers, clerks or lumber men passed, no-one paid her any mind.

Then, from nowhere, a crowd formed on the Spring Street junction yards away. A police carriage, still a horse-drawn one, raced by. Somebody hysterical cried out.

'Murder ... murder on Shore Street.'

Frank.

Frank was looking for Baughman on Shore Street.

Annie ran to the Spring Street junction then south towards Shore Street.

The trouble was easy to find. Uniformed officers poured from the carriage and up the steps of a sordid looking rooming house. A gawping crowd had already gathered.

Annie barged through the muttering bystanders.

'... Murder ... heard tell it was a knife ... some kinda fight ...'

At the door a stationed constable tried to stop her but she pushed through. 'I'm his wife ... let me through ... his wife.'

The constable's grip loosened,

'Hey, aren't you ...'

She'd broken his grip and was onto the stairwell, shouting,

'Frank ... Frank ...'

She couldn't think except,

You can have shooting ... take it off of me forever ... just let Frank be alive.

Then she heard him,

'Annie! Annie! ... I'm on the first floor ... don't come in here...'

But nothing could have stopped her. She took the stairs in twos and pushed past the constables posted in the doorway.

Frank stood centre of the room, white-faced and grim. His eyes met hers.

'I said don't...'

Too late. Frank was flanked by two men in plain clothes. They had him in restraint.

Baughman ... Mesmer ... or whoever he was sat quietly in a tatty looking armchair. His dark eyes stared ahead, still cold and intense. Annie thought his grin appeared more sardonic than ever.

His throat had been cut ear to ear.

A blood encrusted hunter's knife lay at his feet. On the wall someone had written in his blood:

The Dead Have Their Due.

Her mouth opened but words wouldn't come—she turned to Frank. One of the other men stepped forward and said, 'Ms Oakley—I'm Sheriff Opperman.'

Opperman was silver-haired. He wore a dark three-piece but no silver star, guns or Stetson. He looked modern—more business owner or lawyer than dime novel western sheriff.

'We've arrested Mr Butler.'

Behind Opperman a constable removed papers, a photographer entered and was setting up.

It was like she and Frank had stopped being people—like they were being noted and catalogued in evidence.

She looked Opperman in the eye and her voice was strong.

'Sheriff—you're making one big error here. I have the best lawyers in the U.S retained. If one word of this reaches the press before this ... this misunderstanding ... is ironed out, I'll have your badge mister.'

Opperman didn't wince.

'I've already instructed no press be admitted,' he said. 'Your husband's coming to the Sheriff's Office. He'll be detained until this is cleared up. Or until he's charged.'

*****

Annie waited hours at the Sherriff's Office while Frank was questioned.

She telegraphed a law firm in D.C that had served Cody well in his many legal troubles—she told them to put their best man on the first train to Greenville.

Opperman agreed that she could see Frank.

They kept him in a barred cell, a deputy stood guard. They weren't allowed to touch.

'He was … like that when I arrived …'

'I never thought different. I've engaged the best law firm already, we'll …'

Frank interrupted, 'It won't do any good. Something even worse has happened.'

She made her voice sound calm. 'Tell me.'

'I found Baughman's door open. The sheriff's men arrived a minute later. They tell me that they had a telegram—it was from Baughman. It said I'd made threats against Randolph McGill last night, said he feared for his own life too. Claimed I'd threatened them both with a hunting knife. They went to the McGill mansion. He was … he …'

Annie knew before he said it but still shook when he whispered, 'Randolph was murdered. His throat cut and words on the wall, like Baughman.'

A perfect frame had been built around Frank—the hand that sent the telegram was the real murderer of Randolph McGill and Baughman.

It could only be the Indian manservant.

Like he'd heard her thoughts Frank spoke again. 'Annie … it had to be Baughman's servant. But here's the worst. The sheriff's men spoke with Mrs Borman—the only other person to see him.'

He said the next words in a whisper. 'She's old … confused … doesn't even remember him. But she remembers me hitting Baughman, shouting and making threats.'

Annie felt the room spin. Then she took a breath, she had to get herself in hand.

When she spoke, she sounded in control.

'Frank, I won't lie—this looks real bad. But it ain't over. I'll find that servant.'

'They got men lookin' Annie,' he said it like he'd given up already.

'A man in a golden turban … a man from British India, it shouldn't be hard.

But he's gone already, he even sent the telegram third hand by a kid he'd paid. He ain't here Annie, he left after killing Baughman ...'

She remembered the manservant—more an impression than his actual face. All of the carefully laid on detail, all so easy to recall ... the deferential manner, peculiar diction and accent, the golden, gaudy clothing.

Yet she couldn't see his face when she thought back to him—always in shadows, always quiet, always unnoticed himself.

'No,' she said at last, 'he ain't left ... Not yet. He's watchin'. He was watchin' Baughman's rooming house as you were led away ... and he ain't left town yet. He won't do that until he thinks Opperman's men stop lookin'.'

Frank was pale. An image of a frightened boy running for his life to catch the San Antonio stage flitted through Annie's mind.

'This ain't over,' she said. 'I'm gonna find him before he skips town and disappears.'

Hope flickered on Frank's face like a damp match struck in stormy weather.

She turned, striding from the cell block—she hadn't a second to lose. But before she reached the door Frank called, 'Girl ...'

She turned and their eyes met.

'Well done,' he said it sad and quiet. 'Well done for comin' here today and trying.'

*****

Annie talked with Opperman before she left but it just confirmed her fears. The sheriff was marshalling evidence to prove Frank's guilt rather than investigating.

He told Annie that her sworn statement about the manservant's existence was undermined by her being Frank's wife.

Baughman had documents, letters and a journal going back years—none of it put him in a good light, nor Frank either.

'The man was a snake ... plain evil,' said Opperman. 'His effects show he's not just been a vaudeville performer or a medium. At various times he's been an ordained minister in Tennessee, an Indian Agent on a Little Rock reservation and a faith healer in Baltimore. Every place he went, in whatever guise, he left promises broke, money taken and lives ruined. Your husband gets mentioned ...'

'Things from years gone,' yelled Annie. 'The word of a dead swindler ...'

'That's as may be,' said Opperman. 'But explain two dead bodies to me ...'

Annie left the sheriff's office in a cold fury.

She'd extracted a promise from Opperman to keep his men watching at the automotive stage, the railroad station and roads out of town but she knew Opperman had no real faith that Baughman's manservant even existed. He'd already convicted Frank in his own mind.

She stepped from the sheriff's office, blinking as she emerged from jail-house gloom into weak sunlight.

The streets of Greenville seemed just the same, folks passing by and conducting their business—yet everything was changed.

Frank's life depended on her success in the next few hours.

She looked out on the streets of her girlhood—her territory, just as much as the woods where she'd hunted game.

Her senses heightened, just like back then.

She returned to Meeker's Ward, starting on South Street where Baughman's murder was discovered and Frank had been arrested.

The rooming house was still a busy crime scene, she bitterly counted a half dozen deputized men entering and leaving regularly—men who could be searching for Baughman's real killer. A mean looking crowd of Meeker's residents still clung on outside the murder scene like a lingering stench.

She surveyed South Street, knowing in her bones that the manservant had watched from some nearby point—the mouth of the alley over yonder or the communal stairwell of that Methodist Mission or ... any one of a dozen hiding places.

She knew he'd watched Frank been led away.

She pictured him standing in the dark corner of the McGill drawing room, taking a pressing of Randolph McGill's keys and making facsimile copies as they'd all gawped at Baughman's phoney theatrics.

He'd seemed so harmless no-one had paid him any mind. Now she recognized his dangers as plainly as she knew game in the woods—he was a planner, a watcher and a stone cold killer.

But his camouflage was the most dangerous thing about him—she knew on some level she was misunderstanding him, who and what he was.

She thought back to the incident with the picture, when he'd asked Randolph McGill about *The Battle of The Fallen Timbers*. Baughman had scalded him—he'd reacted in his fake-humble servitude ... but for a split-second a curtain had raised in her mind, showing him to her ... letting her understand the whole thing.

But then, just as quick, it had been snatched away.

Still boiling with frustration she tried every flophouse on South Street, then Shore, Dayton and as far north as Meeker's Avenue—following the same plan they'd had when trying to locate Baughman, except this time it was the Asian servant she described to the bored, suspicious reception clerks.

She went to houses that let space to anyone—deep into Meeker's worst streets—without a single moment's discomfort.

Nobody had seen him.

She started the long walk back to the Grand on Broadway—depressed by the growing feeling that something she already knew was slipping from her.

She looked back towards the dirty, maze-like streets.

Where was he?

She stopped at the railroad intersection on North Broadway as a freight train roared past on the Dayton and Union railroad.

Not on board there for sure—he'd made a point of telling her how little he liked train travel.

She shuddered ... something they had in common. Since the crash nothing now scared her more than trains—except the thought of being without Frank.

Foot-sore and soul-weary Annie took the Ohio Grand's elevator car to her suite.

The room was quiet without him. She saw Baughman's letter—the one with the Mesmer 'all seeing eye' design—still on the bureau.

She picked it up. The eye seemed to mock her.

The dead will have their due—Baughman's revenge. She recalled a cold-eyed face that seemed to be smiling even with its throat cut.

Exhausted, she got ready for bed. Tomorrow would be her final chance to find Baughman's servant. If she had time she'd hire a regiment of Pinkertons but she knew he'd get out of Greenville soon. She ignored her greatest fear, that he'd gone already—that it was too late to help Frank.

*****

Annie dreamed again—worse than ever—dreams that sent her straight to Hell.

She walks on broken rail track, screams of dying horses and her pain more real than before. He's next to her ... the sneering servant laughs. He whispers, 'I am never travelling by train.' She tries to shout but...

Now she's in McGill's mansion, it's dark and everything is different sizes—a clock ticks, someone's laughing. In the blood-drenched drawing room Baughman smiles. He stares at her and his throat is cut. He stands and points— 'The Dead Have Their Due' is written in his blood. It's written next to the Fallen Timbers painting. His butchered body stands and staggers towards her. He whispers, 'What you see isn't what you think, not in the form you think'.

Annie screams...

But now she's staring into different eyes. Harder than timber, older than time—but good eyes. Sitting Bull ... she's young again ... Little Miss Sureshot ... standing in his Tribal Tent ... was this in Paris, France maybe? He's speaking kindly to her in broken English. Indians of mixed tribes surround them. One sneers ... sounds angry. Sitting Bull roars a rebuke—a single word like a gunshot ...

She wakes.

And she knows. She knows the answer to all this, what she has to look for and where she has to go.

And she knows which gun to take.

*****

Daybreak. Annie waits and watches at the Martin Street railroad depot.

She'd come early, resisting the temptation to call in on Opperman. A single deputy was stationed at the platform's far end—honouring the sheriff's reluctant promise that all the ways out of town be watched. He sat dozing on a fold-out chair and didn't even look in Annie's direction.

Her post-crash fear of trains had gone—replaced by a deeper fear.

Early on the passenger platform stood empty, the trains that roared by hourly carried freight or livestock.

She stepped back into the doorway of the platform's only building. She mustn't be seen.

Morning faded to early afternoon a crowd formed with the suddenness of sea-mist. She cussed quietly. So many people filled the platform she wished she had gone to Opperman for help.

The Union City train was due. In the milling crowd stood hard faced lumbermen, expensively dressed ladies on shopping trips and prosperous business types. To Annie's dismay a noisy and excited class of elementary school children, dressed for some special school day out, emerged onto the platform marshalled by a schoolmarm who'd have had more success playing shepherd to felines.

Then Annie saw him.

A roughneck American Indian in canvas trousers, boots and lumberman's jacket; his hair worn long, his face surly and closed—the deferential manner discarded along with the golden turban.

He looked like casual labour, ready to board a third-class carriage perhaps to a North Ohio timber-yard.

Her hand closed around Sureshot.

The crowd, including the Indian, were looking down the track a way—towards the still distant train.

Annie stepped forward from the doorway.

'You ain't leaving mister ... you ain't makin' my Frank pay for what you did.'

He turned—his skin dark enough to pass as British Indian.

He didn't pretend,

'How did you know I'd be here?'

The musical tone of India was gone but he didn't sound American Indian—he talked like an East Coast stockbroker.

The crowd fell silent sensing conflict about to begin. The deputy rose from his seat at the platform's end—too far away but moving closer.

'I figured out Baughman's words,' she said. 'Show business is misdirection

… remember? Maybe you see what you think—but it ain't in the form you think. I thought you was an Indian—and you are … just a different kind of Indian. Your interest in the painting—the Indians at Fallen Timbers—might have been a foreigner's but when Baughman scolded you he used Athapaskan, language of the seven tribes. I heard the same word used long ago by Sitting Bull. You also made a big show of tellin' me you never travel by train. So, I figured the train would be the best place to look—once I saw you were a murderer and a liar.'

He smiled, although sadly.

'You are most clever madam,' he said it in the British Indian accent. 'It is but one of a thousand voices I can do.'

Then in old Mr McGill's patrician snarl,

'Isn't that right Randolph … my boy.'

The whole crowd stared, confusion and fear on the faces of the now silent children.

'And this is my voice,' he yelled in his high-class East Coast accent.

Annie saw anger on the faces of some of the adults, anger at a red-skin talking like an educated man.

He turned, snarling now at the silent crowd.

'Taught me by do-gooding missionaries at an East Coast Indian School—what good's this voice to an Arkansas Choctaw the white world hates?'

'That's where you met Baughman—the reservation?' She remembered Opperman's words … Baughman had been an Indian Agent at Little Rock.

His face twisted,

'He saw I didn't belong …I'd returned to the reservation but they hated me there worse than the whites. He saw I was quick and clever, made me steal and cheat … and other things I'll never tell. He corrupted me—and McGill's folks stole this land from my kind. That's why I killed them.'

Tears filled his eyes and he said quietly,

'But your kind always win.'

Annie saw the Union City flyer getting closer, its roar almost drowning out their words.

He screamed, 'My name is Nahotabi.'

A hunting knife is suddenly in his raised fist, the nearest child seized and the knife raised high—in a quicker motion, an arc of movement beyond thought, Annie swings Sureshot and—like Cody always said—makes the right shot at the right time.

The knife flies from Nahotabi's hand, its blade broken.

His eyes meet Annie's and then he jumps, proud and strong with a battle cry from the platform and into the path of the Union City flyer.

His dying scream and the howl of brakes applied too late fills the platform.

The crowd cry out and everyone looks away.

Everyone except Annie Oakley.

*****

Frank looked out of their suite's window.

Annie sat at the dresser's mirror, brushing her white hair freely.

After dinner they'd think about what came next—go through the invitations to resume shooting.

Frank spoke low and quiet as he looked out on Broadway. 'I can't help thinking about Nahotabi. He was a kid like me ... quick hands, a talent for performin'. He just met the wrong man. Only difference, I had the blessing to meet the right woman.'

She combed harder. 'Iris Matheson?'

He laughs now, comes to her and places strong hands on her shoulders. 'The best of everything's ahead of us' he says. 'I feel it surely as ...'

'As death, taxation and the Good Lord's judgement?'

Frank's hands run through her long white hair, his lips rest gentle on her neck and he whispers softly,

'Surely as us Annie ... as sure as you and me.'

Reaching for the Moon
N. M. Cedeño

As midnight neared, a red Corvette raced into view, glided off the road, and rolled to a stop at the edge of the bayou where I stood waiting under the soft yellow glow of the full moon. The driver, slim and athletic, climbed out of the car with an efficient but unenthusiastic air. He had a chagrined lift to his lips, not a smile by any stretch of the imagination. Meeting me wasn't the highlight to his day that meeting him was for me. After all, how often does a private investigator like me get to meet a national hero, an astronaut, one of the mere handful of people who'd left the planet?

What I knew of his biography, culled from the pages of *Life Magazine*, ran through my head. He was a test pilot and married with kids. The Life article presented him as a squeaky-clean Boy Scout with a middle America 'aw-shucks' quality, living with the ideal family in a picture-perfect house near Clear Lake, not far from the Manned Space Center south of Houston. Selected by NASA with the second group of astronauts, the man in front of me had already been to space as part of the Gemini program and was aiming to go to the moon on an Apollo flight.

Being an incorrigible skeptic, I wasn't betting that NASA would accomplish its audacious goal of landing on the moon before the decade ended, especially after the fiery end to Apollo 1. I also didn't believe the Life biography was accurate in its depiction of my client. Anyone who needed privacy so badly that they wanted to meet at midnight by a bayou near an oil refinery south of Houston had something to hide. This astronaut got himself into trouble, skidding into an oil slick of scandal that would embarrass him and NASA if I didn't help him out of the mess. Space travel wasn't anything I'd aspire to do. Resolving blackmail, on the other hand, was my specialty.

I straightened my favorite pale blue guayabera shirt over my ample torso and extended my hand as he approached me. "Mr. Jones," I said, using his previously supplied cover name even though no one would overhear us in the middle of nowhere by a bayou, "I'm Gordo Reyes." *Gordo* was more of a description of my belly, but it's what people called me since childhood. No one called me by my given name of Juan.

He shook my chubby hand. "Thanks for meeting me." He gestured to his car. "Do you want to talk in the car? If we stand here the mosquitos will carry us away."

The thought of sitting in an astronaut's Corvette almost made my head explode, but I kept my excitement in check and nodded agreeably. "That works for me." I walked over and slid into the passenger seat with my brain dancing a jubilant cha-cha as 'Mr. Jones' returned to the driver's seat.

He studied me with an icy expression on his face and grim determination in his eyes. "You will keep everything I tell you completely confidential?"

"Absolutely."

He sighed. "Where should I start?"

"At the beginning."

His eyes narrowed as he shot me a look of annoyance.

I must have failed to squelch the ever-present humor in my voice. I'm a good-natured guy, as a general rule. But I try to rein in the comedy when I'm dealing with new clients since they are mostly too stressed to appreciate the humor in their situations. I cleared my throat and tried to be serious. "I mean it, sir. Start at the beginning and don't leave anything out." I pulled a pencil and pad of paper from my breast pocket and prepared to take notes.

'Mr. Jones' stared out the windshield at the rising moon. "I wanted to see the Polynesia Room in Galveston. A friend of mine told me the history of the place, about all the mobsters and the stars that visited in its heyday. So I drove down to the island last Saturday evening to take in the scenery."

I knew the Polynesia Room well. It had a colorful history as an illegal gambling establishment run for decades by a local Sicilian mob family. Big name Hollywood stars went there to perform and to party in the 1940s and early 1950s. The Travio family had run all of the illegal gambling on Galveston Island from Prohibition until the mid-1950s. But ten years had passed since the Governor and the Texas Rangers managed to bring the lawless 'Free State of Galveston' to heel. With the principal mobsters dead and a law-and-order government running the state, the family member who still ran the Polynesia Room mostly kept his nose clean. "What time did you arrive?"

"I made a reservation for dinner at 7:30 for me and a friend."

"A reservation. Okay." Then, whoever had targeted him knew he would be there and had time to plan. "Who was the friend? Did he see anything?"

'Mr. Jones' pinched his lips into a flat line before replying. "I'd like to leave my friend out of this."

My eyebrows rose. "A friend of the female persuasion who isn't your wife?"

He nodded curtly. "My wife and I haven't been on the best of terms for some time, but the image is important for NASA."

"I understand. Tell me what happened at the Polynesia Room."

"After we ate, a woman came up and asked if she could get an autograph. That's not unusual. It's happened a few times since my Life Magazine profile came out. I signed the napkin she offered me, and she walked away. A few minutes later, I paid the tab and went to hit the head before the drive back, while my friend went to powder her nose. As I came out of the men's room, the woman appeared and grabbed my hand. She asked me to dance." He paused and clenched his teeth.

I could see the muscles in his jaw rippling. "What did you do?"

"I tried to be polite. We're supposed to be calm and not lose our tempers with civilians. I pulled back and said that I was sorry, but I had somewhere to be."

"How did she respond?"

"She moved in closer, said she wanted to take me to the moon, and winked at me as she shimmied up my leg. Then a guy jumped out from behind a potted tree and took a picture."

"Ah, a compromising photo. An old scam. That doesn't sound too bad though. You can always say she climbed on you and that you were in a public place."

The astronaut banged his palm into the steering wheel in front of him. "No. It's worse than that."

"How's it worse?"

Red flamed up his neck and cheeks. "I was stunned and still trying to politely extricate myself." He hung his head in defeat. "She was holding my hand, remember? She planted it firmly on her breast just as the guy snapped the photo."

I turned in my seat to look at him. "That's worse all right." My skepticism kicked in. "Are you sure you didn't put your hand there yourself?"

The astronaut's eyes bulged out of his face. He looked like he was going to blow a gasket. "No, dammit. I was set up."

I put out my hands, palms down. "Calm down. I believe you. I had to ask. Then what happened?"

He slammed his hand on the steering wheel again. "She winked at me and shoved a note into my hand. Then she walked away and vanished. I left with my friend as quickly as I could." He reached over, opened the glove box, and produced an envelope. "Here. Read this. She was wearing evening gloves when she handed this to me. No fingerprints."

I opened the flap and peeked inside. A sheet of scented stationery lay folded in half. Its jasmine fragrance tickled my nose and wafted through the air in the car. Drawing the paper out between two fingers, I opened and read the note.

> ***If you don't want the photo on the front page of the Houston Post – along with a napkin that says I LOVE YOU with your signature on it – you will deliver $10,000 to me at 9 pm next Saturday night. Meet me outside the place we first met.***
>
> ***XXXOOO Jane Doe***

The blackmail plan was straightforward and simply executed. I could have laughed at how easily the poor chump had been framed. But he wouldn't appreciate me laughing at his misfortune, so I turned a chuckle into a cough and pretended to reread the note. Then I tucked it back into the envelope and handed it back to him. "Destroy this and don't worry. I'll take care of everything from here."

"I don't have that kind of money laying around to pay her off!" he said. "Even if I did, I couldn't take it from my account without my wife exploding."

"You don't need to give her a dime. I can handle this without paying her off. All I need is for you to describe the woman in detail." I held my pencil ready to take notes.

His eyebrows came together as he studied me. "You aren't going to harm her, are you?"

I reassured him. "She will be exactly as I found her when I leave her. No violence needed. You were directed to me because I specialize in resolving this kind of thing, and I know the ground rules in Galveston. I have a much more elegant solution. This lady made mistakes, starting with the location she chose to conduct her little scheme. Now, describe her."

'Mr. Jones' drew me a verbal picture of a girl in her late twenties, round in all the right places and narrow at the waist with platinum hair in a Marilyn Monroe cloud of waves and curls around her head. She had blue, china-doll eyes with extremely long, dark eyelashes and delicate, arching eyebrows. She sounded like a knock-out.

"And did you notice anything about the man with the camera? Had you ever seen him before?"

'Mr. Jones' stared ahead thoughtfully. "He was dressed like a waiter. He may have worked in the restaurant."

We talked for a few more minutes as I tried to elicit more details from 'Mr. Jones' memory. Then we parted ways. As he roared off at speed in his Corvette – clearly working out his frustrations – I puttered along in my Ford pick-up, planning a trip to Galveston Island.

*****

The ferocious sun beamed down like an unseen omnipotent hand was holding a giant magnifying glass over Galveston Island, and the humidity was like a blanket, smothering and uncomfortable to someone my size. My fault for arriving late the in afternoon.

My first order of business was to identify the woman behind the blackmail scheme. After parking near the Sea Wall close to the pier where the Polynesia Room perched over the green-brown waters of the Gulf of Mexico, I walked down the sidewalk listening to the gulls scream and the waves crash in the surf. The restaurant was getting ready to open for the early evening customers.

Even a short walk in Galveston's heat is no picnic for a stout guy. My second favorite guayabera shirt was sticking to my back and sweat was beginning to drip from my temple before I reached the restaurant doors. I entered into the cooler comfort of the Polynesia Room and took in the South Seas décor as my eyes adjusted to the dim lighting.

A woman in an orange shift dress approached me. "We'll be opening shortly, sir."

I introduced myself and asked for a moment of her time.

"I'm Sally. What do you want to know?" she asked in a gossipy way that told me she was eager to spill whatever information I requested.

"I'm a private investigator trying to locate someone: a woman who was here last Saturday night." I described the Marilyn Monroe look-alike, and the woman's eyes darkened.

"That's Cheryl. She calls herself Cheryl Monroe, but that's not her real name," Sally said with a look of distaste. "She's part of the floor show."

"A dancer?" I asked.

"She sings. Poorly, if you ask me, but our male customers like to look at her."

"Does she have a friend who works here? A waiter she's friendly with?"

"That sounds like Bill Sharp. He's wrapped around her finger. If she calls, he comes running. What's this about?" Sally asked, looking at me with curious eyes.

I winked at her. "I can't divulge the details, miss. Is the boss in? I need a word with him."

"The boss? You mean the owner, Mr. Minetti?" Her eyes widened.

"That's the man I mean."

"He came in a little while ago to go over the books." She tilted her head toward the back of the restaurant.

"Thanks, honey, you've been a great help. Can you do me a favor and don't mention to Ms. Monroe or her friend that I asked about them?" I gave her a big grin and stuffed a sawbuck into her hand.

Sally glanced at the money before tucking it down her dress. "I never saw you at all."

I sauntered to the back of the restaurant and asked, respectfully, for a moment of the boss's time. With mafia guys, even semi-retired ones, a little respect and caution goes a long way.

He granted me a few minutes during which I explained the scam that had been initiated at his place of business the previous Saturday. I left with what I needed: addresses and work schedules for Cheryl Monroe and Bill Sharp and, more crucially, the boss's backing. Then, all I had to do was kill some time until I could search Cheryl and Bill's homes after they came to work.

*****

With the moon shimmering off the waves in the Gulf that night, I let myself into Cheryl Monroe's apartment with a quick and highly illegal lock-picking maneuver. After 20 minutes of searching all the usual places that people like to stash important things, I found an envelope under the mattress. It contained the signed napkin and the compromising photo of 'Mr. Jones' with his hand squarely on Cheryl's boob and a shocked look plastered on his face. Much to my annoyance, I didn't find the film negative for the photo.

So I left Cheryl's place and broke into Bill Sharp's apartment. There, I encountered the kind of hazard that people in my line of work have to face on occasion.

"Down, boy!" I said firmly to the dog growling at me from barely four feet away. On the plus side, it was a chihuahua, so it couldn't kill me. On the minus side, it was a chihuahua, so it had a seriously bad temper and a yap to match.

The tiny terror leaped forward and snapped at my ankles as I did an impromptu flamenco dance. I considered kicking the dog, but I didn't want to injure him. He was only doing his job after all. I danced into the kitchenette of the one-bedroom apartment and opened the icebox.

"Are you hungry?" I asked the pooch as it nipped at my heels. I found a chunk of cheese and broke off a piece.

The dog ceased his assault of my feet and retreated, nose quivering with interest.

I held up the cheese. "Do you want some cheese?"

The dog sat and locked his bulging eyes on the cheese, which I tossed to him.

He caught the piece and lay down to gnaw on it.

While he was distracted, I searched the apartment. Mr. Sharp's camera was in his closet, but the negative took me half an hour to find, hidden in a cookie jar in the kitchen. I waved goodbye to the chihuahua, noting the damage he'd done to my trouser legs, and left.

With the napkin, the photo, and the negative in my pocket, I drove back to the Polynesia Room. As soon as I entered, the boss saw me and signaled for me to join him in his office.

"Did you find what you were looking for?" Mr. Minetti asked as he seated himself behind his heavy mahogany desk.

"Yep." I displayed the photo.

While the frown that wrinkled his face from forehead to chin was formidable, the look in Mr. Minetti's eyes was cold-blooded and sent a chill through my veins. The boss's mafia side, though ostensibly dormant for a dozen years, hadn't lost any of its edge. Ms. Monroe and Mr. Sharp had crossed the wrong man.

"I'll deal with them," the boss growled.

"Yes, sir," I said in as level a voice as I could muster, "but, remember, 'Mr. Jones' would prefer that this not be a killing matter."

The boss eyed me like a falcon with prey in its sight.

I swallowed but held my ground. "He doesn't need the trouble, sir."

Mr. Minetti nodded noncommittally. "I won't allow this sort of thing to happen in my establishment." His eyes went to the door. "Vinnie!" He called out and a man stuck his head in the office. "Bring me Bill Sharp and Cheryl."

"She's finishing the floor show, boss. I'll bring her as soon as she's done." The man vanished.

Five minutes later, a wet dish-rag of a waiter and a show girl, looking like a memory of Marilyn Monroe, came in the door, escorted by Vinnie.

"Thank you, Vinnie. Stay close," the boss said, tossing a contemptuous look at his errant employees.

Vinnie vanished outside the door again.

I leaned against a wall, waiting to see what developed, hoping I didn't have to witness anything I'd then have to hastily forget.

Mr. Minetti let Cheryl and Bill stew for a moment, giving them a stare that should have turned their knees to jelly.

Bill broke first as sweat began to bead his upper lip. "What's up, boss? Somebody complain about the service? What did I do?"

The boss narrowed his eyes. "This girl is new in town, so maybe she don't know how things are, but you've been around long enough to know what's what, Bill. You remember how my cousin Rose kept the peace in this town? He kept the family business and our customers safe from harassment, safe from crooks. What did Rose do to people who dared rob a customer who'd won big in one of our establishments?"

I stifled the urge to laugh from sheer terror. Rosario Travio had been the Travio family enforcer. Papa Rose, called "the Iron Glove," had died in 1954 after he and his brother Sam moved most of the family business interests to Las Vegas. The Galveston properties and businesses were left to cousins, the Minetti family, to control. The boss was a Minetti, and he was invoking the memory of the brutal Rose Travio.

The color drained from Bill's face. "We didn't rob a customer, boss!"

The boss extended his hand toward me. I pulled the photo from my breast pocket and handed it to him.

The boss brandished the photo. "Then what do you call this? Blackmailing a customer in my restaurant? And not just any customer, but an astronaut?"

The boss turned his eyes to Cheryl whose face had flushed as the realization that she'd been caught red-handed hit her. "And you," Minetti spat, "I gave you a job so you wouldn't have to work on your back, and this is how you repay me? No loyalty to me. No loyalty to your country. You want the Russians to beat us to the moon?"

"But, boss!" she pleaded with tears in her eyes. "We never meant any harm. It was just a bit of fun."

I gave her performance a C. She didn't remotely convince me that she hadn't known the boss would be angry. She only regretted getting caught.

Minetti pounded his fist on his desk. "Shut up!" Then he called out, "Vinnie, get in here."

Vinnie appeared at the office door. "Yes, boss?"

"Escort Cheryl and Bill out of town. They leave tonight, and, if they ever return to the island, take them night fishing and see how well they work as bait. You got me?"

"Got it, boss." Vinnie shoved Cheryl and Bill out of the office and followed them with an eerie gleam in his eye, closing the door behind him.

I was left alone with Minetti once more.

Slowly he stood up from his chair and returned the compromising photo to me. "What kind of person blackmails an astronaut? Where's the patriotism?" He shook his head, clearly puzzled. "Stupid people cross their bosses. I've seen it happen before. But this? This is a new low."

Coming from a man who just threatened to send two people to sleep with the fishes, this seemed funny to me. But self-preservation told me it wasn't a good time to laugh, so I said, "I don't know, sir, but I want to thank you for your assistance on this matter. 'Mr. Jones' will be very relieved to see the end of it."

The boss smiled magnanimously. "Tell 'Mr. Jones' that I hope he beats the Russians to the moon. He has my full support, and if he ever visits the island again, he can have dinner on the house." He paused, looking me over. "I'm a legitimate business man, Mr. Reyes. The fact that I have relatives who were known for a certain kind of activity can be handy at times. Vinnie knows how to follow my lead and how to play along with a bluff."

"Of course, sir. I understand," I said as convincingly as possible, while not believing a word. I respectfully said my goodbyes and left the Polynesia Room with the napkin, the photo, and the negative in my pocket.

Outside, in the cooler evening air, I looked up at the clear night sky above, and the moon looked down on me as I walked to my car. I wondered if someday 'Mr. Jones' would look down on us from up there. It seemed impossible, but what did I know.

*****

Leaving the salt air and sand of the island behind, I returned to Houston. The next morning I called to schedule a meeting with 'Mr. Jones.' He said he was working on flight simulations until late, so we planned to meet that night in an isolated location near Clear Lake.

I arrived at the appointed place early and waited. The mosquitos were out in clouds. Once again, a racing Corvette approached and stopped by the side of the road. Without waiting for an invitation, I opened the passenger side door and climbed inside the car.

"Good evening. I have something for you." I placed the napkin, the photo, and the negative in his hand.

He looked at me in complete surprise. "How did you do that so quickly?"

I laughed out loud at the shocked expression on his face. I figured I'd earned the right to laugh. "It was simple. You aren't from around here, or you'd have known that your blackmailer made a crucial mistake by running her scam in the Polynesia Room. The mafia family that used to run Galveston protected their customers and the town residents from all but their own chosen illegal vices: booze and gambling. They were known to kill anyone who dared rob their customers or their businesses. They felt it was their civic responsibility to look after Galveston. A branch of that family still runs the Polynesia Room. The owner won't stand for his employees running scams on his customers."

The astronaut sat trying to process what I was telling him. "You're saying you got these things back because a mob guy won't allow anyone to harass his customers?"

"That's it in a nutshell. The girl worked at the Polynesia Room as a singer. She talked the waiter into helping her blackmail you. They were hoping their boss didn't get wind of the scheme, because they knew he would, um, frown upon it."

"So you informed him?" 'Mr. Jones' looked at me with shock in his eyes. His jaw was close to dropping open.

"I did. In return for informing him that some of his employees had gone astray, he gave me their addresses and work schedules. While they were at work, I searched their homes and found the materials we needed to recover. Once I had those, I showed them to the boss, who promptly fired the lady and her assistant. Then he ran them out of town. It turns out the boss is also a patriot who would like to see you astronauts beat the Russians to the moon. He said if you're ever back on the island, dinner at the Polynesia Room is on him."

"The mobster is a patriot?" The astronaut ran a hand threw his short hair. "Well, as much as I'd like to thank him for his help, I'll be steering clear of Galveston. I've been selected for a mission. If this mess had gone public, I might have lost the flight."

It was my turn to be amazed. "You're going up there?" I pointed to the creamy whiteness of the moon, glowing high in the night sky.

'Mr. Jones' smiled at me and shrugged.

"That's the goal, Mr. Reyes. That's the goal."

Portfolio Diversification
Edward St. Boniface

From the nefarious adventures of *Black Hand Incorporated*, Corporate America's favourite executioners.

> *Money is a work of the imagination. And I've got a big imagination.*

From the bestselling Wall Street confessional memoir and business diary: *Funny Money: Have A Gas Grabbing Your Stash* (Vol III) by Phil Pheidon, prominent former Wall Street stockbroker convicted of repeated gross financial misconduct, abuse of fiduciary trust, asset theft and multiple fraud in 1970. Case brought as a joint class action by client investors, the Internal Revenue Service and the Securities and Exchanges Commission, New York City. Trilogy published by Cosmopolis University Press, 1972. Quote above refers to Pheidon's early pioneering use of numerous 'pyramid scheme' unsecured loans in structure to repackage unviable-risk debts as tradable portfolio assets.

Series of transcript-excerpts between narrative from *Black Hand Incorporated* company confidential archives, special financing records, surrogate tax liabilities & investment strategy sub-section. Original spoken audio dialogues all captured using replica micro-miniaturised tape recording device once the property of the Central Intelligence Agency. Device carried by company president in all transcripted dialogues. All matters discussed are *strictly classified*, company archivist's eyes only. Location of dialogue is the main boardroom, company headquarters, Blackwells/Welfare/ Roosevelt Island. Duration from approximately 10:47am–12:29pm on 17.09.1973. Conversation already in progress. Present are company senior officers and controlling directors Gary Banomena (*Company President*), Survind

Juggerghazi (*Deputy Company President and chief financial officer, various other company titles*), Warkentin Westgate (*various company titles*) and Dag Ulköln (*various company titles*). Subject of following discussion: proposed investment strategies for *Black Hand Incorporated* (using company cover LLPs), one other participating guest individual hereafter identified.

"…needless to say, we call it *Fuckspeak*."

Even when I review the transcript of the recorded session later, that punctuating moment is indelibly etched on my memory and I have to smile. Everyone's mouth is hanging open at the intelligently articulate and terrifyingly energetic stream of profanity we've been hearing for the last hour in our company boardroom, mixed up with a very high-quality lecture on prudent corporate investment strategy from our invited guest. Even Survind has temporarily lost his normally unbreakable composure and stares at him like a stupefied fish.

Ron '*Bozo*' Callabozo ('*It's my official industry handle and that's the way I like it*'), licensed stockbroker, professional investment counsellor, freelance fiduciary agent/advisor, chartered accountant and certified actuary, pauses to take a drink of water. Adjusts with skilful care the overhead projector he's been using to illustrate a detailed plan for what he calls *Portfolio Diversification*. To, in effect, infiltrate our now unmanageably large accumulated monies from secretly funded murderous exploits into respectable dividend-return enterprises.

RON '*BOZO*' CALLABOZO: "And that, gents, is pretty much the whole Kitten Kaboodle. Given your large pool of off-the-books capital, we now have to do a big job of what's generally called 'money laundering' in the financial biz brainiac world. Converting the non-declarable into respectable earning assets that will pass the tax-man's most stringent tests. And incidentally giving a big yahoo's (*deleted*)-you to those (*deleted*)ers the (*deleted*)-witted (*deleted*)ing IRS. It will not be easy and will be expensive. But with me you will get top of the line (*deleted*)-hard professionalism. The Bozo hath spoken."

Trucker trumps me by smoothly rising, just as I'm about to clear my throat, and speaks for all of us without missing a beat. Recovering himself almost instantaneously, he recaptures the initiative I simultaneously realise we had lost over the last hour to Callabozo's clever linguistic shock tactics. This profane world of razor-sharp creative finance and brutal clarity is new to me.

Wall Street's new universally accepted vernacular; apparently.

SURVIND ('*TRUCKER*') JUGGERGHAZI: "We hereby accept you as our exclusive financial advisor, Mr Callabozo. Colleagues?"

I agree. We all agree, at once, in unison. Callabozo isn't surprised.

R ('*B*') C: "Ron, please. Or Bozo. Well, like I described it's going to be a big job. It's hard to take money from no discernable source and transmute it into (*deleted*)ilicious-hot gold ingots stamped Legitimately Earned. At the same time it's not impossible. Look at the silver-plated Kennedys and the coltan-plated Vanderfellers. Mr Juggerghazi here gave me a brief summary of the (*deleted*)ed-up financial position. You have no receipts or invoices or actuarial documentation backing any of the cash?"

S ('*T*') J: "We do not."

R ('*B*') C: "And you can't provide client correspondence or the usual balance sheets for a tax return."

S ('*T*') J: "Assuredly not."

R ('*B*') C: "Or accounts."

S ('*T*') J: "Ditto."

R ('*B*') C: "No (*deleted*)-in-the-muck problem."

(*Collective pause*)

GARY BANOMENA: "What does the solution all boil down to?"

R ('*B*') C: "International travel."

WARKENTIN WESTGATE: "No *way*."

R ('*B*') C: "*Yes*, way."

DAG ULKÖLN: "There are a lot of reasons we can't do that, Ron."

R ('*B*') C: "And there's one stark staring reason why you can't afford not to."

(*Longer collective pause*)

GB: "Pray elucidate, Bozo."

R ('*B*') C: "You guys are smart and subtle operators or you wouldn't have come to me in the first place. Most people take one brief look at my consultation estimate and ascending fee structure and dive back down the free-(*deleted*)-fall elevator shaft *Toot Sweet* to get away fast enough. But you gents didn't even blink at it. So I know you mean biz."

GB: "Keep elucidating."

R ('*B*') C: "The cash is metaphorically slow-burning its way through your safe deposit boxes. Or mattresses. Or pickle jars in the basement, wherever you're stashing it."

S ('*T*') J: "Implying, perhaps, that we fear its federal seizure?"

R ('*B*') C: "Not immediately. But you've clearly all discussed it. The (*deleted*)-you-triple-hard-in-the-face bleak conclusion is that sooner or later it's inevitable."

GB (*long pause*): "Bleakly conceded."

R ('*B*') C: "Tax evasion, concealment of assets, mail fraud associated with same and half a dozen other charges I can think of connected with such a case are mostly federal offenses. And they will slap every single one of them they can think of on you. Potentially twenty years each charge consecutive, with a severely limited appeal process. That's assuming you've got nothing else to hide. Either way, you're all eventually staring at six-foot five tattooed Buckaroo the I Want To Be Your Special (*deleted*)buddy in a little sewer-perfumed cinderblock two-bunk in Joliet or Canaan or Beaumont or Terre Haute or Penascola. Maybe sharing with someone marginally less pleasant who'll want you to meet his other (*deleted*)buddies first at their daily Encounter Group in the showers. Every way I angle it, you're major league (*deleted*)ed-up."

WW: "So how does hopping on a Concorde work into the evasion equation?"

R ('*B*') C: "Hah, hah, hah! I like the take on that, Warkentin. Prefer to fly Club Class myself if I go transatlantic. We'll discuss the luxury booking details later. First and foremost you (*deleted*)ety-split need to get your money into a respectable foreign bank outside of federal jurisdiction."

DU: "Meaning jurisdictionally what?"

R ('*B*') C: "London or Geneva or Vaduz. The Swiss banking code is tight but in my experience any top private Western European bank is good cover.

The English have some of the best. All those oil sheik royal families have a fortified house and a very solid petrodollar-fattened bank account in London against the day their great unwashed subjects rise up. We just use the same banks they use."

GB: "I always wanted to see Big Ben."

R ('*B*') C: "Wanna see some classic (*deleted*)-tick-(*deleted*)-tock clocks? I'll take you to the London Horological Museum too. And in the evening, Soho. It's even more depraved than the New York one. (*Deleted*) it; in all the literalistic and nuanced imaginative sizzlin' re-iterations of that (*deleted*)tastically double-(*deleted*)ing versatile word."

DU: "But going by what you say, we'll have to smuggle the cash over there."

R ('*B*') C: "Yep. All can be arranged for an unreasonable price."

S ('*T*') J: "What kind of sums are we talking about?"

R ('*B*') C: "Any sums you're talking about."

WW: "Could we write off our fares as a business trip, Trucker?"

S ('*T*') J: "Yes, I believe so. We've only used two of our tax-deductible travel expense allocations this year so far. However, we will need to file appropriate documentation to justify the claim."

R ('*B*') C: "You'll have it. The London banks I'm thinking of present you with whole books of contract in perfect cold incontestable legal-ese. Once they've underwritten you they'll issue credit certificates to die for. Once you've got them you can come back to Wall Street and they'll fall all over you. Every kind of top level investment scheme with (*deleted*)-Daddy Warbucks preferential opportunities at improbable dividend rates will be offered. But we won't take any of 'em."

GB: "Why won't we take any of 'em?"

R ('*B*') C: "Invest in tax-free. Invest in equity. Invest in *charity*."

GB (*short pause*): "(*deleted*)ing A; Bozo."

(*Similarly-phrased agreement from other participants.*)

*****

So on Callabozo's advice we flew to London. Survind and Warkentin and I had never been out of the United States apart from Canada and Mexico. Dag had been to Denmark and the other Scandinavian countries on family visits, a few summer holidays in France with friends of his Dad; that was about it.

London startled me with how different it was from my expectations. Coming from my Midwestern background, New York had always seemed like the apex of cosmopolitanism. But London had once been an imperial capital, and many peoples of that lost empire had gone there to find their fortunes.

Even in New York I rarely saw someone who resembled Survind with his Bengali heritage, but in London I saw them everywhere. Every nation seemed to be represented. All of them bustling in this thrown-together imbroglio that made New York's more strictly defined neighbourhoods seem almost organised.

Admittedly my prior impressions of London were almost entirely movie-based. Mostly the London-set works of Alfred Hitchcock, although I'd looked up a fair number of near contemporary documentaries. *The London Nobody Knows* presented by James Mason was especially resonant and informative, but had some seriously deranged stuff in it that just confused me.

Frenzy, Hitchcock's last feature, had come out only the previous year and had been set right in the heart of Covent Garden fruit and vegetable market, now vanished to a new location called Nine Elms Lane. I regretted not being able to see the place as it had been. London and its surroundings were otherwise pretty accurate as portrayed, but of course all cinema is inherently stylised.

So now we're in the different-pitched, disorienting clangour of the real thing, naïvely annoying tourists stumbling awkwardly through an urban Babylon fundamentally different to the one we know back home and continually wrong-footed. All the traffic goes the wrong way. No intersections, just these treacherous narrow stripe-painted walkways the natives call *Zebra Crossings* although we're visibly nowhere near the Veldt.

Nobody speaks English.

At least no kind of English I can readily understand. Almost every single utterance made in this country, birthplace of the language I thought I was commonly heir to, seems qualified by some kind of weird self-contained colloquialism. Time and again I hear double-negatives like '*I wouldn't say no!*' or surreally inexplicable things like '*Are you holding folding for a pound from the till, then?*' if I take out my wallet to pay for something and use a too-high denomination bill.

Exploring the totally unfamiliar heightens your natural alertness, though. It's not hard to remember we're far from home in potentially dangerous territory. Utterly exposed to unaccustomed perils.

Not least because we're using our real passports as private citizens. We couldn't afford to trust forgeries of any kind for a transatlantic trip. Slightest suspicions aroused could stall us and unravel everything.

At the same time we also couldn't afford not to risk this. Callabozo was right and saw straight through the problem with frighteningly immediate acuity. Only way to convert our illegally gathered cash into tradable credit was by exactly the means he proposed.

All of us kept up our genuine identities at the heart of our cover operation in telephonic security. From the beginning we used a core shell company in our real names. Building a series of dummy corporations and transient companies around it helped us to stay invisible, but keep our official accounts straight.

We had to do this, since social security numbers with no activity on them and all the other details of tax records and efficient bureaucracy of the society that formed us would turn their attention to family and friends next if they couldn't find us. I was prepared to be a cipher forever, but Survind and Dag and Warkentin didn't want to become fugitives and estranged from their families and pasts otherwise. So we compromised and had stand-in false identities for our contractors and clients, and a far more extensive selection for our true operations selectively decimating corporate America.

Between them, Survind and Dag used their remarkable business and banking expertise to keep us solvent in the eyes of the authorities. We had to endure occasional tax inspections and other official harassment like any other business, but on the whole it worked. We changed sub-contractors who did most of the real work fairly often, but that was usual in an industry of freelance and single-job projects.

Paralleling this with our real work in *Black Hand Incorporated*, which is how the illegal cash reserve built up, of course. We received our payments in large denomination bills or through illicit bank accounts from which we always drew out our fees in cash. All of it stored in our company safe deposit boxes at the very secure Vanderfeller National Commerce Bank on Herald Square.

Ten boxes in our early years, a full row in the vault. By the time we talked to Callabozo we'd had to add a second row, ostensibly for archived client circuit diagrams and confidential contracts. Only five established years of robust executive removal business had left us with multiple millions we couldn't move into legitimate investments, stock and shareholdings, property or anything of that nature.

Now however we really did have an urgent need for that capital. A collective decision had been taken to move company offices and Survind had found us a large under-construction private business compound already selling units in advance just outside Albany. We'd gone there for a viewing and were so impressed that we make the decision there and then to set up in the place.

Buying in and getting the top floors we wanted, along with permissions for certain special requirements like our necessary company labs and additional space and floor reinforcements for large safes was going to cost a lot of money. No matter how we worked our finances in different directions, we couldn't afford the fees without loans. Far too risky exposure and it would have fundamentally compromised our security.

Unlocking our huge cash reserves was an imperative. So we had to find a way. Or more specifically, someone who already knew the way and could guide us through its pitfalls.

Trucker and Dag already had plenty of experience concealing our illegal monies. On a fee by fee basis it was relatively easy to hide profits. Once we had the cash secured in our safe deposit boxes we simply drew on it as needed, transferred from company boxes to our personal ones on designated paydays and stayed resolutely prudent with all our accounts.

But to credit-convert most of the cash reserve, the multiple millions it signified now, was an entirely different order of magnitude. This was something requiring written and personal endorsement from senior officials at a bank with faultless reputation. In other words, we had to reach bankers with an impeccable veneer of respectability whom we could also bribe for our purposes.

Meaning an intermediary who would act as our fixer. Contact those bankers, arrange the deal and safely bring us through the many dangers to avoid the merest official suspicion. All of that was going to be expensive and we'd have to sacrifice a good slice of the reserve to make it work.

Over our careers so far we'd risked our lives and faced lethal dangers many times, in spite of doing everything we humanly could to avoid them. This really was different, though. Vulnerability abroad meant we had effectively no escape routes if things went wrong.

Still; I'd always wanted to see London.

*****

(*Transcript resumes, location of dialogue a luxury suite at the Buckingham Villiers hotel, Soho, London, from approximately 08:33 to 08:51, 02.10, 1973.*)

GB: "London is a (*deleted*)ing hellhole, Bozo."

R ('*B*') C: "Hey Gary, it's only our second day."

GB: "Those smarmy English pigs call that a burger? It was a strip of old shoe leather between two rancid stale old buns. If you tried to pass that off in the Big Apple you'd get fed through your own meatgrinder. And when I ask for a refund they threaten me with someone called Bobby in the goddam plural? Ketchup was like industrial waste. That hellish so-called mustard burned my taste buds out of operation. And that was no relish, either. On top of everything else, they don't know what a real *pickle* is! (*Deleted*)ing hell; like they say here. Bunch of wally-wankers. Why am I even talking like that? Am I going native?!"

R ('*B*') C: "Cool off, Gary. Fast food isn't great here, admittedly. I'll take you to some places where the food will send you to paradise, I promise."

S ('*T*') J: "In this world I hope, Ron. We've already been poisoned by Perfidious Albion once and as you point out, we haven't been here forty-eight hours yet."

R ('*B*') C: "Limey cuisine at its best is surprisingly good, but you really have to know where to go. They just don't understand how to do middle level quality restaurants here, that's all. It's a class jealousy thing. I'll arrange something at a private home in South Kensington I know for tonight instead of the hotel."

GB: "Jest hope my palate can recover in time. I couldn't even taste my breakfast this morning. What was that poison factory called?"

WW: "…'*Wimpy's*', I think."

GB: "Popeye should sue."

R ('*B*') C: "You'll be fine. Okay, Now that we're all rested up and lost the jet lag I have some people to see about your money in what they call the City of London. As distinct from the London we're in here. It's actually run by a private corporation, and where all the best banks are. Centuries-old setup; they know how to do *that* kind of thing here, at least. It'll take me the rest of the day but I'll meet you gents back here for 19:00 and we'll go for dinner. You won't be disappointed."

WW: "Okay if we see the sights in the meantime?"

R ('*B*') C: "Booked you a private tour guide, waiting in the lobby if you want him. He'll drive you around the town in a proper Rolls Royce and raps on like Noel Coward."

DU: "Hot Deppity Dawg. Hokay; let's jest pound the pavements and strategically starve ourselves for the day in anticipation. What do you say, guys?"

WW: "I'm in."

S ('*T*') J: "I've waited a lifetime to do a trip like this. If we have time I'd like to see Kew Gardens."

R ('*B*') C: "That's the spirit. Gary?"

GB: "I wanna meet the Queen. Or *Queen* the band."

(Uproarious general laughter)

R ('*B*') C: "You know, the Limeys have still never forgiven us for Yorktown. Or being there for D-Day. Overpaid and over-sexed and over here, right? We're all a bunch of tobacco-chewing *lassiez-faire* rapacious barbarians to their lordly cultured sophistication. So be prepared for a little *(deleted)*ery-up-your-nose snob stuff now and then."

WW: "Fair enough. I'm a dumb Hoosier backwoodsman, anyhoo."

DU: "I'll put on my Norwegian charisma."

S ('*T*') J: "I for my part will smile sweetly, and try to do nothing that might provoke any post-colonial guilt."

(More laughter.)

R ('*B*') C: "I like it. Gary?"

GB: "Let's do it. London Bridge is falling down my fair Bozo; so let's get there before the emergency services. By the way, does everything around here really grind to a halt about 14:00 for a massive tea party like in those *Lipton* commercials?"

R (*'B'*) C: "Pity us all if it does."

(*Chuckling as all five present head for door of the hotel suite.*)

*****

True to his word, Callabozo had arranged for our cash to be smuggled over on an entirely separate cargo flight to London. This was the part where I was really worried about us being ripped off. It would have been almost easy to divert our money and then Callabozo could have swiftly lost us in unfamiliar London Town.

Survind had been more than meticulous in his vetting, though. Despite his huckster's persona, Callabozo was as shrewd and cunning an under-the-counter operator as they come. In his long and very successful career he had laundered sums for clients far in excess of anything we were bringing to the table.

Just because someone doesn't have to cheat you is no guarantee they won't. So I wasn't at ease until we could finally count our greenbacks in the smart London hotel suite we finally made our tourist-gawking way to. Callabozo had it shipped up to the private apartment via the hotel's freight elevator in small crates marked '*Copies Of The Holy Bible*'.

Each billfold was cleverly hidden in the sealed spine so that the book barely had to be damaged to retrieve them. We were left with a sizeable and saleable lot of American-vernacularized Good Books that were apparently very popular, some London evangelical churches favouring them over the King James version. Callabozo would also arrange that small return on the side, he promised.

And for only a small extra fee; gents.

Thus spoke Bozo.

*****

(*Transcript resumes, location of dialogue a private partner's office in the Southwark Brothers Mutual Capital Bank, Croesus Mews, the City of London. Present are two bank partners, Gary Banomena, company president and Ron Callabozo, broker and advisor. Dialogue takes place between 13:07 and 13:24 on 09.10.1973.*)

CULTIVATED ENGLISH BANKER'S VOICE ONE: "…and these are your credit certificates, gentlemen. Each of them as you can see countersigned by myself and my partner here."

CULTIVATED ENGLISH BANKER'S VOICE TWO: "All of them valued in American dollars as specified, at the rate of exchange for the date on each note. We also converted a smaller sum, at higher fees, into American treasury bonds issued this year. Those are a little more difficult to get. With them, the prepared letter of credit for your Internal Revenue Service. It states that you have opened an account with us for investment purposes in London, with an additional attached certificate made out in Pounds Sterling. I have added a copy of our investor's guidelines and some personal recommendations as to reputable brokers. Of course the certificates otherwise are not mentioned."

R ('*B*') C: "What did I tell you, Gary?"

GB: "Ludicrously and monstrously and agonisingly expensive, but worth it."

CEBV1: "Should any become lost or damaged or stolen, our fees include a replacement and secure couriering service to your offices in New York within a week of notification. Numbers of any such certificates so claimed on will of course be changed to prevent misuse."

CEBV2: "We also have private agreements with several respected investment banks in New York. For reasonable fees there, you can re-convert our certificates into certificates of equal value endorsed by those banks. That, unfortunately, is not something we can arrange here for you."

GB: "Can you do all that magic for Monopoly Money as well?"

(*Pause, then polite laughter.*)

CEBV1: "A fine game. My grand-children insist I play it with them after dinner whenever I visit. I make sure to regularly land on the '*Go Directly To Jail*' corner square. That always makes them burst into laughter. And they're surprising good at manipulating me into landing on squares where they've purchased those little red plastic hotels. I always leave that house absolutely strapped."

CEBV2: "Mine invariably force me to play that MAD MAGAZINE board game, the one where you draw losing cards and have to do humiliating things such as squawk like a chicken. I've gotten quite good at it. They cannot get enough. We live in an increasingly deranged world."

GB: "Tell me about it. I saw *Jesus Christ: Superstar* last night."

CEBV1: "Personally I prefer the popular musicals of Lionel Bart to those of Andrew Lloyd Webber. He's far more clever and deft with melody, and his stage musical cues changing scenes are far more subtle. Webber just crudely bludgeons a story along without any finesse. There's an excellent revival of *Oliver!* playing at the London Phasmodrome just now. I strongly recommend it."

GB: "I have a cast recording of the songs at home but I never saw it onstage. Thanks, I'll check it out. Do we have anything planned for the evening, my devious friend?"

R ('*B*') C: "Not apart from counting the day's take as carefully as old Fagin."

(*Laughter*)

R ('*B*') C (*continuing*): "Reckon I could scare us up some tickets. I'll talk to our concierge at the hotel."

CEBV2: "Ron tells me you're a jazz aficionado, Mr Banomena?"

GB: "My favourite, yes."

CEBV2: "I'm a member of *Ronnie Scott's Jazz Club*. Mention my name on the door and they'll admit you. If you have another day or two in London, Bill Evans is doing a week of nightly spots from 7pm. He plays for about an hour before the resident band takes over again. I guarantee you a good night's music there. I'll call Ronnie to make sure you're welcomed."

GB (*pause*): "That's very generous, sir. I don't know what to say."

CEBV1: "And with that I think our business is concluded, gentlemen. It has been a pleasure."

GB: "Next time I'll bring gold."

(*More laughter, sounds of chairs scraping on wooden floor as participants rise.*)

*****

Simple as that. At a stroke, the increasingly toxic problem we hadn't addressed for years and couldn't see a way to resolve was smoothly and professionally alchemised into millions of untraceable respectable dollars we could invest. All at an impeccably polite loan shark's rate of twenty-five percent.

Still, each of us was a millionaire by a very wide margin out of it. We all lived well and the others had homes or expensive apartments, but it was getting a lot harder to live a cash-only lifestyle. And each of us went in terror of suspicion falling across our path and the company safe-deposit boxes impounded.

Now we could buy into whatever we wanted.

And Bozo spoke.

*****

(Transcript resumes, location of dialogue main boardroom, company headquarters, Blackwells/Welfare/Roosevelt Island, from approximately 11:09am-12:50pm, 21.10.1973)

R (*'B'*) C: "Okay; now to the real nitty-gritty hard-core (*deleted*)ery of the biz at hand. My primary major investment recommendation, apart from more treasury bonds and a balanced portfolio of low-risk indexed large companies like Bell Telecommunications and Woolworth's, both super-solid market (*deleted*)ers, is simple. Sink the greater part of your collective treasure into the *Cosmo-Slotnik Foundation*."

GB (*short pause*): "Once again, elucidate?"

R (*'B'*) C: "They're *zero* risk."

S (*'T'*) J: "Charitable organisations pay no dividends, Ron."

R (*'B'*) C: "Now that, gents, is where most investors and investment experts miss the Moon-rocket. Telling you an open corporate secret here. Not only can you write off all company donations against your tax bill, your collective contribution counts as tax equity for an equivalent amount."

DU: "We're doubling our money, in other words?"

R (*'B'*) C: "Yep. As long as you have other appropriate collateral and verified securities to match, you can raise loans against it. You're in one hell of a better position to negotiate debt repayments and get extensive credit leeway on major acquisitions."

WW: "So that's a long term investment on all fronts."

R (*'B'*) C: "Might sound counter-intuitive Warkentin, but it's a straight invitation-only sweet orgy(*deleted*)-fest of a deal. No, it won't give you a good short-term gain like most of the things I counsel, but you're a growing business and you're only five or six years old. This will shore you up for the future. Equity credit reserve you build up from this will eventually give your company the best kind of financial security there is."

GB: "Regale us with the Cosmo-Slotnik connection, Bozo."

R ('*B*') C: "You go to any of their places here in New York?"

GB: "Sure. We all go to their *Cineaste's Cineplex* in Bedford Stuyvesant pretty regularly for repertory screenings. I bought a lifetime membership for all of us a few Christmases ago."

DU: "I love that. You can walk in anytime and park yourself in a reserved seat even if it's full."

S ('*T*') J: "We also attend musical and occasional theatrical events held in the relatively new *Cosmo-Drome* over at Coney Island. We have a company membership there too. It's surprisingly large."

R ('*B*') C: "Fee-Fi-Fo (*deleted*)er's bigger than the Kennedy Centre. Lobby measurements are only short of it by a few feet. All the auditoriums are larger. Keep going, gents."

WW: "Back in 1969 they endowed this seriously well designed and equipped public sports and health centre right beside their main Arts Centre in Williamsburg. It's called the *Cosmonasium*. Even got a full-sized stadium and Olympic-sized pool attached. I take my little boy down there to do all-day classes on the weekend. I can barely drag him out of the place at the end of the day."

R ('*B*') C: "I go down there too; watch the girlie professionals pumping iron. The gyms are all walled in transparent glass. Amazonian (*deleted*)-tacular XXX-travaganza. *Hoo-Yah!*"

DU: "Their *Cosmo-Cosmic Gallery* over in the East Village has the best planetarium I've ever been to. Seriously good Space-Age exhibits, too. You really feel like you're in the far future."

R ('*B*') C: "Their planetarium shows *All These Worlds* and *The Solaris Effect* won awards. I love a good sky show almost as much as grooving on heavily sweating pink feminist flesh."

GB: "Let's not forget the *Slotnik City College*."

R ('*B*') C: "Over in Battery Park City, yeah. Half the guys I came up with in the firm did their chartered accountancy and financial management free courses as a way out of Hell's Kitchen."

GB: "Or the free *Cosmo-Clinic* over in Bowery."

R ('*B*') C: "They re-located my shoulder after I slipped a disc on the floor of the Stock Exchange. It was a heavy zinc futures bid, as I recall. Donated to them myself ever since."

S ('*T*') J: "Recently I read there's to be a new institute situated in Idlewild Park called the *Cosmo-Slotnik Herbarium, Botanical Gardens And Arboretum*. It will incorporate what they call a fully Vegan restaurant and regular vegetarian cooking classes. Apparently it's meant to be a much larger version of the Orto Botanico Di Padova established by the fifteenth century Medicis in Padua, Italy."

R ('*B*') C: "So they're doing veggie stuff now; too. Wonder if they'll serve pizza there."

WW: "Oh, and they're building this massive research library and study centre for students and journalists and academics and other eggheads over on Long Island. It's even going to have computers linked to universities and other specialist libraries across the world. *Cosmolab* or something."

GB: "This is all adding up to just what, Bozo?"

R ('*B*') C: "Multiplying up your collective equity in a seriously (*deleted*)ulating way. The Foundation has a separately administered fund for each charitable enterprise. Give over a million dollars spread across more than ten of those different enterprise funds in a certain period and they stick another twenty percent of full dollar value onto your equity. You get official certificates saying so, and the IRS recognises them."

GB: "Certain period is what?"

R ('*B*') C: "A decade. Goes up to twenty-five percent after the second decade. They really want you to donate over the long term."

S ('*T*') J: "Prudent and far-seeing strategy."

R ('*B*') C: "*Cosmo* has gently hot-(*deleted*)ed all the way to the top of the game. Since the Twenties when they started out, the *Cosmo-Slotnik Foundation* has become one of the biggest charitable institutions in America. Colossal is what they are. Despite sheer weight and bulk in the do-gooder's marketplace though, it's not really a household name. Maybe here in New York with so many operations, but LA is the only other place where they're similarly represented. And that's when most cities above 500,000 population have at least one art centre or college or local museum or library or medical centre or granny-home from 'em."

DU: "Have you got any contributor's prospectuses with you?"

R ('*B*') C: "Dag; I thought you'd never ask. Brought them in this sack with me, here."

(*Sound of heavy softcover paper books being slapped one by one onto a table.*)

WW: "Wow. I've seen smaller phone books."

R ('*B*') C: "Every single enterprise covered in précis. Of course that's just the digest version. You can request more detailed booklets for each enterprise from their administration and information offices. Those are over at the Vanderfeller Center on Madison Avenue. You know, that huge new high-rise place? They've got an entire (*deleted*)ing floor of the joint. Must cost millions but it's a diamond-standard prestige location."

(*Sounds of paper pages being turned, riffled.*)

DU (*audibly page-turning*): "Didn't know they operated a chain of health-food stores."

R ('*B*') C: "Yeah; *Cosmonuts*. All staffed by leftover hippies from what I can see. There's one down in Greenwich Village and another in Tribeca."

S ('*T*') J (*audibly page-turning*): "Interesting. They're even into mass-market educational publishing and have a stable of liberal periodicals."

R ('*B*') C: "Both *The Slotnik Review* and *Cosmopolity* are worth subscribing to. First class lefty journalism. After two years continuous subscription they send you an annual magazine binder every Christmas. I use them for my favourite (*deleted*)-fantasy girlie mags instead, they last forever."

WW (*audibly page-turning*): "Now this beats all. They sell *water*?"

R ('*B*') C: "Mineral water; yup."

WW: "Same stuff that makes up most of what we call rain?"

R ('*B*') C: "Well, super-distilled purified and filtered water, really. I think there's a carbonated version too. Big new health fad and they're right at the forefront of cashing in on it. Tax-free so far because it also classifies as a health food with the FDA. I think the *federales* are gonna close that loophole 'cos it's selling so fast. Try some *Cosmo-H2O* sometime. It refreshes the palate and purges you out. Kind of like the best (*deleted*)scream-ream you ever had from a Vegas showgirl working her last pair of rubber gloves."

GB: "Anything else? Like plutonium milkshakes?"

R ('*B*') C: "Sure, they're building an experimental nuclear reactor near Albuquerque. The *Cosmotomic I*; I think the brochure calls it."

(*Long pause*)

GB: "That one has to be a joke."

R ('*B*') C: "Yup. Late April Fool!"

(*Uproarious laughter from all participants.*)

GB: "Never mind it's October. I actually fell for that about a nanosecond, and it hurt."

R ('*B*') C: "Hey Gary, you haven't opened your own prospectus. Anything wrong?"

GB: "Nothing's wrong Bozo, you'd convinced me from the beginning. I don't need to review anything and I trust your judgement. We'll collectively invest just as you advise."

S ('*T*') J: "Agreed and seconded."

WW: "If they can make money out of something that falls from the sky, that's all my homely and lonely brain cell needs to know."

DU: "As long as I get to stay a carnivore."

R ('*B*') C: "The zucchinis are crying. Gentlemen, you will not dry-(*deleted*)-our-mothers regret this."

GB: "Warky, Bozo, tell me about that water again?"

*****

Even Survind and Dag, our nefarious financing experts, were surprised by just how successful Callabozo's investment programme proved for us. The moment we signed our first million-dollar pledge and expressed a willingness to pledge for a second decade in advance, they actually gave us twenty-five percent additional tax equity on our first. After a lot of discussion we agreed to put the second required million in a ten-year escrow account we couldn't touch.

During which it earned interest that would additionally be paid to the designated donation recipients on release of our funds to their specified enterprises in the first year of our second donation in 1984. The tax equity on *that* was fifty cents in the dollar. Interest rate was index-linked, but Survind forecast it would end up in excess of between a hundred and fifty and two hundred thousand.

Callabozo himself was surprised in turn. In his characteristic way he mused that we had caught the *Cosmo-Slotnik Foundation* on what he called an upgrading fiscal professionalism curve; whatever that meant. The effect, though, was tangible. Survind reported to me in March 1974 that he had heard from the IRS, and for the next financial year our cover business had both reduced tax liabilities and our code rating had improved by several levels.

Meaning we could launder our own cash now by simply putting it back into our cover business. Entirely new tax schedule enabled us to self-invest much higher sums into our cover capital fund. All Dag and Trucker had to do was invent sub-contractors and work projects and plausibly forge our purchasing invoices and billings and balance sheets.

Adding them to the real ones seamlessly. We had already been doing that on a small scale to launder some of our cash, but the main bulk of it built up too fast. Now we could multiply our own concealment operation many, many times over.

Callabozo's services, or those of someone like him, would not be needed by us for quite a way into the future. He advised us a few more times but after looking at our arrangements pronounced we were financially independent for the foreseeable. But he always met former clients socially and we owed him a lot.

We had to invite him to something.

*****

(Transcript resumes, location a noisy and spacious reception room with animated conversation and a live jazz band playing. Vocalist is performing a spirited rendition of 'I'm Sitting On Top Of The World' *in a combined satirical imitation of the voices of Al Jolson and Jimmy Durante. Occasion is the official opening evening gala of the* Cosmo-Slotnik Herbarium, Botanical Gardens And Arboretum, *location near Idlewild Park, New York City on 30.07.1974. Present are all four senior company officers and Ron Callabozo, who is audibly drinking and inebriated. An occasional low rumble of approaching thunder sounds in the auditory background.)*

R ('*B*') C: "I've been to a fair number of their *soirees* but never a full gala opening gig. What a (*deleted*)- (*deleted*)-(*deleted*)-your dancing toes show. That firework display over the park must have had the JFK control tower grounding planes. *Cosmo-Slotnik* sure know how to put on a shindig. Great band playing."

GB: "Yes, I actually know them and they're performing a request for me. Call themselves the *Caffeine Fiend Combo*. They play a lot down at the *Green Aphid Jazz Club* in Greenwich Village."

R ('*B*') C: "Hey, cool. I'll check out the scene, I don't get down to Hippyville that much. Know what they charge for gigs?"

GB: "Quart of espresso each and they're yours for the evening."

R ('*B*') C (*laughing*): "I love it. This almost beats strip clubs, and I can sure imagine some of the society girlies here up on the pole. Some of them are straight out of *Lolita* to talk to. Not just bedroom eyes but after the monster-(*deleted*) ones. Maybe I should invest in a place for the best young talent to slum it safely and make some heavy Double-(*deleted*) With A Poor Little Rich Girl cash tips on the side. Think some of them would be game for it?"

WW: "These uptown girls sure know how to wow you with style. And they don't exactly inhibit what they say either. I don't think you'd have any recruitment problems."

DU: "Sounds like a growth industry from the bottom up to me."

R ('*B*') C: "Hah, hah, hah! In fact, at a conservative estimate I'd say about eighty-five percent of the people here, including the pouting sophisticated Pretty Baby (*Deleted*) Me But You'll Pay A Price set, are clients of mine but they don't know it. Mostly I deal with the family accountant or stockbroker or lawyer or sometimes all three at the same time. Only a few of the Richie-Rich upper strata even know my name. It's better that way for confidential dealings behind the scenes. I might as well be invisible."

S ('*T*') J: "We ourselves are clandestine in a way. Everyone takes a telephone contractor for granted. Practitioners like yourself are crucial to the ongoing health of their fortunes, but most of them don't want to know you socially like an aristocrat won't deign to notice his own lifetime-loyal servants."

R ('*B*') C: "Y'know Survind, Trucker if I may, I used to let that bother me. The old Class thing. Snob Factor hits you wherever you are in any walk of life. There's always gonna be somebody you have to answer to that nothing is good enough for. No matter good a job you turn in, there's always something to bitch about with those types. Only one solution to stick them with."

S ('*T*') J: "Ah. And that is?"

R ('*B*') C: "Be the best and hike your prices. Make them pay through the (*delete*)ing nose. Grudge-(*deleted*) them even harder the next time when they come back to you. Invoice everything down to the smallest petty expense-cent, but make sure you deliver at the same time. If they think they can get something for nothing they'll just take a dump on your plate. Screw them harshly at the top (*deleteddeleted*)-level and they'll respect you."

GB: "Maybe we should put up our gasoline-mile charges."

R ('*B*') C (*laughing uproariously*): "You're a gas; Gary. Life is one big expense claim. And a (*deleted*)-buck is a (*deleted*)-buck to me. Wherever it crawls out of. I mean, I've helped tin-pot dictators salt away national assets rightfully belonging to their suffering peoples. Assisted assorted (*different expletive deleted*)-hole greaseball gangsters to get their evil ill-gotten gains and blood money out the bank's back door in pristine certificated form just like I helped you. Those ones will kill you if things go wrong. Didja see *The Passenger* with Jack Nicholson? I been in heavy deep-six situations almost like that. Money doesn't make the world go round, its belief and ideas and popular perception. Get them to believe they can't do without you. Then you're forever anchored against the storm in the unholy ideology of filthy (*deleted*)ing *lucre*. Just look good and let the marks come to you."

S ('*T*') J: "Speaking of storms, I believe there's one on the way here from the Atlantic. Before it hits we'd like to show you something special."

R ('*B*') C: "There's a rich girlie strip-tease going on in a private room?"

S ('*T*') J: "Ha, ha! Not that I've heard, sadly. No, it's more something I take pride in and since we also know nobody here, I need to show it to someone who might appreciate the work. Did you know I'm a trustee of the board of directors for this place?"

R ('*B*') C: "Hey, I didn't. Congratulations. So what's the (*deleted*)ing ambitious story?"

S ('*T*') J: "I manage part of the Herbarium upstairs. A rather specialised section. Shall we head on up there and see what's waiting?"

GB & DU & WW: "Yeah."

R ('*B*') C: "Since I don't even know what that is, it's all gonna be new like a virgin (*deleted*). Lead on."

(Footsteps of company officers and Ron Callabozo go through gala reception, conversation waxing and waning around them. Passing briefly near the band before coming out in a quiet corridor, entering an elevator and ascending several floors. As the doors open they proceed out into another entirely silent corridor until they halt and keys are turned in a lock, a door opened and closed. Door is locked again from the inside. Acoustics change to a large and silent interior space which is glass-roofed. Thunder is now noticeable and gradually growing in volume in the auditory background.)

R ('*B*') C: "Oh man, the scent in here is gorgeous. Just like some of the girls at the *Come On Aphrodite* on Seventh. Well, at the start of the night, anyway. Look at those thunderheads through the skylight."

(Distant but audible crash of thunder.)

DU: "It's going to be a drencher."

WW: "We should get a move on."

GB: "Agreed. Before we need raincoats. Trucker?"

S ('*T*') J: "Come over here, Ron. Let me show you my personal garden. I've become an expert on poison plants in my spare time. That's why this display here is roped off. Some of them can give you a nasty rash just from the touching, or even fever."

R ('*B*') C: "Oh, man. That reminds me of the time I had my first summer-(*deleted*) with this bitchy lifeguard girl over on Fire Island. She was like a blonde Barbi Benton but talked like the hideous side of Jersey. It was incredible physically, but the bushes we did it in near the lido pool were all lousy with thorns and poison ivy and stinkweed and I had to get this special all-over ointment from the paediatrician. And on top of that I got hepatitis and couldn't tell my parents how it happened…"

(Footsteps and speaking voices recede away from company president bearing recording device, a pause and then two more sets follow.)

GB (*to himself, inaudible to other participants*): "You shouldn't have done it, Ron."

(In auditory background brief scuffling noises, gargling sounds quickly cut off followed by a faint but sharp crack, a heavy falling object settling onto

the floor, rustling noises and then digging and grunting for several minutes. Afterwards three sets of footsteps return to position of company president.)

GB: "Finished?"

DU: "In every sense."

WW: "Used the garrotte then a karate chop to the neck. It was quick. He's four feet under soil and the plants can eat him for us."

S ('*T*') J: "I have his clothes and all personal effects. Most importantly his key-ring. It is Sunday tomorrow so we will visit his offices in disguise as a cleaning crew. The same for his home, he lives alone in a high-rise apartment near Wall Street with no family. My estimate is that after a year or so only Ron's bones will remain. The herbs and plants in my collection over there are hungry ones. I will keep a close eye on the soil consistency and measure its changing chemistry to be sure. I actually own the poison plant garden personally since I donated it, and my instructions forbid digging it up or other major work without my supervision. I chose species for it that need little maintenance. This solves one of our long-running supply problems for subtle and lethal but obscure natural poisons. We can be sure the late Ron will stay precisely where he is supposed to until it comes time for us to remove and dispose of the last remains."

GB: "Good work. We'll incinerate his things back at headquarters to be sure. Let's scram to the service elevator and back to the car before it really starts bucketing down out there."

DU: "Just sorry it had to happen this way. I liked the guy despite the '78 speed motormouth sewer-level gibberish. He had a kind of genius and really helped us when we needed it."

WW: "I am too, Dag. It wasn't an easy job just now. But you know what he did."

S ('*T*') J: "Company rules are clear."

GB: "I would have vaporised him if we didn't have the rule."

S ('*T*') J: "Even in these circumstances we have to work to stay objective and detached, Gary."

GB: "This was not about revenge, Trucker."

S ('*T*') J: "No?"

GB: "No. It was about professional ethics."

(Four sets of footsteps walk towards and through the door, as it is unlocked, exited, closed from the outside and re-locked, sound terminates abruptly as company president switches recording device off.)

*****

We had to do it, we had no choice. The biggest danger we had faced so far now came from the one time we trusted someone with our inner secrets. Despite what he had made from us, Ron Callabozo tried to sell us out to the one enemy we really did fear.

*****

Transcript-excerpt of phone interception tape recording from *Black Hand Incorporated* company confidential archives. Company president and senior deputies' eyes only. Transcript is on file in context of emergency-level danger to company operations and senior officers. Call takes place on 26.07.1974 from 19:03-19:13 (Eastern Standard Time) between Ron Callabozo from his personal office on the 35th floor of the Nimrod Building, Wall Street, New York City and Michael Tumesne, prominent journalist and political commentator at his home in Hoboken, New Jersey, telephone connection surveilled.

(Dialling tone with repeated rings, phone is answered, Michael Tumesne acknowledges.)

RON CALLABOZO *(audio background)*: "Mike? My name's Ron Callabozo, an independent partner at Minos & Associates Capital. You interviewed me earlier last year on techniques of money laundering and criminal banking. Told me to call you on this number if I had any more pertinent information."

MICHAEL TUMESNE *(audio foreground)*: "Ah, Ron. I remember, we met at a café near Penn station. Yes, I appreciated the insights. I used some in a subsequent exposé article, but I'm devoting a full chapter to it in a new book I'm bringing out. Death industries will be the theme."

RC *(ab)*: "Cool, I'll watch out for it. I called about something entirely different, though. You're interested in tracking possible murder-for-hire outfits, right?"

MT *(af)* *(suddenly alert)*: "Right."

RC *(ab)*: "Now, you must get a lot of cranks approaching you on this thing.

There's a whole universe of paranoia out there. Before calling you I've thought it over literally for months. Tried every angle of common-sense. But I keep coming back to the same conclusion, so felt I had to talk to you."

MT (*af*): "Listening intently, Ron. I seem to remember though, in our conversations before you used a lot more expressive language. What did you call it?"

RC (*ab*) (*chuckling*): "Best left unsaid. That's really something I put on for the customers, Mike. Kind of a professional persona which I use in the industry generally. It's an effective distraction tactic as well. Enjoy it yeah, but it's not really me."

MT (*af*): "Did you do some money laundering for an organisation like I described?"

RC (*ab*): "If so, it would have been for their cover company, or one of them. Now, you understand, the standard practice in this biz is for me to look at the assets and holdings of the client, always under the supervision of their accountant or lawyer. That way I can make the best judgement as to what laundering or conversion techniques to use and advise in detail. In very few cases is the client actually present. Almost the sole exception to that rule is gangsters who have to launder a lot of cash."

MT (*af*): "All of this comes under strict client privilege, I assume?"

RC (*ab*): "That's why I don't want to go into detail for now. If I'm wrong it would effectively be the end of my career, however anonymous I stay in it. Word would get around against me. Everybody talks to everyone else in this world, and there's only a certain number of people who do what I do at this level. Trust and confidentiality and never breaking them are the only way to survive in the long term."

MT (*af*): "Which seems to be against the prevailing tide in Wall Street these days."

RC (*ab*): "Tell me about it. We're on the verge of a whole new round of the Roaring Twenties. All the con men are professionalising themselves in preparation and doing Business Majors. In a few years I reckon all that funny money madness is going to start itself up again big time with the credit boom."

MT (*af*): "So what alerted your suspicions?"

RC (*ab*): "A small group of guys running a large and very successful but kind of nebulous business came to me last year. They had multiple millions in cash they wanted me to get legitimised. They didn't show me a single balance or ledger sheet or any other kind of paperwork. Given their particular business sector there is no way they accumulated that boodle conventionally."

MT (*af*): "If it's not too sensitive, how were they hiding it?"

RC (*ab*): "Simple safe deposit boxes, a perfectly ordinary and appropriate business account. Almost exactly like you described in your article. I had to go with them to their bank to verify they had the cash. At the time I didn't think anything about that, it was just another relatively straightforward job. I did the deal flawlessly, we went overseas to do it, and they got what they wanted. Client file closed."

MT (*af*): "What was it that didn't fit the usual pattern?"

RC (*ab*): "Them. Real businessmen leave it to the accountant, to the lawyer. Because they have a business to run and only have so much time to spare. Gangsters are there for every session without fail. These guys were all there every time and didn't miss the smallest agenda item. I think they may even have been recording every conversation. They stuck together like flies."

MT (*af*): "Did they let anything slip? Stuff that came over as incongruous?"

RC (*ab*): "Overseas travel terrified them. I mean, it was blatant. I had to argue them into it because that was the only way to get what they wanted. It had to be done outside American jurisdiction, and that means even more expense. But once they made up their minds they organised it like clockwork. Clearly they had something big to hide, but it wasn't just the money. That's what didn't fit."

MT (*af*): "Profiling them over the years I think I've come to understand them better. Everything you're telling me fits into my expectations, Ron."

RC (*ab*): "There was this guy who was their chief financial officer. Sharper than a razor. Kept quizzing me about the laundering and then the investments with the money once we were back. He let a few things slip about me and my career which I never mentioned to them. I only realised it later, this guy was subtle. Talked a bit stilted, like an old Bostonian out of a book, but I caught the Midwestern accent there. They all had it. Anyway, they all must have done one hell of a thorough research job on me. Career stuff right from my beginning, or really obscure things you'd only come across in the financial pages. Must've used a press cutting bureau or spent a lot of time in the library or something."

MT (*af*): "Again, that fits. They'd be security-conscious far beyond the meticulous."

RC (*ab*): "But for me the clincher is purely intuitive. And that's why I still can't be sure."

MT (*af*) (*with an edge*): "Please give me as much detail as you can, Ron. It's important. I think these may be the same people that I'm looking for, now."

RC (*ab*): "Okay, it was their headquarters. Anyone in their business sector would operate out of a typical roadside unit for customer visibility or an industrial park. These guys were set up in this really old building which even had its own old-time *chapel*; they showed it to me. Some former hospital or something. It was so obscure and hard to find they might as well have been underground. They were self-evidently hiding, concealing themselves from view in plain sight. Eerie as hell. Place was definitely haunted. And here's the clincher thing. They fit right into it."

MT (*af*): "Example?"

RC (*ab*): "Outside the place they act like a military unit or something. Even when they were tourists overseas and seeing the sights. They stay close, look out for each other continually and keep glancing to their company president guy like he's their commanding officer or something. They're well-practiced at making it look natural, but I'm sensitive to things like that. I feel the tension there. At first I thought they were CIA, fronting some rogue operation or something, but I've met a few and they didn't match the usual profile. A different kind of clandestine."

MT (*af*): "And on the inside?"

RC (*ab*): "Completely relaxed back at base. 'Cos that's what it felt like. They're actually nice guys in the main in that setting and I like them, apart from their company president guy. He's glacier cold. Quick-witted and smart yeah, but there's always a pretty nasty barb underlying whatever he says. Eyes like gun-muzzles that spookily follow you around."

MT (*af*) (*long pause*): "You're referring to them in the present tense. Are you still in close contact with these characters, Ron?"

RC (*ab*): "In fact I'm meeting them in a few days. Again, I don't want to go into details in case I'm wrong about them, because some very specific client privilege is involved with where we're all going. Should I try to learn anything when I meet them?"

MT (*af*): "Absolutely not. If we're both right these are killers, Ron. From what you've described you know way too much about them. There's no doubt in my mind they intend to kill you at some point. If you arouse even the slightest suspicion, they won't hesitate."

RC (*ab*): "Well, to be honest I think they regard me just as a skilful vulgarian who doesn't suspect a thing about them. That's another way the professional persona is useful. Maybe not a clown, but not dangerous either. They also know I have all the records and probably have taken precautions in case of a suspicious accident or fatality involving me."

MT (*af*): "So you do have all this information prepared?"

RC (*ab*): "You bet, it's in a small parcel which I've locked in my desk here in the office. There's a letter instructing my secretary to have it couriered over to you if anything bad happens. And there's a duplicate in my desk over at my town apartment. So worry not."

MT (*af*): "Ron, the only thing I'm worried about is you. Don't meet these people again."

RC (*ab*): "Oh, it's gonna be a public place with lots of people around. I'm not driving with them or anything. Given some of my clientele, that's damn well the last thing I'd do. There's no good reason for me to go to their freak-out headquarters anyway, and I won't."

MT (*af*): "Please be careful. They're devious and may even have you under surveillance."

RC (*ab*): "Well, that's happened to me a few times. There aren't any signs of it I can detect and I haven't gotten that crawling feeling I usually do if I am being watched, but I'll stay alert. "

MT (*af*): "Would you call me when you get back from it? I'm working on the book at home right now, I'm normally up late and often right through the night. I'll be here."

RC (*ab*): "Sure. Glad I called you Michael. If they are who you think they are, I'm proud to help as long as my name doesn't come in. I've helped some bad people but I get a seriously ugly vibe from Gary. I've passed along stuff to the FBI and the CIA and the Treasury people too for particular scumbag clients, but I think these spooky guys are, like, spook-plus or something. I get the distinct impression they're at least two steps ahead of any kind of law enforcement."

MT (*af*): "No officials I talk to even half-believe these characters exist. You've helped me more than you know, Ron. Take good care of yourself."

RC (*ab*): "Talk to you soon. Unless they query my last fees invoice; of course!"

(*Ron Callabozo ends call, telephone receiver replaced and connection broken, dialling tone takes over. Michael Tumesne lingers briefly before audibly replacing receiver.*)

MT (*af*): "God help me, I've never been this close. Please Ron; don't fall into their evil hands. If there's a *Zeitgeist* to any age, these unholy monsters are the Devil's mirror of it."

Revenge on the Menu
Jan Glaz
California 1988

LaDonna pulled into Cozy's parking lot, popped a few uppers, minus water, and checked her face in the mirror. Make-up intact, she injected a wide smile, opened the car door, whacked it shut, and strolled into the eatery. She'd revved up a best behavior persona for the past few months, which meant allowing insults from co-workers, from her boss and from the low-class patrons the eating establishment catered to. She, in essence, allowed her ego to diminish into a door mat because she needed the job.

As she marched to her assigned station, in an unusual action, the owner, Nick, who the gals nicknamed 'Snicker-drooler' for dripping saliva and mini-snorts, stepped up to greet her wearing a more wicked expression than usual. "LaDonna," he hesitated, "I'm taking on a new girl tomorrow, she has a following. I'm forced to cut your section to minimum, nothing personal but your low on the hiring pole my other servers have seniority. I'm running a business here and the new girl's, well, revenue."

Suddenly LaDonna became seventeen and it was Pete's face, not Nick's, piercing her soul. She ignited into a burst of hate. Ugliness gushed out of her steamy lips, "Mr. big shot owner," she flamed, as she waved her hand at the other servers busy standing like petrified wood. We all know you're a miser and a cruel-mouthed pig who sexually harasses the staff. They won't tell you, but you should shower more often. God only knows you need to dig down into your fortune and by a toothbrush." And then she thundered, "I quit", followed by every obscenity she could think of.

The bulbous face of her boss lit from its daily dead white to a starchy orange-red. He lunged at her with hands extended in an effort to rip every slander from her tongue. LaDonna jumped back to avoid a blow. Nick screamed, "Get out of here before I call the police."

Satisfied with the foulness she'd dished up, she spun towards the exit.

Safely inside her car LaDonna allowed her temper to drive, gunning the vehicle whenever possible. That was risky, her license had been revoked. She was planning to junk her junk of a car and taxi to work. Then, as soon as her driving privileges were reinstated, she'd hunt up a better paying job followed by a brand new flaming red convertible that she'd seen. The sporty car was at the top of her goal list. Her outburst had stymied that plan, pronto.

Arriving home LaDonna screeched her car to a halt, parked, and then stomped her way to the door of her female cave. Safely inside the apartment she went atomic, let out a banshee yell, swung her arm backward and in one grand sweep, flung a row of cheap wine goblets into oblivion. Crying began with each step she planted between chunks of splintered glass. She knew depression was part of her personality and she had plenty of reasons for the condition. It was impossible to bury mountains of uncaring, cruel people. The sick side of her couldn't detect that her illness was expanding as she aged and that lately any slight to her ego easily opened wounds that brought her to the brink of madness.

After a quick check of funds she realized she could weather a much required bout of seclusion. Priding herself on being practical, she'd saved for these occasions. Not from her miserly waitress earnings but from a variety of rich guys she met. Her hobby of choice, just a hobby, because she had satisfaction from her skill as a waitress. Customers preferred her. Years of experience gave her the confidence she deserved and desired. This wouldn't be the first time she quit a job, and most likely, it wouldn't be the last.

Her kewpie-doll phone, inlaid with mini precious stones, began playing a tune. A nifty gift from a prosperous stranger she met in Las Vegas, she barely recalled his face, a married, extravagantly wealthy type. They spent a few memorable days drinking, drugging, gambling and sexing.

"Hello!" Anticipation raced through her veins, "who's this?"

A male voice answered, "Hi, it's me, Sam. I told you I would call tonight and I kept my promise." LaDonna felt herself grow passionate. But she didn't recall any Sam man, or any promise. The next words she heard shocked her back to reality.

"Come on Judy, stop playing around, and talk to me."

Her heart sank as she pushed the receiver back into kewpie's cradle. Sam was a wrong number, but it rang again. She yanked the receiver into the air and yelled, "You have the wrong number, idiot!" After setting Sam straight, she went to her liquor cabinet and gulped down a load of whisky.

The next morning LaDonna picked herself up from the bedroom floor. Urine had soaked her carpet and vomit had crusted her hair into knots—no big deal. She grabbed the flat of her bedroom walls to steady herself and walked into the bathroom. One glance at her face in the mirror set tears streaming into the hollows of her cheeks. She saw her mother, the mother, who was not a mother. Gaping at the reflection, she shouted, "You're as crazy as her!"

In an unlocked chamber of LaDonna's mind she tried to fool herself and swore that, unlike her mother, who died in an asylum, God blessed her with beauty and a photographic memory. It shaped her into special and whenever she rode into the depths of hell, she managed to rise again.

As she wobbled into the kitchen, her kewpie doll sang a cheery song. Her voice shook, timid and weak, she heard herself answer, "Hello".

"Hello, is this LaDonna Jenkins?" a female inquired.

"Yes."

"LaDonna, my name's Cheri, I'm a manager at the Bountiful Restaurant, our hiring manager, Brenda, asked me to call the most recent applicants and last week you applied for a job. Three servers are not showing up today. Are you available? Do you feel you can handle the day on short notice? If so, Brenda might agree to start you as a fill-in server."

LaDonna's voice grew monstrous, "Of course I can. Thank you. What time shall I arrive?"

"As soon as possible, we'll be swamped due to the Labor Day holiday."

Time to race into survival mode. A hurried shower led to styling her hair into curly. She had to pencil-in fake eyebrows because two days prior she singed off her real ones while drunk and frying bananas. For face flavor she gobbed on generous helpings of bright coral lip balm and glued on a set of thick, violet eyelashes. She scurried to her closest. Resting neat and clean on a hanger was her lucky outfit, whenever she wore it to an interview it never failed to impress. She chose a pair of chocolate toned shoes and then selected the perfect jewelry to add an air of refinement. Surely, being accepted, she must pack her server sneakers into her stylish tan calfskin purse.

LaDonna had plans to stay on at the magnificent Bountiful, it was a latent desire. Waitresses who had the good fortune to land a position raked in the dough. The restaurant hugged the ocean and resembled a ship from a bygone era. Diners were served in elegant settings both below and above board. She'd done her homework by becoming a now and then customer in order to memorize and note their various menus. Every few months she filled out another application.

She decided to call a taxi instead of taking a chance that some wise-guy cop might pull her over. With the promise of this job she was sure to reinstate her driver's license and purchase her dream car.

"Hurry driver, you should have taken the side route, expressways are jammed at this time of day!"

The seasoned driver shot his eyes upward and on seeing his fare in the mirror thought 'another lunatic'. The cabbie knew taking side streets would add untold miles to her arrival, but he learned not to wage a customer war. He swerved the car's tires left and followed her command.

LaDonna was a sweaty mess by the time the taxi pulled up to the Bountiful. There was an endless line of people anxiously awaiting a seat.

"The fare's $17.85 Miss."

LaDonna handed the driver a $20 dollar bill and kept her hand out for change. No way would she leave a tip when she had to provide the route. To further host her dissatisfaction with him she slammed the cab door, and then rushed towards the Bountiful.

"Excuse me, excuse me, I work here!" LaDonna shouted, as she tried to push and bump her way up a ramp filled with would be diners.

"Get in line like everyone else," a disbeliever shouted. "Yeah, lady," shouted another.

She became frantic and thought, 'I'll find the back entrance'.

A hefty rear door was locked, but there was a small window. She shoved her narrow face inside the pane, banged and shouted. Finally, a man in a white apron streaked with fresh blood, opened the door. Immediately she told him her name and that she was there to see Brenda.

"You're here for a job?"

"No, I'm hired," she replied, "Please open the door."

The man seemed bewildered. "You're not at the server's entrance ma'am, you're at the cook's quarters." He opened the door and said, "Follow me."

They walked through the lower galley and up a flight of antique stairs. "The center door is Brenda's office," said her escort, as he walked off.

She snooped around and located a bathroom, brushed her hair and practiced facial expressions. She'd been so depressed she almost forgot how to look professional, confident and successful. After a few long breaths she walked head high towards Brenda's door and administered a medium knock. Loud would be too aggressive, and soft too needy. When there was zero response, she tap, tap, tapped it again. Nothing—so she let loud ones fly. "Bang, Bang, Bang!"

The door opened and an annoyed female confronted her. It was her first glimpse of the mighty Brenda who had the power to make or break a server. Brenda was as tall as a Viking Shield Maiden. The woman's obviously dyed black hair was permed to faux Jamaican. Gold circular earrings pierced each earlobe, they glistened like two rising suns. LaDonna heard the goddess speak.

"And you might be?"

"Hello Brenda, your manager, Cheri, phoned me this morning and requested my help as you are three servers short. My name is LaDonna."

"Well then, enter."

Brenda eloquently seated herself and reached for a large ocean blue cup with an etching of the 'Bountiful' ship set among rolling waves. She delicately took a sip of its contents and then carefully placed it so the name Brenda, cast in gold leaf lettering, faced LaDonna. Her voice became docile.

"Oh, yes, yes, I have your application… somewhere?"

LaDonna observed a platter overstuffed with goodies, it fought for space on a desk piled with disarranged folders and loose papers. Brenda flipped through the papers.

"Ah! Ms. Jenkins, I see you've applied many times." She pointed to a seat opposite her desk and LaDonna sat down like a timid child. "Our lines are longer than usual today and we can't turn the tables fast enough. Cheri suggested you, and another wannabe waitress, Rita."

Brenda handed her their lunch menu and asked her to take time to study it. "Cheri will assign you a wait section as soon as you are prepared."

"I'm familiar with your lunch menu," offered LaDonna, "and your basic breakfast and dinner menus, as well."

"I'm impressed," Brenda said, as she placed the menu back on her desk. "Well, let's suit you up in one of our uniforms, it may not fit, but if I hire you as an alternate, I'll make arrangements for a perfect size. I'll walk you to the servers quarters."

The uniform was similar to a sailor suit, with a skirt instead of pants. A crisp white cap embroidered with the Bountiful's insignia completed the look. Both items were too large for puny LaDonna and she appeared as a castaway stranded for months on a deserted island.

When she emerged from the quarters, a tiny, delicate female, with a brass name tag "Manager Cheri" pinned to her sailor's blouse, greeted her. Frizzy strands of reddish hair peeked from the edges of her snug cap. She motioned and LaDonna shadowed her into the main seating arena to a section comprised of five elaborate tables set with hungry faces impatiently ready to spill out their choices.

Like an actress upon a stage LaDonna said her lines, smiled, and chatted a bit. She questioned guests for preferences and wrote down their orders. Her mind imagined her audience of customers gazing at her in awe of her beauty and skills. 'I'll put these other pussy waitresses to shame, meow... meow!' she whispered to herself, smiling, as she lugged a huge tray of items to one of her tables.

LaDonna prided herself on recalling all manner of details, like who wanted non-menu items or who preferred bread with ends cut off. Paying high prices made for fussy patrons. Rita, her competitor, seemed flustered and confused. The menu was complicated. 'Rita's toast', thought LaDonna.

But Rita wasn't toast, she was Cheri's friend and Cheri kept rescuing her throughout the lunch rush. LaDonna's jealousy streak reared its revengeful head. She could've used Cheri's help locating items from areas unknown to her, instead she had to take unwanted time to browse around, or ask another server, and that broke her swift rhythm, but somehow, she managed.

Rita happened to be what LaDonna labeled a "looker". Classy pretty, with bouncy blond curls styled neatly around her cherub face and gentle eyes, plus she had a sensual sway to her step, she didn't walk, she glided.

At the end of the shift Brenda called LaDonna and Rita into her quarters and said, "I'm going to hire both of you part-time. It's a trial period that may lead to a permanent position for one of you. If you girls would like to try, then welcome to the Bountiful."

LaDonna was livid with envy. Rita didn't deserve a chance, she was slow and Cheri had to take most of Rita's orders along with a few of her own. If it wasn't such a great opportunity, she would have rejected the offer, immediately. Instead she allowed her lips to curl into a relaxed smile. She looked into Brenda's uncaring eyes and then, pretending to be sparkly, said, "Oh, I'm so thankful to be given a trial servership aboard the ship Bountiful."

Rita expressed similar emotions of gratitude before extending a hand to LaDonna. Like two prize fighters ready for round one. It wasn't a fair fight, Rita had a buddy to speak up for her, manager Cheri. All the happiness of her luck hired as a server sunk into a grave plot in her heart. She excused herself from Brenda's office.

The next day as LaDonna entered the main dining room Rita approached her and said, "We're like two race horses at the gate." LaDonna didn't respond. She knew Rita planned to collect a stable of regular customers. People who ask for you, prefer you above the rest. And yes, they slowly start tipping you better, and give nice gifts at holidays. Rita spotted Cheri and walked over to complain, loud enough for LaDonna's ears. "What's with that LaDonna? I tried to joke with her and she brushed me off." Cheri answered, "Don't worry, eventually Brenda will catch her behavior and she'll become an ugly memory."

Ladonna didn't covet making friends. The longest relationship she had was with Leon, a customer at 'Burgers n Such', her second server's job. In her heart of hearts she wanted to marry Leon. And then, fearing marriage and the baby they conceived, Leon disappeared. He left no forwarding address and no other choice but to abort the child. Thus, Cheri's dislike didn't faze LaDonna because she'd been there too many times.

"Follow me girls," said Cheri. They were each assigned five tables in the lower dining room.

LaDonna snapped to attention. "Good morning, my name's LaDonna and I'm pleased to be your server." She hoped not only to create a following, but to steal regulars from the seasoned servers.

Rita was busier with a whopping nineteen customers seated by Cherie, LaDonna had been given fourteen. "Blatant favoritism," LaDonna silently quipped and thought, well, I'll play your game, Cheri and Rita. She decided to mess with Rita's orders. The place was super busy, nobody would pay a mind to anything LaDonna was doing. As she nonchalantly walked over to pick up her customers food, in a wink of an eye, she dipped into Rita's orders, moving sliced tomatoes from one plate to another and adding sliced onion where none should be.

Rita couldn't handle five packed tables. She was naïve, banking on Cheri's expertise to back up her nimble brain. Not only was she slow, she at times messed up who wanted what, so with a little extra adverse help from LaDonna, she'd soon appear even more dimwitted than she was.

LaDonna zipped near Rita's table to collect the evil consequence of her slide of hand performance. She heard a customer say to Rita, "No dear, my friend ordered tomatoes, where are they?" And another corrected, "My husband didn't want onion and the omelet has slices of onion."

LaDonna performed her tables like a whiz kid. One man complained about his raisin bread, "I expected more raisins?" She hurried back to the kitchen and shuffled through 3 loaves of bread to find slices that were stuffed with more raisins, then she not only replaced it, she gave him an extra slice. Tricks of the trade to build profitable word of mouth and return business, guests would tell others: "Oh, ask for LaDonna."

After the breakfast crowd subsided, Bountiful servers gathered to gossip while waiting for the lunch rush. LaDonna shunned any type of camaraderie and stood in a corner munching a dry cinnamon roll. She felt disliked and besides, she feared slipping up and divulging her server secrets.

At days end, LaDonna entered her apartment and slammed the door: not once, but four times. Downed a load of pills and a whiskey brew. Tried to sleep, but instead opened a box buried under her everyday items. Inside were the remains of a local newspaper clipping: Pete's murder. She read the heading: "Restaurant owner bludgeoned to death." Today she had toyed with the idea of doing away with either Rita, Cheri, or Brenda. Upon that thought, thunder shook her windows, a flash of lightening scanned the pupils of her eyes and for a split second she thought she saw Pete's brutalized body.

Her memory quickly recreated the spring of 1979. She had packed a few clothes along with money her mother had hidden and boarded a bus from Illinois to Indiana. Upon reaching her destination she stopped for a bite to eat at a joint called "Pete's Place". In the window was a sign Help Wanted—No

Experience Necessary. The owner, Pete, hired her on the spot. She was excited, it was her first job. Pete came off protective, advanced her pay and located a one room rental. Eventually he won her trust with his fatherly concern.

About three months after her hiring, father Pete descended into a lurid fiend. He kept, accidently, bumping into her. "Excuse me" he would say, and while he said the words, he would pat her on the rear. One day he asked if she would join him for dinner at his home. "You must be lonely, no parents, friends, or siblings," he said. She wished she'd never told him about her personal sorrows and declined his every approach.

One of Pete's customers, Leon, her future heartbreak, told her a family style restaurant called "Burgers 'n' Such" would soon have an opening for a server. LaDonna applied on her day off and was hired.

The following day she marched into Pete's office to say, "I'm leaving, this will be my last day." Pete begged her to stay for two more days. "You could have given me notice," he pleaded.

She agreed, "Fine, two days, then, I'm out of here."

The next afternoon he drove up with a truckload of supplies and asked her to help him stock the back room after hours. He said he would pay her double time. Once again, she accepted.

In the evening she met Pete in the back room. He waved as he slit open a box filled with pickle jars, and said, "LaDonna, come grab some of these to shelve." She bent down to pick up a jar and he put his hand up her skirt. As soon as she turned to stop him, he whacked her, spun her around, and then secured her wrists with tape. He kept moving fast, demanding, "Don't scream or I'll shove something down your throat." She did scream, and he shoved a rag into her mouth. She saw he was glistening wet, sweating hard from the excitement he was causing himself. His sweat dripped over her face and she started to heave, but they were dry heaves. She began kicking him, but he was swift and wrestled her young body to the floor where he viciously stole her virginity. He removed her bindings and told her to dress, and then coldly quipped, "You're fired, get out of here".

Weeks passed before she had the strength and conviction to report him to the police. It would mean reliving the horror she'd been fighting to kill. At the inquiry, Pete avoided her gaze and talked squarely to the authorities, "This girl's a psycho like her mom who died in the looney bin." He went on to invent a pack of lies about her. He said he caught her hanging around his place after closing, making out in the dark with guys who she'd given free food, his food, but he forgave her time and again because she was like a daughter to him. The police listened intently, their male mindset acknowledging the existence of rape accusations from other wanton females.

"Officers, she begged me to become her lover." Pete spit on the floor. "Me! Her father figure!" One interrogator raised his eyes in disbelief, like hey, she's not your daughter and it's obvious the young woman is gorgeous. Pete caught it and to halt any defensive truth in LaDonna's favor, he added, "This nut case girl had her eye on being Mrs. Pete, on my business, my money, and when I flat out refused and asked her to leave… next thing I know, she claims rape."

Without evidence and only LaDonna's accusation, Pete signed a statement, and the rape charge was dismissed. Pete had a clean police record, but she knew otherwise. While he was pulling off her clothes, he said he had raped before and would again. His exact words, after he told her she was fired and as she limped out of the restaurant, she would never forget: "Young girls are always begging for it, I believe in giving gals what they want."

Almost a year later, LaDonna decided to give Pete what he needed, what God wanted. Pete's last night on earth was as starless and black as his soul. A giant tree lived in back of Pete's business. She recalled a short wood plank with rusty nails nestled along the side of the building, it was still there, she hid in back of the tree and waited. He never changed his routine. He drove up, and as usual, unloaded his truck. She crept up behind him while he was bent over, fuzzing with boxes, and using a force that only unrequited rage can produce, whacked him over the head. He fell instantly. She wasn't sure he was dead until reading it in the neighborhood news. He would never rape again. The police never solved the case. Never questioned a petite rape victim named LaDonna.

*****

Cheri phoned. "Rita called in sick. Can you take her section for the lunch and dinner crowd?" LaDonna slammed her purse to the floor and kicked it across the room. "I'll be more than happy to help out," she lied. She'd planned a day of shopping, a pricey dinner, and then hit the night spots for a bit of dancing, maybe wind up with a male encounter. Now the suspense of that thrill fell to the floor, kicked out of sight with her handbag.

A pep rally was in town, the Bountiful was jumping. Cheri greeted her upon arrival and thanked her, but she didn't seem sincere. In short time, tips were bulging from LaDonna's pockets, but the prosperity saddened her, because she realized that she'd been Cheri's second choice. Rita had been scheduled for the event. Cheri knew it would garnish big money. Before leaving, LaDonna requested a day off. It was the date that she would pick up her sports car.

On the way to the dealership, she retrieved her newly reinstated license and kissed it. She paid the taxi driver and entered the showroom.

Her salesman greeted her, "Follow me Miss your dream car is in the back lot." The young man escorted her through rows of vehicles sitting like orphans.

"I see it!" she shouted!"

Handsome it was, her spiffy tomato red convertible topped with a gravy brown roof. He handed her the keys and she gave it a spin. "I earned every inch of this car," she told him after she signed the necessary documents.

At home the kewpie answering machine reported a message. Cheri had called to inform her that she was assigned the late shift instead of breakfast and lunch, then added, "Rita will be at the station next to yours, if that's a problem call me."

The next day, as soon as LaDonna arrived, Rita began gloating about Charlie, a wealthy, prized customer. Brenda frowned on dating regular customers. Charlie had propositioned her for a date, more than once; she rebuffed him. Evidently, Rita, willingly obliged.

"Please, don't mention this to Brenda. Charlie asked me to move in with him, it happened the night you filled in for me. I'm debating the move. I can't risk this job on a maybe relationship."

"Men like him are fickle," LaDonna's jealousy answered, "if I were you, I'd take a pass on this one."

"It's truly a risky decision because I'm up for a management position. The pay is through the roof, higher than any ever offered a fledging server. Brenda called me in yesterday and told me that manger Scott was leaving, and that I was her prime choice to fill the opening."

Rita's words pierced her to her core, her psyche began bleeding profusely. Scott was a manager equal to Cheri. Enraged, she asked Rita, "Do you have manager experience?"

"Heck no, I can barely handle my tables, but Cheri informed Brenda that I would make an excellent manager. Cheri's so great! She's been devoting her personal time to coaching me, and wow does she know her stuff."

The news of telling Rita and Cheri about the thrill of buying her new car faded into nothingness. LaDonna went into a daze, she could barely function and took her customers' orders correctly, only out of habit. An envious tune played repeatedly inside her mind; no experience as a manager, about to live with Charlie. Cheri stepping in to ensure Rita's success. LaDonna recalled clearly listing managerial experience on her resume, she had been hired as a manager more than once, and yet she was not even considered for the promotion. Evil people were a constant that LaDonna could not seem to avoid. Why had fate given her such a life? After contemplating her own question she became convinced that God had sent unworthy people into her life because it was her duty, her responsibility, to dispose of them so His righteousness could prevail. She welcomed her chance role as a crusader, for the cause of the Almighty.

Her shift ended, it had been the worst day of her life since she moved to California. She gunned her new sports car all the way home, she even ran a red light, just because she could and she blew a stop sign for the same reason. Great tears soaked her hands as she navigated the steering wheel. Safely home, she tackled a few shots of whiskey and tried to analyze her latest problem.

Who's to blame, was it Rita? LaDonna's mind answered, 'no'. Rita could not help it if Cheri favored her. In reality Rita had not been personally cruel. It must be Cheri. Then she calculated that Cheri can advise, but only Brenda can promote. The perpetrator in the crime against her sanity was the one and only Brenda. All three added to her misery, but Brenda had authority to seal it. The gossip that loomed over Brenda was that she'd unjustly favored and fired other employees. Brenda was in bed with Satan.

The next day was April fool's day, and it was the day she would cease being Brenda's fool. The first chance she had, she would administer poison. The ingredient was not easily obtainable. It was a quark that she managed to generate a hefty supply from a keeper of poison in order to rid society of a rat holed up at the 'Capricorn Steak House', a midwestern job she held for three months.

As she brushed her teeth and rinsed, she began to reminisce how she had neatly done away with a chunk of society's human rubbish. Dressing in pink hot pants, and a skimpy jersey top she visited Lou's Garden Center. LaDonna had purchased a box of posies at Lou's a week earlier, a bevy of living flowers that unfortunately died off rapidly. At that time, she made a mental note of one employee, the one she hoped was at work; he was. His eyes remembered her and he rushed forward. "Can I help you?" He ran his gaze up her long bare legs.

"I hope so," she answered, "I have rats, I need the strongest possible poison, fast working."

"Ricin is a poison we use here, but never sell to the public. I've something else you can purchase for rats." The old guy was coming onto her heavy, staring unabashedly at her popping breasts instead of her face.

"No I'd prefer, the non-public variety. Gee, it's so hot in here," she said, as she innocently fussed and pulled on her blouse to expose a bare chest. The guy's expression changed to dreamy soft. LaDonna was an excellent seductress, they made a date, sex in exchange for poison.

While driving to the Bountiful on fool's day, LaDonna had second thoughts about doing in Brenda. 'I'm content. I have a coveted job, the envy of many servers'. She tried to advise her ego to wait, after all, she presently had car payments. Why rock the ship?

That decision didn't bear fruit. Less than two weeks later Rita approached LaDonna during her break. "Brenda wants to talk to you, ASAP." The demand unnerved her but she bolstered her courage and tapped on Brenda's door.

"Enter," was the response. LaDonna obeyed.

"Hello LaDonna, please, have a seat."

LaDonna sheepishly obeyed.

Brenda reached for her employee files and retrieved a folder. LaDonna became hopeful that within was her resume stating her highly rated managerial excellence. Being offered the promotion would wipe away for good the murderous hate bubbling in her veins.

Brenda's expression was stern as her eyes shot sabers towards LaDonna's, and her lips clenched like a tight fist, opened wide. She declared, "I wish to inform you that I've decided to promote Rita and I have a replacement set for her vacancy. I've hired a male server full time, based on his wait experience at one of New York's finest restaurants, he'll rise up our ladder quickly. Unfortunately…" LaDonna's hands tightly squeezed the sides of the chair as Brenda's death sentence passed between her ears. "There's been reports coming to me from other servers about you. They've told me that not only are you standoffish, but that you are also farming their regulars. They've lost customers to you that they've built over time. Brenda handed LaDonna a sheet that listed the staff's objections. LaDonna scanned them into her photographic memory before stating, "I don't agree." She placed the page back on Brenda's desk. "The accusations are preposterous. Don't they strike you as a jealousy hunt?"

Her boss gathered the reason sheet and placed it back inside a folder, she continued, "Our server, Irene, has been with us near twelve years and she is known to be forthright and honest. She claims one customer she's served for nine of those years has been requesting you as his server."

"Brenda that customer may have observed my actions as a server, my manners and efficiency opposed to Irene's bolstered his desire to request me."

After listening to the explanation, Brenda exposed the incident she believed as the most reasonable proof for Irene's claim. "Irene has our chefs make a menu item we no longer offer. The man's been a patron since our ship first sailed on still waters. He only orders this particular meal if Irene is on the floor because I gave her alone permission to have the chef prepare his specialty. How you came upon the details involved in preparing that meal suggests to me that it was a premeditated move, a plan to acquire Irene's customer. He ordered it from you, and without my permission, the chef prepared it, the date is right here on his check. I questioned the chef and he assumed you had my permission. After that meal the customer began requesting you. The cook on duty continued to prepare this meal, until shy Irene nerved up and approached me to question why I now allowed you the exact privilege."

"Ms. Brenda one morning, when server Irene was on vacation, he happened to be in my section. He said he was hoping to request Irene because he so wanted his favorite dinner. He also told me he didn't know exactly how to explain it. I'd seen the plate waiting to be picked up by Irene many a time and being curious I deciphered the contents, plus, I instructed the chef to add a splash of extra flavors to some of the ingredients. I thought the spice concoction would enhance his enjoyment, which it did. And from that day forward he insisted on being seated in my section."

Brenda's assurance turned sour. She slammed her right hand on top of her desk. "Well, that explains just one of your many tricks that my employees have witnessed."

She took a second to think and produced a rebuttal. "Brenda, the Bountiful is known as a restaurant that caters to its customers, it's the backbone of its success and as your server I am only following our "mission statement" not stealing regulars. I happen to go the extra yard that your other staff neglects to perform."

Brenda's expression softened. She ate the bait and then spoke with all the authority her position granted, "I see your point LaDonna, but as Captain, I run a tight ship. We support each other's endeavors similar to a loving family. Your actions in regard to my employees, though good for our clients, are too self-based. I don't want to lose you because you're a superior server, and I can always count on you to answer any staff emergencies. You're outlandishly dependable. When you sat down I had no intention of complimenting you, firing you, maybe? Truth be known, customers I've interacted with have raved about your professionalism.

"What I propose is a second trial period to give you a chance to raise your likeability level with co-workers. I'm sorry, I'll have to cut your hours until you've proven yourself."

"Brenda," LaDonna begged, "I recently signed a loan for a new car. I wish you would have warned me about my co-worker likeability."

Cold hearted Brenda continued, "I'm not a mind reader, LaDonna. How am I to know you bought a car? I'm warning you, that's why you're sitting here. Yes or no, do you agree to my proposition?" After delivering her heated statement, Brenda waved LaDonna's job application like a fan to cool herself.

"Yes, or no… I've spent enough of my day with you."

LaDonna tried to block off her emotions, to no avail. Gobs of pent up tears dripped onto her starched sailor collar. Brenda sat with her eyes riveted on LaDonna, and said, "Well, I'll give you two more seconds. Are you going to accept, or quit?"

"I'll try," LaDonna whispered between her sobs. Once again, she was being treated like a doormat, abused like her mother abused her, like Pete ravished her and Leon abandoned her.

In an unlikely move, Brenda stood up and offered to shake hands. LaDonna didn't reciprocate. Brenda accepted LaDonna's missing hand as payment for bad employment news, and said, "I know you LaDonna, you have gumption and you can be exactly the type of employee the Bountiful will someday be proud of, both at the stern and bow of our ship."

But it wasn't gumption LaDonna's mind was festering with as she stood up to leave, it was poison.

"So, it's settled, LaDonna, you'll begin part-time employment one week from today, when Scott leaves the floor."

*****

Brenda's bashing had left her stunned, weak, and beaten below ground level. Her earlier decision to do away with Brenda's style of evil now took precedence. She dug out a crucifix that had belonged to her mother and as usual the object brought her to a terrible mountain of sorrow, to the brink of all that she could bear. She clasped the cross to her chest. If there was ever a doubt about her past executions today she was convinced that God had sent unworthy people into her life, and it was her duty, her responsibility, her calling, to dispose of them in order for His righteousness to prevail.

Day after day LaDonna began to size up Brenda's eccentricities, her mind held each nuance. The spectacular Bountiful cup with her name embossed in glittering gold was the only cup she would drink from, and she had to have it filled with 'fresh brewed coffee' the first drips out of a 'just' cleaned coffee maker. Brenda's fetishes harbored extreme quarks. LaDonna observed that Brenda was just as finicky when it came to her sweet platter. Only the cooks' just baked goods could be placed upon it. Tale was that she fired a few people who had the audacity to try and fool her. In the server's quarters LaDonna once overheard Cheri tell Rita of an incident. Cheri claimed that Brenda once spat her chewed contents, a mixture of cake and coffee. "Yuk! It splattered over her desk, I was elected to do the cleanup." Brenda had scolded Cheri and told her that the cake was old, and she was to make sure it never happened again… or else!

It was quite a show seeing employees jumping through hoops, fussing over Ms. Brenda, their queen bee. Usually, Cheri carried in her sweet tray and her newly brewed coffee. If Cheri wasn't onboard when Ms. Brenda was at the helm only one of her most prized managers had access to delivering her food. LaDonna wondered if Brenda suspected foul play, if she didn't, she should have.

Coffee seemed the best route to travel poison to Brenda. LaDonna used poison in a drink at the Capricorn Steak House, to kill a rat. She became wise to a longtime cook. He'd been selling drugs to minors and then enlisting them. He made a huge mistake by talking about his crime during work hours.

She had forgot a package in the back room and returned for it. Upon entering, she heard murmuring in a small storage cove. Larry the cook and another male. She planted her ear near the door hinges and learned that besides dealing drugs, Larry was also into trafficking child pornography.

LaDonna couldn't risk turning in Larry. No way did she want a crime ring stalking her, nor did she savor the idea of Larry escaping conviction, or being handed a reduced sentence for good behavior. At first opportunity, LaDonna handed Capricorn's sinner a glass of his favorite, sweet, lemony iced tea, with a splash of poison. When he didn't arrive at the steak house as scheduled, a well check discovered he was dead. Heart attack. No one suspected foul play.

The plan is to drop a dose of poison into the waters of Brenda's blue cup on a day when the Bountiful is extremely busy. She recalled that Cheri or the manager of choice is at times diverted. When that happens they momentarily walk away from her cup, return, and then carry it to the queen's abode. In that scenario, LaDonna would have a chance to ease over to Brenda's cup.

It was months before the play was on. She fiddled in her pocket for the handkerchief laced with a generous dose of death. On the pretense of sneezing, she lifted her hanky to cover her nose and then in a split second dropped the contents into Brenda's cup. She had a spoon and quickly stirred Brenda's coffee. If she had been noticed stirring Brenda's brew, she had an excuse. She purposely placed another cup of coffee near it, so she could exclaim, "Oh, I'm stirring the wrong cup."

The scene went off smoothly, in fact, too easy. Unknowingly, Cheri delivered Brenda's justice with a smile on her face. The day after LaDonna's most magnificent caper was her day off, and most likely, the day the evil Queen Brenda would die her rightful death. LaDonna envisioned a drive into the ghetto to buy heroin. A drug she usually avoided, but it would be her reward for a deed well accomplished.

About thirty-six hours after Brenda's ingestion, LaDonna's Kewpie phone jingled a sprightly tune. She answered.

"Hello?"

"Hello… LaDonna… its Cheri! Oh my God! Brenda is dead!"

"Oh my God, Cheri!!! Was she in an accident?"

"No, she became deathly ill and went home. Her condition worsened, she was rushed to the hospital where she died. Everyone's freaking out. The Bountiful is closed."

"Thanks for letting me know, Cheri. I'll pray for her family."

"She has no family. I'll call you as soon as I find out about the funeral arrangement. There's more… it came out that Brenda owned the Bountiful, she had kept that fact a secret."

Cheri began to baby-ball. "I'm so upset I can hardly function. My life, all our lives, are at a standstill. The Bountiful died with Brenda."

LaDonna hung up the phone and voiced to herself, 'Good riddance to bad rubbish dear Cheri, and good riddance to you and Rita too!' She sank down to her knees and said a prayer, "Thank you God for allowing me to do your will." Thrilled, she reached into her cupboard for a bottle of whiskey.

Brenda's funeral produced buckets of employee remorse, not for Brenda per se, but for the loss of a nice paying job. LaDonna strolled over to her former boss, resting stiff inside her perfect box. She knelt down, motioned the sign of the cross and lowered her warm face near Brenda's cold body that now matched her cold soul. "I hope you know what I did," she whispered to the corpse, "I did it for the people in this room, the ones you have hurt, and those you would have hurt. May God have mercy on you."

After Brenda's demise LaDonna took time to scout around for job openings. An exclusive dining club would soon be opening in New York City. The club was searching for highly skilled waitstaff. An acclaimed swiss chef, Anton Museman, was slated to run the kitchen. She called their number and set up an interview. After all, she was more than qualified. To disappear she'd need to jump her apartment lease.

While packing, the kewpie phone fell and smashed to pieces on the hardwood floor, causing a small pouch of poison to escape its hiding place. No way could she put humpty dumpty back together again. As she gathered the poison and the phone's remains into a trash bag, the loss of kewpie triggered an avalanche of crying.

Walking to the buildings dumpster a thought of God passed her mind. She set the bag down. Her hand scoured through kewpie's mess until her fingers located the satchel of poison. She placed it, temporarily, in her pocket.

LaDonna then shoved her belongings into the trunk of her prized car, seated herself at the wheel, revved the engine and screeched away. Turning onto the freeway, she bellowed at the top of her lungs, "Good bye California, hello, New York!"

Honeyguide
Eleanor Luke

The day I discovered the Honeyguide, I was seated in the front row at a zoology lecture. Wrapped in my old green duffle coat, I wore black fingerless gloves and a purple hand-knitted scarf.

Nineteen years old and no-one would say I was a beauty. But I'd been assured by the two boys I'd slept with since starting my degree that I had gorgeous eyes and a good pair of tits. I don't mean I was told by both boys at the same time. The sex, fast and fumbling, happened on separate occasions, and indeed, with each boy separately. Don't get the wrong idea about me. If anyone had even mentioned the word threesome, I would probably have thought they were referring to a triple-fingered Kit Kat.

I had a terrible cold on the day of the lecture and the contrast between the January air outside and the hot lecture hall had a disastrous effect on my nasal passages. I blew my nose hard, held my breath—as if that would help—and tried to focus on what the lecturer was saying.

'The Greater Honeyguide, otherwise known as the African Cuckoo, though a typical brood parasite in that she lays her eggs in other birds' nests, at times displays a remarkable, mutualistic understanding of humans…'

That was interesting enough, but what came next really spoke to me.

'However, the female Honeyguide can sometimes display brutal behaviour towards other females, destroying its own species' eggs to eliminate any competition…'

I connected instantly with the lecturer who was speaking so passionately about this murderous little bird and scribbled down questions I could impress him with. But then, my nasal congestion moved to another level.

I'd pinched a roll of toilet paper from the flat I shared and stashed it in my coat's oversized pocket. At regular intervals, I would tug on the roll, rip off a piece, and once used, place it in the empty pocket on the other side. I had quite a system going and I doubt, with hindsight, that the lecturer had even noticed me or my streaming nose. But then I tugged too hard on the stolen loo roll causing it to fly out of my pocket, except for a strip of tissue which remained firmly lodged around a toggle on my coat. The toilet paper began to unroll, coming to a standstill at the lecturer's feet.

He didn't notice at first. But as giggling spread around the lecture hall, he stopped and looked up from his papers. If I'd been quicker to react, I would have cut the tissue umbilical cord quickly. But the absurdity of the situation caused me to freeze.

He held up the toilet roll. 'Does this belong to anyone?'

I gave him a wide smile. 'I believe the paper trail leads back to me.' The entire audience howled with laughter.

At the end of the lecture, as the students were filing out, he gestured to me to come over to his desk. He was arranging his notes, his large hands smoothing the sheets of paper with slow strokes.

'Jason Duchenne.' He held out one of those hands to greet me.

'Melissa Hart. Pleased to meet you.' I allowed my hand to linger in his.

I was struck by how tall he was, a good head and shoulders above me. He was older than he'd appeared when I'd been sitting a few feet away fiddling with the loo roll. He had wavy, black hair, flecked with splashes of grey. Every now and again, he'd sweep back a couple of unruly locks. His dark complexion contrasted with his eyes which were the most intense shade of blue. *Robin's egg blue*, I decided, feeling pleased with the accuracy of my description. Though he seemed smartly dressed from a distance, up close I saw that beneath his dark grey blazer, he wore a T-shirt with a picture of a parrot emblazoned on the front.

'Did you enjoy the lecture?' He stood opposite me now.

'Very much,' I replied. 'I have a question, if I may.'

'Go ahead.'

'That African bird, the Greater Honeyguide, how does she destroy her rival's eggs?'

He gave a mischievous grin. 'Can't you imagine? They puncture the eggs with their beaks.'

He formed a beak shape with his long fingers and imitated the puncturing of the egg by making a hole with his fist and inserting his fingers in and out. The message was unmistakeable.

I smiled. 'Fascinating.'

'They're highly intelligent birds, you know. They've been known to develop mutually beneficial relationships with humans.'

'How so?'

'Well, they feed off beeswax. But to reach the wax, they need to get the hive open. How do you think they manage that conundrum?'

'Let me think.' I moved closer to him and picked a stray thread off the lapel of his blazer. 'If it were me, I'd find a strong man to help me.'

He hesitated, surprised by my boldness. 'Spot on,' he said, then took a step back. 'They guide men to the bee colonies. The men open up the hives to get the honey. Then the clever little buggers feast on the wax and larvae left behind.'

'Amazing that such a small creature should be able to manipulate a grown man,' I said at last.

He narrowed his eyes and thought for a while before answering. 'I'd never thought of it in those terms, but you're right.'

He asked me why I'd chosen to study zoology and nodded when I gave my explanations. I knew he wasn't really listening though. His gaze kept dropping to my chest. I should have been outraged, but all I could think about was how he could cup one of my large breasts in a single strong hand. He ran his fingers through his dark hair and asked me whether I was in the habit of carrying loo roll around. I noticed the ring on his finger but pretended not to. We chatted for a while and he pressed something into my hand as I got up to leave. It was a packet of tissues. He always had a sense of humour. I'll give him that.

*****

After the lecture hall incident, whenever our paths crossed on campus, Jason took to waving a white hanky in my direction. He would find reasons to summon me to his office during tutorial hours and engage me in conversations. I'd let him play the role of wise university professor while I played mine, lowering my chin slightly and casting my eyes downwards. Slowly, I'd glance up at him, under fluttering lashes. His speech would become breathless and he would shift in his seat. It was just a question of time.

One evening, as I was walking back to my flat, a heavy carrier bag dangling off each arm, someone called out from the other side of the street.

'Need some help with those bags?' Jason grinned then whipped a white hanky out of his pocket, waving it in anticipation of his surrender.

He crossed the street and signalled to me to give him a bag. 'I was just on my way to an Indian shop round here. They have ingredients you can't get anywhere else.'

'Yeah, right. Some coincidence, Mr Duchenne.' I smiled at him. A fine drizzle was falling and in the dying light of day, the rain dressed him in a silver sheen. How unreal it felt to be face to face with the man I fantasised about all the time. It also felt so right.

'I swear that's the truth! I'm not a stalker you know!' He waved the hanky frantically, a grin on his face. 'Honest!'

I giggled and he looked relieved.

'I'll help you with the bags, then I'll be on my way.'

'To the Bombay Emporium, right?' I plucked a name for an Indian shop out of the ether.

'Right.'

As I led him back to my flat, I allowed myself to bask in his glow. And him in mine.

We stopped at the front gate of the Georgian townhouse, once a mansion, but now divided into low-rent student flats.

'Thanks so much for helping me, Mr Duchenne,' I said, enjoying the pantomime.

He smiled and cleared his throat. 'So, Melissa, do you live with other students from uni, then?'

'Yep. A couple.'

He glanced at the house. 'I'll be getting home then…I mean, to the Bombay Emporium.' He looked so disappointed.

'My flatmates are post-grads. Geology. Off on some field trip. God knows where,' I replied. 'Probably shagging each other behind a rock.'

He took a while to react, as if he unsure whether to be shocked or amused. I made a circle with my thumb and forefinger and poked my fingers in and out of the hole, a sweet smile on my face. He roared with laughter. 'They're not here, then?' he said when he'd finished laughing.

'Nope.' I offered him a drop of hope which he lapped up greedily.

'Need someone to help you unpack those bags?'

'Why not?'

I opened the door, threw my bag on the floor and gestured to him to do the same. Then I took his hand and led him upstairs to my room. He looked a little surprised at the way I took control, but he let himself be guided.

'So this is where you spend your time, is it? Is this where you come up with all those offbeat ideas you like to fill your essays with?'

He looked around the small room, eyes moving from the kettle on the bedside table, to the dream catcher at the head of my bed and the sketches I'd decorated the far wall with. He walked over to study the drawings up close.

'Did you draw all of these?' he asked.

He glanced around counting how many I'd stuck to the wall.

'Yes. I sketched them.'

'They're very impressive….and all of birds.'

'Not just birds,' I said, twiddling a lock of hair around my finger. 'They're brood parasites. The ones you mentioned in the first lecture.'

I took hold of the index finger of his left hand, and as I tapped each sketch with it, we reeled off the names of the birds in unison.

The Plaintive Cuckoo, the Shiny Cowbird, the Brown-Headed Cowbird, the Grey-Bellied Cuckoo, the Asian Koel….

We reached the last one.

'The Greater Honeyguide,' we said, our lips close but not touching.

I leaned in to kiss him, but he stepped back. He reached out and smoothed back the lock of hair that had come loose from my ponytail. 'Not yet,' he whispered. 'I need to see you first.'

He led me over to the bed and undressed me slowly. I observed him, starkly aware of my youth and his years. Watching him take each garment off me, with some assistance, and the lustful expression on his face, caused me to feel giddy with excitement and the sense of my own importance. He took his shirt off and unzipped his trousers revealing how hard I'd made him. As I lay on my bed watching this much older man cast his gaze over my body, my perfectly shaped breasts and smooth, cellulite-free thighs, I knew I was the sexiest woman he'd made love to in a very long time.

When he entered me, I was the most powerful woman on Earth and Jason was all mine.

*****

For the next few months, we became one and consumed each other with an energy so powerful that it is little wonder I can remember hardly anything else. We were together as much as Jason's circumstances allowed. His job gave him freedom as there were always seminars to go to in other universities. I became used to him appearing at my door in the early evening. My flatmates were rarely there till later. But if one of them happened to be in, I'd sneak out and we'd have sex in his car parked on a backstreet or on the industrial estate on the outskirts of town. He seemed to enjoy these encounters, the risk of being caught ever present. But I preferred to have him in my room as much as possible. I wanted to savour Jason, let his sweet taste linger in my mouth, to see every inch of him. But more than that, I needed him to see every inch of me.

Jason was with me all the time. And I mean *all* the time. It was as if we'd injected each other with a tiny bit of our own consciousness. In my head, I would have the conversations I was unable to have with him in real life because we only ever seemed to find time for sex. Whatever I did as I went about my day, however insignificant or inappropriate, I did it imagining that Jason was watching me. It was all for his benefit.

I lived and breathed Jason.

There were close scrapes of course. Literal ones, like the time his wife noticed carpet burns on his knees. And other emergencies, like when she found a condom in his jacket pocket. Jason was adamant he'd not put it in there. Adamant when he confronted me, I mean. It was not my intention to make things difficult for him. But I needed to give him a nudge. His wife began to demand explanations for everything. She was always phoning and interrupting us. She'd make him feel bad whenever he arrived home late, interrogating him and turning on the waterworks.

One evening while I was lying on my bed, watching him get dressed, I spoke.

'Jason?'

'What, babe?' he replied, without looking.

'When are you going to leave her?'

His jeans were round his ankles, having never been completely removed. He'd been about to pull them up. The decisive tug never came, though. He spun round to face me, startled, and fell flat on his face in a tangle of trouser legs, immediately scrambling back up again. He reminded me of a Jack-in-the-Box and I almost laughed. I stifled it though, trying to keep a serious expression because I *was* deadly serious.

'Leave who?' he asked, red-faced.

'Your wife, Jason,' I replied. 'Carol*ine*.' I put special emphasis on the end of her name, knowing I was pronouncing it incorrectly.

'You think I'm going to…. I mean, we can't carry on like this of course. But not right now. I mean, not at the moment,' he whined. 'You know we're trying IVF again. I told you about that.'

Yes, indeed, Jason *had* told me about that. He'd gone into rather a lot of tiresome detail about the heartache of the five miscarriages Carolyn had suffered and the stress this had placed on their marriage. He once described having sex with her as like putting petrol in the car, except that the car never quite reached its final destination, juddering around before grinding to a halt and needing to be filled up again. I laughed so hard at the image that it took me a few minutes to realise Jason was not laughing at all. Instead, he sat there with a strange, twisted expression, somewhere between sheepish and embarrassed. I felt briefly repelled by what I now know was a first hint of weakness. But I didn't dwell. I finally understood the nature of our partnership. It was up to me to guide him to freedom.

What could be easier than slipping a condom into his pocket for Carolyn to find?

*****

As the end of the first year of my course approached, my patience was running thin. Though Jason hadn't said it yet, it was only a question of time before he went public about us. But everything in his life, and everyone, seemed to conspire to hold him back, to stop him from becoming free.

The main obstacle was selfish, spoilt, self-pitying Carolyn. Jason had told me she worked part-time for a solicitor in the coastal town where they lived. There were only a couple of solicitors listed in the phone book. So one Friday afternoon, I drove to the town in my old car. I went to a coffee house across the road from her office, bought a large cappuccino and waited.

Half an hour passed before a blonde woman came out of the stuccoed, Regency-style building and walked down the steps. I knew Carolyn was blonde because after the carpet burn incident, coupled with the condom situation, Jason became quite fixated on making sure that nothing could give him away. This included careful shaking out of his clothing to rid it of any of my dark hairs. I also knew she was taller than me because Jason had commented many times on how petite I was in comparison. It delighted him to be with a woman he could tower over. But what caused me to be certain it was her were the dark glasses she wore. Jason had told me about her photosensitivity. Another one of her precious traits, and on this blustery, grey day with a downpour about to begin, it had to be Carolyn. She was not entirely what I'd expected, mind you. A good few pounds lighter than the description Jason had given me along with the IVF sob story. But I took my irritation out on the oversized coffee mug I hurled to the floor when nobody was looking.

I followed her for a while as she walked back to her car. She was good on her heels. She wore a long tan coloured coat, smart and practical. Her hair was tied back in a sensible ponytail with no stray hairs flapping in the wind. Yet there was something about the way she clutched her handbag a little too tightly and bowed her head almost imperceptibly that made me sure this confidence was a well-rehearsed act. I knew what I was dealing with now and that excited me. I tried to match my pace with hers, our feet pounding the ground in unison. My pulse was racing. I'd never felt adrenaline like that and all at once I understood what drove people to hunt innocent creatures. I felt alive. The slightest mistake and the beautiful pursuit would be over. I was careful to control myself, although exhilaration shot through me, sparks flying from the tips of my fingers. I began to feel myself rise, as if I'd sprouted wings. I knew it couldn't be happening but from above, everything, everyone looked small and insignificant. Trees became Bonsai versions of themselves, and parked cars resembled miniature wind-up toys. I could see Carolyn below, a little blonde doll marching through toy-town. I almost swooped down and caught her in my talons.

At last she reached her car, parked down a deserted back street. She was still unaware of my presence as I slid into an alleyway on the other side of the road. She fished around in her handbag for her keys. She found them then spun round looking in my direction. I held my breath and pushed my back hard against the wall, willing the bricks to absorb me. I knew she'd felt my gaze but she turned back to her car, opened the door and got inside. I heard the automatic locking system click down. Sensible woman, I thought.

As I watched her pull away in her neat little car, I felt like setting fire to my own.

*****

The summer vacation was approaching and I was more restless than ever. Whenever I sat down at my desk to study, I would manage to focus for about five minutes before the pages of scrawled notes would turn blank before my eyes. My mind would follow suit, emptying itself of any notion of course work or other tasks. I would grip my chair to stop myself floating away. The sensation I'd had the day I'd followed Carolyn was becoming more frequent.

My parents were expecting me home for the summer. They'd not seen me since Christmas and Dad had rung a couple of times to ask what my plans were. Returning home was out of the question. I was not the same person who'd left for university all those months back.

I needed Jason to tie up the loose ends.

He was busy with end of term activities, marking exams and hearing dissertations for the final year students. I was doing my best to be understanding but the reality was that I was beside myself with frustration.

I hadn't seen him for over a week, when finally, one afternoon, I bumped into him in town.

'Hey, Melissa!'

I tried to hide my irritation at the generic way he'd greeted me. Like he was a barista at Starbucks.

I smiled. 'Hello, Jason.'

'Doing some shopping, are we?'

I cringed at his use of the 'we' pronoun. '*I've* just been to pick up some photos.' I clutched the plastic folder close to my chest. It had been a bad idea to mention them as they were supposed to be a surprise. I wasn't sure what I'd do if he asked to see them.

I need not have worried. 'Cool,' he replied. 'We should get together soon.'

I gritted my teeth, infuriated by the strange way he was talking. Like I was just anyone. But I relaxed a little when he suggested coming round the next evening with some take-away Indian food. It would be my chance to give him the surprise.

It was a hot and humid June. I had a shower before he arrived and made quite an effort with my appearance. An expensive conditioner for my hair and a fruity smelling lotion for my body. I put on a short, sophisticated summer dress, a cornflower blue that contrasted perfectly with my dark hair and slight tan. My breasts looked larger than usual. As I studied myself in the mirror, I felt satisfied with what I saw. Perhaps a little turned on. I imagined the thrill Jason would feel when I opened the door and I momentarily allowed myself to imagine I was him. He wouldn't be able to take his eyes off me, like the first time we made love. He would realise he had to be with me.

Jason kept me waiting, though. He was an hour late when I heard a faint knock. I took a deep breath, opened the door wide and stood there, allowing him to feast his eyes on me.

He pushed past and trod on my bare foot in his haste. I was in agony but I countered the pain with more pain, biting my lip till it bled.

'What are you doing? Someone could've seen me,' he said.

'You're late,' I replied, more loudly than I'd intended.

'Am I?'

'And where's the food?'

'I didn't have time to pick anything up. There was a last-minute faculty meeting.' He walked over to the window and drew the curtains. 'I had a bottle in my office though.' He held out a bottle of Lambrusco.

I closed my eyes and took a deep breath. Something was wrong. This was not going according to plan. I couldn't understand why Jason was trying to derail the evening. He placed the bottle on my desk and fished his phone out of his pocket, checking for messages. It was as if I didn't exist. I figured he must be feeling stressed, so I resolved to make him feel better. I gave him the present, wrapped in white tissue paper. It had seemed like a good idea at the time, a nod to our private joke. But the package looked tatty now, like it had been wrapped by a four-year-old. What on earth had possessed me? My cheeks were burning.

'This is for you.' I handed him the present. A large chunk of the tissue paper stuck to the palm of my hand.

'A gift wrapped in loo roll. Well, that has to be a first.'

My chest went tight and I clenched my fists. I imagined tearing the remaining tissue off Jason's present and hurling the contents at him.

Instead, I closed my eyes, took another deep breath and smiled.

'I wanted you to understand how much you mean to me.'

As he unwrapped the gift, I tried to ignore his twisted expression. Why couldn't he just pull himself together? We both knew how this would end.

He opened the album. As he leafed through it, his blue eyes narrowed. Then they widened with each turn of a page, until they were bulging. I felt like I was watching a cartoon version of Jason. He looked so peculiar. I wished I could rewind, press play again and get the right reaction.

'All the photos are of me!' He stood there, mouth agape. 'But, when did you take them?'

He was overdoing the disbelief now.

'Have you been spying on me?' he asked.

Spying was a foolish choice of word. The photos were almost always of him in public places. Leaving his house in the morning, sipping coffee at the refectory, chatting with his colleagues on the way to the lecture hall, stopping to buy cigarettes at a newsagent, coming out of a bank, parking his car outside his house. Alright, there was one of him sitting at his computer in his living room. I couldn't resist. And then there were the photographs of him in post-coital doze. But they were taken in my own bed and in my room. I felt indignant at his shock. I'd put so much work into this.

'What the hell is wrong with you, Melissa? This isn't normal behaviour!' He spat the words at me.

'Not normal behaviour? Really? I would say it's not normal behaviour to be fucking one of your students while your wife's at home trying to decide what colour to paint the nursery!'

'Don't even mention my wife! I was clear from the beginning. I told you I wasn't leaving her. It would kill her!'

I had to suppose that was just a figure of speech.

'I wanted to show you how much I love you. That's all.' By now tears were rolling down my cheeks, almost unsummoned.

'Love?' he said. 'Who said anything about love?' His face crumpled.

'I know you love me, Jason,' I said quietly.

'Melissa, listen to me,' he walked over and put a hand on my shoulder. 'I'm very fond of you. But love? I *love* my wife.'

The extent of his delusion became clear. I removed his hand from my shoulder and faced him. I needed to look him in the eye.

'Jason, you don't love your wife,' I said slowly. 'I will admit that she's in better shape than you led me to believe…' I stopped abruptly wondering whether he was following everything I'd said.

He exploded. 'You've been spying on Carolyn?'

'Only the once,' I edged away from him. 'Well, maybe twice…'

'What the hell is wrong with you? This isn't normal. Do you hear me? This is what crazy people do! Stalkers!'

'Stalkers' was what did it. I threw myself at him, pounding with my fists, hissing and spitting. It was not supposed to be like this. He'd ruined everything.

Jason allowed me to vent my fury for a while. I was much smaller and weaker than him. I suppose it must have been comical to see. Then he grabbed hold of my wrists and threw me hard on the bed. For a moment, I actually thought he was going to make love to me. Instead, he spoke.

'It's over. Do you hear me, Melissa? Over!'

He kicked the album to one side and left.

*****

For a while, I was furious. I didn't leave my room for two days. I didn't eat or sleep. I barely drank, except for the bottle of wine Jason had brought with him that evening. When I finished it, I smashed it against the wall and imagined what I could do with the pieces. I pressed one particularly jagged piece against my thumb, to test its usefulness and marvelled at how little it hurt to bleed. I caught sight of my reflection in the glass, distorted and with a red hue. I didn't recognise the defeated creature looking back at me.

Jason had made a mistake and despite everything that had happened, I could forgive him.

*****

The end of term was approaching fast and Jason was busier than ever. I'd given up any idea of passing my exams. But that was the least of my concerns. I needed to find a way of letting Jason know everything was going to be alright. I would help him to understand me better. All I needed was a way to get his attention.

He refused to see me during his tutorial times, and although I thought he was behaving childishly, I could handle it. I would turn up at his office every day at 4.00 just in case. The first few days, he ignored me, barging past and slamming his door. After four days of this, he softened.

'How are you doing?'

'I forgive you, Jason.' I spoke calmly and smiled to show I understood.

'You forgive me?' For a moment, he looked as if he was going to burst out laughing, but I think he realised how out of place that would be.

'You forgive me. Well, thank you, I guess.' He made his way to the office, but stopped short of going in. He turned, that old twisted expression etched on his face.

'Well, I suppose I'll see you around then,' he said.

I held his gaze and waited before replying. 'I told you… I forgive you, Jason.'

'I heard that and I'm very grateful for your forgiveness.'

He was avoiding eye contact and I had to resist the urge to scream. I began to float upwards, with Jason assuming clockwork toy proportions. I imagined tossing him into my rucksack. Leaving him at the bottom, with the biscuit crumbs and old receipts. I would let him out once he'd had time to reflect.

'I thought we could have a meal tonight. Would you like that?' I said.

He opened his mouth, closed it, opened it again. I stared back at his idiotic fish gestures and, for a moment, I doubted he was all there.

'That's not a good idea. I mean, that's definitely not going to happen. I told you, we have to stop this. It's over. We had our fun and we weren't found out, were we?'

I left without responding. This was going to require more effort than I'd envisaged. But I knew he could be persuaded and I was almost certain I knew how to do it.

*****

I waited for a day I knew Jason would be tied up at the faculty until late. I knew Carolyn was usually home by 5.00. I went there with every intention of talking calmly to her. It was a question of explaining to her that her marriage was over. That she'd lost her husband somewhere in between the visits to the fertility clinic and the outings to Sainsbury's. It was no wonder the man felt unfulfilled and bored. I realise now that taking the photo album with me could be interpreted as malicious, but I wanted her to see what he meant to me. To see what it looked like when a woman devoted herself to a man. All I wanted was for her to understand.

She'd seemed a little on edge when she opened the door and I introduced myself. 'Hi, Carolyn. I'm Melissa Hart, one of Jason's students. Can I come in?'

I didn't wait for a reply. It was best to get this over and done with. I pushed past.

'Jason isn't here. I can take your number and ask him to ring you when he gets back.'

'He has my number,' I said.

She was trotting behind me as I made my way to the kitchen. The mental plan of the house I'd managed to put together from my photographic outings was remarkably accurate.

'I said Jason isn't here. Would you mind leaving, please? I have things I need to be getting on with.'

I sat on a high stool at the breakfast bar. She was maintaining a safe distance, but a globule of her saliva landed on the end of my nose. It made me nauseous. I wiped it off with my sleeve and tried to compose myself. I was there for a reason and I could not waste this opportunity.

'I know this may seem a bit strange. Me turning up like this. Sit down. I need to explain.'

I gestured to the stool opposite and smiled. With some hesitation, she obeyed.

I put the album down in front of me. She reached over for it.

'Not yet!'

I slammed my hand down on hers and she yelped. She was afraid. I would have to play this carefully. If I'd been her, though, I would have made a run for it. It was her curiosity, as well as stupidity, that kept her there. She must have known that she wasn't going to like the contents of the album. But the temptation was too great. All those nights Jason had returned late or not at all, the carpet burns, the condom, the stray hairs and the scent of a woman she knew was not her. All of her worst fears were about to be confirmed. As painful as that was going to be, at least she would know she was not going crazy. I was doing all of us a favour.

'Look, Carolyn, Jason's a good man. You know that, don't you?'

She looked at me, eyes wide, and opened her mouth to speak.

'Please!' I put my hand up to stop her. 'You must let me finish. It won't take long. Jason has given you the best years of his life. He's been patient with you … overly patient if you ask me.' I paused and fixed my stare on her, like a stern mother chastising an uncooperative child. She stood up, red-faced and trembling.

'Oh, for God's sake! I was going to explain to you that he doesn't love you anymore, but since you are behaving so rudely, just take a look for yourself.'

I pushed the album over to her. I'd made some graphic additions to the version Jason had seen, but it had to be done. And there was no denying that the photos were beautiful. How could they not be?

Each page she turned heightened my satisfaction. My prey was there in front of me about to be devoured. But then it felt too easy. When she started to cry, I had to do something. I reached into the deep pocket of my duffle coat. She wasn't even looking at me when I took it out and placed it on the table.

'I'm pregnant, Carolyn. I am going to give Jason the child you couldn't give him. He doesn't need you anymore.'

I smiled and gestured towards the pregnancy test strip. I was surprised by how quickly I'd become pregnant. I'd only stopped taking the pill for a couple of weeks before Jason had his little blip about not seeing me. But our child wanted to be born, a child of love. Not like the unborn creatures Carolyn had presented him with. The mistakes, the little tragedies, the guilt trips that kept *my* man by *her* side for so long.

And that was when she ran for it. A bad decision, as it turned out. I was smaller, younger, more agile. I could see she was heading for the front door. I hadn't managed to lock it. I sprinted past her and threw myself against the door, turning the key and putting it in my pocket. So she ran upstairs. I followed close behind. I could easily have grabbed her, but I didn't want to risk her falling on me. I had our baby to think about. I didn't want to kill her. I just wanted her to calm down and agree that I'd won. If she'd done that, if we could have reached some kind of agreement, it would have been easier all round.

She ran to the bedroom and tried to close the door. But once again, I was too fast for her. She fell back on the bed. For an instant, I took in the scene before me. This was their room. The bed they shared. I could see Jason's burgundy checked shirt and tan trousers, the ones he'd worn the day before, hanging over a chair. The novel he was reading and a pair of his glasses on the bedside table. I felt so angry, so insulted. Repulsed by the thought that they had copulated countless times on the bed she was scrambling across, screaming. My prey in its final moments, terrified but unable to escape. I grabbed one of her ankles and pulled her towards me. I knew I didn't have long. After all, she was taller than me and, in theory, stronger. I punched her hard in the face. She was stunned. There was a lot of blood. I punched her again, in the stomach this time.

'Will you please be quiet, you stupid cow? Just be reasonable! For once in your life!'

She kicked me. It was enough to throw me off balance and she ran for it, through the door and onto the landing. I ran after her. She was heading for the stairs and that was when I knew what I had to do. I caught up with her and rammed her back with both of my hands, exerting more force than necessary. But I could afford no mistakes.

At last, she was quiet.

I was certain she was dead when I reached the bottom of the stairs and saw the unnatural angle her head had adopted in relation to the rest of her body.

There was no suffering.

I sat for a while, looking at her. Her eyes were open so I closed them. Then I yanked her wedding ring off and slid it down my finger.

The phone began to ring on the table by the front door. His number flashed up.

'Carolyn?'

'Jason, my love, Carolyn's gone. I had to get rid of her to make space.'

'What the fuck! Melissa? What have you done? Put Carolyn on the phone now!'

'She can't talk right now. But I have news,' I said, trying to inject some calm into the situation. 'We're having a baby, Jason.'

I surveyed my work while he got his head round the news. He was screaming. It was a lot for him to take in all at once.

 I should have been annoyed that for the first time in history, it had been left to the Honeyguide to destroy the hive herself. Instead, I felt proud. I was a living, breathing example of evolution.

'You crazy bitch! I want to speak to my wife!'

At last, I spoke the words I'd waited so long to say.

'Jason, I *am* your wife.' The words slid from my mouth as easily as the ring onto my finger. 'Won't you come home now and have some honey?'

Matters of Assurance
Momodou Bah

This was the information available to the public: The man's name was Charles Millar, thirty-eight years of age and married. He had two children, Emily and Michael, whose pictures and snippets of video caught by cameramen near the family's home were shown during the news coverage a few days before. There was also the mother, Cheryl, who had clutched the children's hands while she furiously battled past the vulture-like reporters to the waiting car across the street. It was reported that Charles was Cheryl's second husband, and the sorrow and loss she must be going through was also briefly discussed on the news—her first husband had died in a car crash just three weeks after their marriage, and now her second husband, although married much longer, had been murdered.

The police had also made a televised statement: The victim, Charles Miller, was found a few streets away from where he lived with his family. He had been stabbed multiple times in the stomach and back. The motive of the killing was unknown; the killer himself, because it's always a *he*, was unknown, and this particular fact, despite their futile attempts at reassuring the family and themselves, doesn't seem likely to change anytime soon—on top of an unestablished motive, there were no fingerprints, no DNA, no weapons of any sort at the crime scene, and former-friends, co-workers and acquaintances that were known to be minor or serious adversaries to the victim, all had strong alibis.

Nothing was known thus far in the investigation, now exactly two days after the killing; but it was hoped that the line of enquiries around the area, most importantly in the street that the crime took place, would be the breaking point for the police to, if not get a name or a description of the killer, then at least a clear picture of what happened that night, whether that be a before or after recollection from eyewitnesses.

Now it all depended on them, the eyewitnesses, if in fact anyone did see something.

But I believe that someone in fact did, and yesterday, once most of the police had cleared from the crime scene, I went to a home which stood opposite from where the body was found and asked the woman who answered the door if I could interview the old man who lived there. It's in connection with the murder, I said, but the woman said that the old man was due to be interviewed by the police rather than a reporter and insisted I go away. But after some much talking and attempted bribery, none of which went anywhere, the old man finally rolled to the door in his wheelchair and, after studying me for a moment, smiled and held out his hand and accepted without any further questions.

*****

The restaurant was a few minutes' drive from where I lived and from where the old man lived. I arrived first. After waiting for about ten minutes, I saw the woman who had answered the door roll the old man into the restaurant and on to where I sat.

'Thank you for coming,' I said.

'No problem,' the old man said. He turned and addressed the woman: 'Thank you, Mary. Hopefully this won't take long. I'll call you once we're ready.'

'You don't want me to stay with you?' Mary asked.

'You can wait over there.' The old man pointed at a far corner in the restaurant. 'This will be a private matter, I think.' He looked at me and added, 'For now, anyway.'

Without further questions and delay, Mary walked over and sat down where the old man had pointed out.

'My name's Bill, by the way. I don't think you asked that yesterday.'

'Oh, yes, I didn't,' I said. 'And my name's Andrew. I really appreciate that you came in today. I asked many others, but once they told me that the police already talked to them, the door was slammed into my face before I could go on. Sometimes being a reporter is hard.'

'So, you're a reporter, huh?' Bill asked.

'Yes, work for the Echo. And I hope there's some valuable information in you somewhere, because there's a lot riding on me getting details on this story.'

At this, Bill had an amused look on his face. 'So you think I have something valuable to reveal?'

'We reporters are taught to have faith and hope for the best wherever we can, no matter the circumstances.'

'Well, then, I guess I can rehearse what I'll be telling the police tomorrow.'

'You're talking to them tomorrow?'

'Yep, tomorrow morning, actually.'

'Well, before that I hope to get the first scoop of information.'

'Right. Well then, we don't want Mary waiting long,' Bill said. 'Ask away.'

I looked over at Mary for a second, whose space at the corner was directly beyond where we sat. Her shoulders were hunched, her face set in a permanent frown, and her dark eyes looked on constantly and unflinchingly in my direction, as if frozen in one gaze. Her nose dilated, in, out, in, out, which brought her whole upper body moving on along with it. It was the image of contempt and hostility, for me in general or for my job, I didn't know.

I turned back to Bill and started interviewing him.

'Because you said you hope to rehearse everything you'll be saying tomorrow, can you recall everything you saw, every detail, whether small or substantial. Before or after this crime took place.' Before he responded, I produced a notebook and a pen from my pocket and placed it in front of me. 'Start from the beginning,' I added.

'From the beginning…,' Bill began. 'Well, first thing is that I always sit at my bedroom window. It's a pleasant substitute for when sleep doesn't come easy. I would sit there at nights and think about all the wrong or right things in my life. The lovely things mostly, really. Other times I only sit and gaze into the darkness. Might sound strange, but it is quite lovely for an old man like me.

'Anyway, that night when the murder took place, I was doing exactly that—gazing into the darkness. It was like any other night—peaceful and quiet, making it easier for me to think. Then, out of nowhere, when I turned my head for a second or so, I saw something down on the road. Movement. I didn't know what it was at first. So I continued looking, and slowly, as my eyes adjusted, I started making out silhouettes down there in the dark.'

'Silhouettes?' I asked, scribbling in my notebook.

'Yes,' Bill said. 'Two, actually.'

'Descriptions?'

'Oh, no descriptions, I'm afraid.'

I looked up. 'What do you mean?'

'You see, the lamppost by my house is busted. Has been for several days. Those two silhouettes were inside that darkness, so I couldn't see any faces.'

'Nothing? Nothing at all?'

'Nope,' Bill said.

'What happened after, then?'

'Well, slowly, it became clear that something…that something was happening. So I quickly pushed my already open window a little bit more and that was when I heard the muffled groans of someone down there. I was about to say something when everything just stopped. I continued looking and I started thinking—now I know it's a silly thought—that, you know, teenagers were down there and had stopped because they heard the sound of the window opening.'

'Teenagers?'

'Yeah. You know, doing teenage things out there in the late night.' Bill smiled. 'I hope you know what I mean.'

'So you thought teenagers were what… being indecent down there?'

'I guess. Look, nothing gave me reason to believe that it was murder, all right? I mean, you couldn't just jump to that conclusion out of nowhere without being given blatant evidence.'

'Oh. All right.' My thoughts swirled: Was he telling the truth right now, or was he playing with me? 'What happened after?'

'Ahh, well,' Bill said, looking to the side, as if in deep thought. 'Oh, yes—the silence continued until about thirty or so seconds later. Then, while I was still staring into the darkness, expecting something to happen, one of the silhouettes got out of the darkness and made his way out the street. He had a hood over his head, and his hands were in his pockets.'

'No description here as well?'

'Just told you—black hood over his head and hands in pockets.'

'And what about the other silhouette? You said there were two.'

'By that time I had made up my mind,' Bill said. 'Teenagers being naughty and indecent. Like I said, there was no way I could simply jump to a murder conclusion. No way. I just thought that the other silhouette probably went the opposite way, and I didn't realise. Now I know I was completely wrong.'

'And that's it?' I said. 'That's your statement of what you saw that night?'

'Yep. You think it would assist the police in anyway?'

Silence fell over us. We both leaned back in our chairs. Bill's eyes darted around the restaurant, scanning the place, avoiding my eyes. The occasional glances my way was to the notebook next to me, and he glanced at that for half a second, as if trying to read it but not daring to, then he would look another half second to my face before looking around us again. Something was not right.

'Okay, Bill,' I said, capturing his attention again. 'I have mixed feelings right now. You know, before you sit down and talk to an eyewitness, sometimes it helps to get a little background, you know? That's what we're taught, and I use the skills I learnt well.'

'What do you mean?'

'Well, first off, I don't think you're being upfront with me right now. You see, I asked the person who lives directly opposite you. That individual said that if anyone could have seen something it would be you.'

'Who said that?'

'He didn't tell me his name. The person who lives directly opposite you on the other side of the street.'

Bill looked off for a second, seeming to be in deep thought. Then he said, 'I already said what I saw that night.'

'You know, I don't believe that. I don't think you're completely opening up right now.'

'And it's because of what the man living opposite me—directly opposite— told you?'

'I asked about the lighting, actually,' I said, leaning closer to him. 'I knew it would be a major factor in a crime late at night. And the man said that yes, the lamppost is broken but there would've been enough light for you to at least get more description than what you provided. And, correct me if I'm wrong, but wasn't your light on? Wouldn't that have assisted in your vision?'

Silence. Bill looked down at the table, as if something entrancing suddenly caught his attention. He stared for about ten seconds before looking up. 'I told you everything I saw. I omitted and made up nothing.' He seemed to be choosing his words with such care that I doubt his mind jumped anywhere else other than his next words. 'The light's not good enough for me to see anything distinctly. And no, the light in my room didn't assist in anyway.'

'I'm sure that man I spoke to lived there long enough, even after the bust lamppost, to see what it looks like in the night. And considering the desperate scale of this murder, and the fact that the murderer is still out there, I don't think he would be lying to me.'

Instead of answering, Bill studied me with what appeared to be great care. His eyes darted this way, that way, up to my dark unkept hair and down again. But mostly, they zeroed in on my eyes. They stayed there, staring, his expression blank and unchanged, for ten seconds, twenty, thirty, until finally I got uncomfortable.

'Is everything okay?' I asked.

He blinked once, as if the hypnotism which seemed to have captured him finally released him. 'All I saw I told you, okay?' Bill said. 'There's nothing else.'

'What are you hiding?' I said. 'Don't you understand the urgency of the case? Or is it something else? Did you know the man? Are you an acquaintance, a friend? Is that it, because if it is it'll do you well to let on right now? Just tell me what you know, without omitting or making things up.' I paused and leaned across to him. 'Bill, who else lives with you in your house?'

Bill started wheeling his wheelchair backward.

'Wait. What're you doing?'

'I think this interview is over,' Bill said, now gesturing to Mary.

'I haven't got what I wanted.' I stood up. 'Once you tell me who was there then you can go.'

Mary was at his side now, glaring at me. 'Everything okay, Bill?' She asked.

He stared at me again, though this time only for a second. 'Take me home.'

Without a word, Mary grabbed the back of the wheelchair and began turning Bill around to face the door. Then he was being wheeled away.

'You know I can tell the police this, right?' I called after them. 'You could get into trouble, Bill. Just tell me who you saw?'

But by that time Mary had rolled him out the restaurant.

It was clear, as soon as I introduced the information the man who lived opposite him gave, that he wasn't being truthful with me. It occurred to me that he was rehearsing, like he had mentioned at the start, the perfect lie, a way to flatten the truth and cementing the false testimony in his mind, which he would then pass on to the police. They were not likely to fuss over the lighting, and even if they were, they would probably forget about it if he let on about the lamppost. But why? That was the main thought. Why was he omitting what he really saw? What was he hiding, and what right and courage did he have to hide it? It didn't make sense. Which, I guess, was the reason why I broke into his home later that night.

*****

I waited in my car until the trickle of people walking past, once coming in groups and passing by incessantly, finally slowed and soon only one or two passed every five minutes or so. It was late at night. My car was parked at the end of Bill's street, where the murder took place. Once a couple staggered past my car holding each other for support and laughing for whatever reason, I peered at the rear-view and watched as they dwindled away. No one else was coming my way. I looked through the windshield and again no one was coming. I got out and walked into the street and up to the house.

He was right—the lamppost by his house was busted. If someone were standing here, no one would be able to see them because of the darkness surrounding the area, and the closest lamppost was a good few metres away. But since I was here, I decided to go through with my plan.

I glanced around. No one was coming into the street. Still covered by the darkness, I scanned around to see if any blinds were open, any that were stirring, but found none. Not even Bill's blinds were open this night. And with that I quickly picked the lock to Bill's front door and slowly made my way in.

It was a quick reconnaissance I had planned, just to find out if Bill was telling the truth about whether he only saw a silhouette or a face. I silently made my way up the stairs, trying hard to keep on the sides so as not to step fully on a creaking stair. I succeeded. I stopped for a while, listening and looking to see if any lights were left on, perhaps under the gap of the doors. After a full minute, nothing happened.

Knowing the window he claimed he was at, I walked over to the door facing that side of the street and silently opened it. I expected to notice stirring on the bed or a bulge under the covers, any sign that someone was sleeping there; but as I entered the room I noticed nothing. I stopped walking again, listening. Nothing again. All that remained now was to inspect whether a face could be clearly seen from this window or not. If not, I walk out of here and forget about all this; if yes, however, Bill must endure another round of questions, this time a more thorough and vigorous examination. I already knew that the former was in his best interest.

At the window, I parted the blinds slightly and looked out. He was right— from here, you couldn't see anything where the body was found. Darkness completely shrouded that one area like a large drape. I nodded, satisfied, and turned to leave.

That was when the phone started ringing. Only a second or two was wasted, in which I was considering the other people in the house, who might hear it. I lunged for it and picked it up. It was an old type of telephone, which meant I couldn't ring it off without picking it up. And I was just about to do that, slamming it down and bolting from here, when Bill's unmistakable voice came though.

'Hello, Andrew?' he said.

My mouth was frozen; no words came out.

'I know it's you, Andrew,' Bill said, 'I saw you walking to my house from the start of the street. And if you don't believe me, look out the window again. Straight opposite this time.'

So I did, as if controlled like a puppet. I parted the windows, again slightly, and peered out. And there, the very opposite house, the blinds were now parted fully, and Bill was sitting there on his wheelchair, a phone plastered to his ear.

'Nothing is stolen,' I blurted. 'I only came to check if you were telling the truth about what you saw.'

'Look, Andrew, I don't care for that. I need to explain something quick. All right?'

I was lock-mouthed again.

'I realised when you said you spoke to the man who lived right opposite my house,' Bill went on. 'That was your mistake. The person who lives opposite my house is my carer, Mary. Close with her family, which makes it easier to come over if I need anything. Maybe if you hadn't mentioned it, I wouldn't have suspected. You see, I was telling the truth: I only saw a man walking away with a hood over his head and hands in his pockets. I didn't see a face, nothing to identify him. But you didn't know that, or at least wasn't absolutely sure. That lack of knowledge gripped you. It was all a matter of assurance, wasn't it, to dispel those doubts that gripped you? Same for me. So I decided to stay at Mary's tonight, just to check my theory. I thought it was all ridiculous until I saw you walking into the street with that same hoodie over your head.'

'I don't know what you're talking about,' I said as calm as I could. 'Now—'

'Can you see those cars driving near the house?' Bill asked.

I had no other choice but to look.

'Good luck,' Bill said, and was gone.

The police had driven in silently and in tandem, like a group of ninjas, undetectable and inconspicuous as they drove into the street. Then the sirens came on, shattering their concealment, and blue and red lights filled the night sky.

Nude With Snow Geese
Eve Fisher

Up here in Laskin, South Dakota, we take our wildlife very seriously. Most of us plan our whole year around the hunting and fishing seasons, and the only real division is whether you go ice-fishing or not. My personal stand is toleration: just because a man chooses to sit hunched over a small hole in the ice out on the middle of Lake Howard in a blizzard, doesn't mean he's not a decent citizen. Maybe you wouldn't want him in the family, but that doesn't mean you can't help him thaw out over a drink at the Norseman's Bar. Especially if he's buying.

And we've never had any of those animal-rights activists, other than the yearly crop of students protesting against that and everything else their elders do. There's something that hits them in high school, makes them crazy. This year they're piercing themselves something awful; you can't even look at them down at the Tastee-Freeze without wondering how in the world they can stand to eat ice-cream with all that metal on their tongues… But they get over it, and the holes will close up and heal over, which is more than you can say for a tattoo.

Anyway, we all hunt and fish, and talk about hunting and fishing, and we buy pictures of hunting and fishing. Laskin's the proud home of Earl Nelson, who as anybody can tell you is one of the top wildlife artists of all time. His *Snow Geese Over Lake Howard* has sold thousands of prints. And the original of his *Snow Geese Sunrise* hangs in the courthouse.

Or rather, it used to. See, what happened was, well, remember I was talking about high school students? Well, back a few years ago, one of them, boy named Dave Jacobsen, turned out to be a pretty good artist. Wouldn't think it to look at him. Big, burly kind of guy, and half-cousin to the Davison clan, so you wouldn't expect him to have any interest in any art other than maybe a little chainsaw carving on the side. My neighbor, Mr. Gustafson, did a real nice chainsaw carving of a squirrel on a stump. Course the squirrel's kind of big, but when you're working with a chainsaw, you can't get much fine detail going.

Anyway, Dave did real well at art in high school, and he could draw wildlife like you wouldn't believe. His mom, Mabel, took some of his work over to Earl to look at and Earl said he had promise. So Dave went on to art school, over in Minneapolis, but he came back home after a year. Said he didn't like the city, he didn't like the school, and he sure as heck didn't like his professors. That all might have been true, but he also couldn't afford it.

Dave came home and went to work down at the goose farm where, if nothing else, he could study goose anatomy in some detail. He painted at night. And come the State Fair, there was two paintings of Dave's right in there with Earl Nelson's, and you couldn't rightly tell which was whose, Dave's was so well done. Well, Earl got Best in Show and a couple of other prizes, as usual, but Dave won People's Choice for his *Slippery Morning*, which showed a flock of geese flying over a frozen Lake Howard, coming in for a landing, three or four of them already down and one of them landing just slightly wrong and sliding on the ice. I'll tell you what, you've never seen a goose look so embarrassed. I took one look at it and I started laughing fit to be tied. You betcha. I voted for it myself.

Now I'd always liked Earl, and I thought he was a nice enough guy, but you know, he didn't take it kindly. The vote or the picture. Said the picture was nothing but a joke. Which it was, but that was the point, wasn't it? And it was done real good. But Earl didn't approve of it, not one bit, and he talked about it all over town.

"There's some things you just don't joke about," Earl said. And a lot of people agreed with him or said they did.

The next dust-up was at the Geese Forever Club's annual October Pancake Feed and Art Show. Earl had a new original he was going to make prints of, "Freedom of the Snows," with snow geese and snow drifts and a sunrise and a line of bare cottonwoods to show where the lakeshore was. Real Christmasy, and people were signing up like crazy for a print. And Dave had an original that he said HE was going to make prints of, *Late Night, Early Hunt*, with snow geese and snow drifts and a sunrise and a line of bare cottonwoods, only different than Earl's of course, and a small group of hunters, who all looked a little hung-over but happy and were banging away at the geese and getting them. And his prints cost only twenty-five dollars, not a hundred and fifty like Earl's. So people were signing up for that one, too, though not when Earl could see.

But Earl knew. And he wasn't happy at all. Oh, he talked good, about how there was room for both of them in the wildlife art world. But you could tell it galled him. I mean, here was this whipper-snapper half his age showing up at all the same shows and getting lots of attention. And he kept winning The People's Choice.

"Oh, sure," Earl said, after Dave had won the popular vote at that winter's Governor's Awards, "people vote for his stuff. It's humorous, if you like that kind of thing. But do they buy it? No. Can he make a living at it? No. He's young, he'll learn. A gimmick'll attract attention, but if you want to stay in for the long haul, you've got to have more than that to make folks pay their hard-earned dollars for your work."

After the Governors' Awards, Dave kind of dropped out of sight and spent all his time working by day and painting by night. Then spring came, and he quit the goose farm and got himself booth space at every fair, festival, and art show in South Dakota. He had prints of *Slippery Morning* and *Late Night, Early Hunt* and about ten other paintings he'd done. Granted, they weren't big prints, like Earl's, done down in Sioux Falls on an off-set press or whatever they use these days. Dave was running them off his computer, so they were just eight and a half by eleven, and that's why he was charging so little. But they were all on glossy paper and looked real good, and every one of them had a joke in it or at least a smile, and at twenty-five bucks a pop, almost everyone could afford one. He did real well.

In the fall, he headed down to New Mexico, which is chock-full of artists and art galleries and art shows. He did real well there, too, because when he came back to Laskin in February there was no talk about going back to the goose farm. Instead, Dave rented himself an apartment and said his plucking days were over. He was just going to paint and do shows, like an artist should.

And Earl was looking more and more like a man with an ulcer. That March at the big Hunters' Exposition over in Mitchell, Earl still won top prize, but Dave once again won people's choice. Dave was heard to say that he'd rather have the people rooting for him than the judges. Earl went over and took a long look at Dave's painting and kind of sniffed. "Nice coloring," he said. "But the boy can't draw people worth a damn."

And then it got nasty.

Dave had been painting like crazy down in New Mexico and he wanted to show everybody all of what he had done. So he decided to have an open house at his place, and he invited everybody in town. Especially Earl. Of course we went. Curiosity and free food.

But I'll tell you what, we were all in for a shock when we walked in because right there, as you came in the living room, hanging over the couch was this big painting that was nothing else but Earl's *Snow Geese Sunrise*. The same one hanging in the courthouse. Only standing by the big cottonwood was no hunter in a camouflage hat and flak jacket, but a tall, blond woman with nothing on but a pair of gum boots. She didn't look particularly cold, either. Dave called it *Nude With Snow Geese*.

Earl about blew a gasket when he saw that, you betcha. He stood and stared at that painting and you could about see the steam coming out of his ears. The rest of us were wandering around, looking at the other paintings. There were maybe a dozen regular pictures of geese and pheasants flying around, but there was also a bunch titled *Nude Hunting Pheasant*, *Nude With Brook Trout*, *Nude With…* well, you get the picture. We certainly did. Dave had taken every hunting and fishing scene you can imagine and redone them with naked women in them. Poor Mabel could hardly tell where to look.

Dave was standing with a drink and a smile in front of *Nude With Brook Trout*, when Earl walked up to him, thumbed back at *Nude With Snow Geese*, and said, "That's my painting and you copied it."

"So sue me," Dave said.

Which is when Earl decked him. It barely rocked Dave, who was grinning from ear to ear, which, of course, just made Earl madder, so Joe Hegdahl got one side of him and I got the other, and wrestled him out of the place. Outside we let him go and he let loose with a string of obscenities that seemed to calm him down some.

"Yeah, sure," Joe said. "Come on, Earl, let's go get a beer."

Over a pitcher of red beer, Earl suggested that Dave had done it on purpose to spite him, that Dave had it in for him, and that Dave was going to come to a bad end. We agreed with all of it. Eventually we got enough beer poured down him to take him home on, and when we deposited him at his place he seemed likely to sleep.

It was the next day that the storm broke. It seems that one of the county commissioners had seen Dave's *Nude With Snow Geese*, and had instantly decided that Earl's painting, *Snow Geese Sunrise* had to come down off the courthouse walls because what if someone came in that had seen Dave's painting and started making fun? Or worse yet, got offended? Now if the logic of that escapes you, let me assure you it escaped all of us, but this particular county commissioner was known for escaping logic entirely, so that was nothing new. He was also known for a temper about as equable as that of a Rottweiler with a boil on its butt, so when he made a decision that didn't cost money most people found it easier to do whatever he said. Down the painting came.

Earl, who had just gotten his mind made up to approach the matter with dignity and decorum, blew another gasket. He went to see Jim Barnes about suing Dave, the county commissioners, the courthouse, and the county. He was hopping mad. Jim, who's honest as they come for a lawyer, told him he didn't have a case. Now Earl was boiling mad. That night he went down to the Norseman's Bar and, instead of holding forth to all and sundry and letting it all out, sat at the bar and brooded over boiler-makers, which never set well with him to begin with. Across the bar Dave was telling Ron, the bartender, what a great idea it was to mix nudes with wildlife.

"You get the best of both worlds. Every guy likes naked women, ever guy likes ducks. And geese and elk and everything else. So you put 'em together, you got sure fire sales. I'm going to make a killing this summer in prints. You betcha."

From across the bar, Earl's growls built up into a long howl of outrage. "You—" well, I can't print that. "You stole my painting! You stole my work!"

Dave looked across at him and said, "Mr. Nelson, the rules are that if you change something three ways, it's yours. I made it bigger, I did it in acrylic, and I put a naked woman in it. Tell me, how do you like the way *she's* drawn?"

Earl threw his glass across at Dave, who ducked, and glass and red beer went all over Ron's back wall.

Dave looked at the mess, said, "Get a life," and walked out of the bar.

Earl lunged across the bar, Ron grabbed Earl, and Dave was long gone. Ron worked on calming Earl down, and Earl claimed he was calmed down, but he was crazy mad. You could tell it the way he snarled and stumbled across the snow. And when he reached his truck, he wrenched the door open, pulled his thirty ought-six out of the gun rack, and laid it beside him as he drove off into the night.

Dave was shot that night in his studio, right in front of his new picture, *Nude Viewing Mount Rushmore.* (Dave was branching out a little.) He wasn't killed, but the bullet went through his arm, nicked his chest, and nailed George Washington on the nose. His model, Melody Turner, went shrieking out into the night, which is why Dave didn't bleed to death. A naked woman running down the street doesn't need to be screaming to attract attention in a small town, and the cops and an ambulance were at Dave's in fifteen minutes.

Once the shock had let up, the general feeling in Laskin was that Dave had it coming, especially since he hadn't died and would still be able to paint. We all felt sorry for Earl, who'd been pushed to the breaking point, and only wished he'd managed to get a shot off at the county commissioner, too. Maybe one with more lasting impact. And we continued to feel the same way even after it was found out that all Earl had shot that night was a dead stump in his back yard.

You can't have police and emergency technicians romping through your house without they find stuff that maybe you don't want found. It seems that Dave, besides doing a fairly good business at selling prints at twenty-five dollars a pop, was also doing a very good business selling dope for considerably more. All those booths and shows were a real good excuse for a lot of traveling and a lot of cash in small bills. As it turned out, the shooter was Fred Davison, Dave's second cousin twice removed, who hadn't liked his latest purchase, and I'm not talking about a print.

Dave's currently in the penitentiary in Sioux Falls doing five to ten. I took Mabel down to see him last Sunday. He was looking fit, and he swears he's learned his lesson.

"Once I get out of here, I'm going legit all the way," Dave said. "I figure I can make a living easy, selling prints over the Internet. You wouldn't believe the interest I've generated already."

"That's right, honey," Mabel said. "I shipped five orders of 'Slippery Morning' this week."

"See?" Dave said proudly. "I know I can do it." Later on, as we were leaving, he whispered to me, "I appreciate you bringing Mom down here to see me. If you'd like a print, say, one of the Nude series? Melody's running those out for me. Mom, well, they kind of embarrass her. Just let me know, Mr. Stark, and I'll be happy to let you have one for free."

Well, I couldn't do that. I'll have you know I paid for my copy of *Nude With Snow Geese*. It's in my bedroom right now. I'd have put it up in my study, but I don't want it out somewhere that Earl might see it. He's a touchy sort of guy and you never know what'll set him off.

The Jumper
John M. Floyd

"The smartest thing?" I asked.

"That's right," Rufus said. "What's the smartest thing you've ever done? Simple question."

I thought a moment. Ten feet beyond the log where Rufus Olson and I were sitting, the muddy waters of Lake Beaudark lay flat and still in the midday sun. The black swamp on the far side shimmered in the haze. It was July in Georgia, and hot as the hinges of hell.

"You mean like *wise* smart?" I asked.

Rufus smiled and tossed a pebble into the water. "I mean like *clever* smart. What's the cleverest thing you've ever done?"

I had to think about that awhile. Clever wasn't something I knew a lot about. If I'd been clever, I probably wouldn't have been sitting there on a log beside the lake with Rufus Olson.

"I don't rightly know," I said. And then I asked him the question I knew he wanted me to ask. If he hadn't, he wouldn't have brought up the subject in the first place.

"What's the cleverest thing *you've* ever done, Rufus?"

He pursed his lips and stared out over the lake, as if actually trying to remember.

"I guess it was something that happened when I lived in Atlanta," he said, after a minute or so. "There was a jewelry store downtown, I forget the name, but I walked in there one Christmas and asked to see some of their finer merchandise. Wanted to buy a little something for the wife, I said."

He paused, scratching his chin.

"The salesclerk was a little bald headed guy with glasses. As soon as he heard the words *finer merchandise* he pulled out a big flat box, set it down on the countertop, and opened it up. Inside that display box, Raymond my boy, was the fanciest jewelry I ever saw. At least a dozen diamond necklaces, lined up so they overlapped each other in the case, gleaming and winking like a million crystal chandeliers.

"'Perhaps one of these,' the clerk says, real prissy. 'Perhaps,' I told him. I took my time, looking at each one. Pretty soon, when he figured he had me hooked, he offered me a silver cigarette case—everybody smoked back then, you know. I opened it and took one out, and he lit it with a matching silver lighter. Then I went back to studying the necklaces, trying to remind myself not to dust my ashes on the carpet.

"About that time, just as a clock in the corner was striking the hour, we heard a commotion outside. We turned around to look, and saw through the big storefront window that a crowd was gathering, and was staring straight up at the tall buildings on the other side of the street. All of a sudden a woman called, 'Look out!' and we heard a scream—a long, horrible, bloodcurdling scream."

"'Oh Lord,' the clerk says, under his breath. 'It's a jumper.'

"And sure enough, a second later, the crowd outside scattered like leaves in a storm, and those of us in the store saw a body falling through the air. There wasn't a lot of traffic right then, and we actually saw the body hit the ground. It didn't bounce or splatter or anything, it just landed—THUMP— on the far sidewalk.

"Right quick after that, half a dozen bystanders ran to the body, gathering around it in a huddle, almost. The two other men in the store groaned and shook their heads. My clerk was pale as a ghost, his eyes glued to the window."

Rufus paused again, staring down at the ground between his workshoes.

I sat and waited.

"That was when it happened," he said. "All of a sudden, as all of us watched through the window, the crowd around the body began to spread apart. They all backed away together—and they looked…scared. No, more than that; they looked terrified. And when they had backed away far enough, we could see the body again."

I stared at him, absorbed. "And?"

Rufus raised his head and looked at me. "And it moved."

In the sticky heat of the July sun, I felt a cold shiver run down my spine.

"It what?"

"The body moved," he said. "First one leg, then the other, then a hand fluttered a little.

Finally, as we stood there with our mouths hanging open, the man on the sidewalk rolled over, propped himself up on one elbow, and looked around."

I swallowed. "You're not serious."

"I am. And I'll tell you, Raymond my friend, you would not believe the reactions of the people around me. One of the men in that store fainted dead away, and so did most of the women outside, and everybody started running in all directions. Every place of business in shouting distance emptied like the whole block was on fire. I guess that was to be expected—this was the city, after all, and crazies do jump from tall buildings. But coming back to life, afterward? Now, that's something to see.

"And that's just what he did. After a minute or so he sat all the way up, an average-looking guy in a gray suit, blinking at everybody like he just woke up from a nap. He didn't seem to have a scratch on him. Pretty soon he stood up, wobbled for a second, smiled real dopey-like at everybody, and just walked away. The crowd parted for him as if Jesus Himself had returned to earth and was setting out to gather the righteous."

Rufus fell silent again. I stared at him a moment, stunned.

"Then what?"

He glanced at me. "Beg pardon?"

"What happened then?" I asked, exasperated. "That's not *all*, is it?"

"No, that's not all. The crowd finally broke up, looking a little dazed. Several people stopped to help those who had fainted."

"And…everybody just went back to what they were doing?"

"Well, not everybody," he admitted. "I, for one, walked down to the corner of Peachtree and Ellis, and hid for a while inside a hotel restroom. I had, you see, the big flat box from the jewelry store tucked inside my overcoat."

I stared at him in disbelief. *"You stole the necklaces?"*

He smiled. "You bet your booties. I figured I deserved it."

"Deserved it? What do you mean?"

His smile widened. "The jumper," he said, "wasn't a jumper at all. He was a dummy, made out of rags sewn inside a gray suit, and its head was a painted sack stuffed with Styrofoam. It was thrown from the roof of the Hamilton Building by a man named Willy Maddox, who should have been an opera singer. His was the scream we heard." Rufus stopped a moment, remembering. "As soon as the dummy hit the sidewalk, six of our partners, dressed in trench coats, ran to the body and gathered close around it while they cut it apart with pocketknives and stuffed the rags and pieces of suit underneath their coats. Within seconds the jumper had completely disappeared."

I shook my head in confusion. "Wait a minute. If that was what happened—who was lying there afterward? Another of your men?"

Rufus nodded. "A guy named Gus Fedderman. He was the first to run up to look at the body, and under the cover of his partners it was easy for him to strip off his trenchcoat—he had on a gray suit underneath—and lie down on the sidewalk while they dismantled the dummy. When they let others through to look, and the new 'body' began to stir a little, they backed away together and vanished into the crowd."

I sat there on the log for a minute or more, staring at him in awe.

Then a sudden thought hit me.

"How did you clear a profit?" I asked. "All the recruiting, the planning, the setup—and at least eight of you to split the take." I studied him. "Was it worth it?"

He smiled. "The way we did it, it was. You see, there were two more jewelry stores nearby, and a couple of ritzy shops. One man in each place did the same thing I did, at exactly the same time. Three days later, at a park in Marietta, twelve of us split more than seven hundred thousand. The six sidewalk men got half shares because of the lower risk, the rest of us cleared eighty grand apiece. Not bad for those days."

Not bad at all, I thought. And he was right: the whole idea was just about the cleverest thing I had ever heard of.

I was quiet for a long time, watching his profile as he squinted at the calm waters of the lake.

"What went wrong?" I asked him.

He turned and regarded me solemnly. "An oversight," he said with a sigh. "A small lapse of concentration."

It took me a minute to figure it out. "The clerk's cigarette case?"

He nodded. "My prints were all over it."

Both of us fell silent.

"At least you're almost done," I said. "One more year, isn't it?"

"Ten months. It's something to look forward to, all right."

Behind us, a deep voice called out: "Break's over, boys. Back to work."

We rose stiffly to our feet, picked up our swinging-blades, and followed the trusty up the hill toward the road crew. Our leg chains clanked and jangled with each step.

Halfway there, I put a hand on Rufus's arm, and he turned and looked at me. The guard had gone on ahead.

"One more thing," I said. "They got *you*. Did they get the money, too?"

A slow grin spread across his face.

"You're pretty clever, too, sometimes," he said.

Smiling, we trudged together up the hill toward the others.

Midnight Phone Call
Joan Leotta

In my experience, a midnight phone call is always the bearer of bad news for you, your family, or in my case for me or a client. My name is Millie Rozzino. Unmarried, a lawyer and the last of my family line, I stayed in California after UCLA Law to practice labor law among the glitterati.

Not quite the same as defending steel works or miners like the men of my immigrant family, but still, on the side of the worker—a debt I owed my dad. Still, a chance meeting with Martin Rosenbluth, an immigration lawyer, at an ABA function I knew I could continue, even more closely to honor my Dad's memory by working, in my retirement, as an immigration lawyer.

Three years before handing in my paper at the firm where I sipped cappuccino with fellow lawyers, I started brushing up on my immigration law by taking courses at my alma mater and picking the brains of any of my former and then-current classmates and professors.

When the time came to leave, I also left the crazy freeways of LA for San Diego. My pension allowed me to offer my services free. I signed on with San Diego's Puebla Pro Bono Law Office.

When my Dad came across the pond from Italy, the legalities of becoming a citizen were much more straightforward. Dad always said, "American is the best country in the world." Now it's more complicated. Even many legal immigrants seek out lawyers—and for the poor, the non-English speaking refugees and illegal border crossers, the path to becoming a citizen is fraught.

I keep my father's citizenship papers, framed, above my office desk to remind me of my debt to him and to this country and to those who wish to become a part of it.

In the last year of separating child from parents at the border, I got a midnight phone call that sent me reeling. It was the case of Manuelita Escobar and her son Felipe.

Separated at the border as soon as the Border patrol captured them near Tijuana, Manuelita was sent to Oja. Felipe, age eight was bused with some others to a childcare center. Manuelita shouted after him to call his Aunt Lina. She was able to make a call to her American Aunt Lina but after a week, the Aunt had not heard anything from Felipe. Neither did he call his mother.

One-night Manuelita called her aunt and told her that some of the other residents were threatening her. After trying to get the local police, the Border Patrol, anyone to help, Lina called my Office. Like Doctors, one of us is always on call. It was my turn that night, and so, around midnight a very teary Lina was put through to my home number. Through sobs she told me Manuelita's biggest concern was the separation from Felipe, but that the threat to her life by a new resident had made Manuelita afraid even to sleep.

*****

I got dressed, called my favorite translator, Estelle (Lina told me Manuelita spoke no English) and headed over to demand a meeting with Manuelita. After pounding on the door for minutes that seemed like hours, a very disgruntled employee opened the door.

"You can't come in. We open to lawyers at ten in the morning. Not in the middle of the night."

"Listen, buddy. My client called her Aunt. She's being threatened. I need to see her now!"

Estelle is a San Diego native, translates for many different law firms, and is in and out of Oja on a regular basis. She also knows many of the agents—nice people with a hard job, for the most part—on a personal level. She knew this guy too and threw a few choice bon mots at him in Spanish.

"Okay, okay."

While we waited for Manuelita to come to the interview room, I read Manuelita's thin file.

Upon arrival she had asked for asylum, saying that MS-13 had threatened her family. However, one interviewer expressed concern that since Manuelita had arrived without a spouse she might be a victim of spousal abuse and possibly rape along the long road from Guatemala to our border.

After a few minutes, Manuelita walked in, trembling. She relaxed a bit when she saw two women in the room. Estelle told her (in Spanish), *"Lina sent us. Talking to Senora Rozzino is like telling a priest. She is a lawyer and cannot tell others anything you tell her."*

"Tell us how you arrived in the US, and then who is threatening you tonight," Estelle asked her again, in Spanish.

Manuelita picked up the bottle of water we'd brought for her, took a short swallow. Then, in a soft, low, but steady melodious voice, she poured out a horrifying tale:

"Just after my husband, Ramon, and my son, Felipe, and I crossed the border with several other people and our coyote, my husband fell. I heard the crack of bone. His leg.

I told him to hold onto us, Felipe and me, but we were soon far behind the others."

Her voice began to shake, and tears started to trickle down her cheeks. She continued speaking.

"Ramon called to the coyote. When the man came back to us, Ramon told him we would just wait in that spot until daylight. We would then allow the border patrol to find us and take us to a doctor. The others in our group, three men, two women, were now out of sight. The coyote walked up to us and ordered Ramon to move. He shouted that this was his path—no one could be left on it or the border patrol agents would, with their dogs, find where he had crossed, and where he was going. He told my husband to move or die.

"Ramon tried to stand up. I reached out to help him again, but the coyote pushed me away, I fell and got up, and put my arms around Felipe. Ramon fell to the ground and rolled away from me. The coyote again ordered him to get up. Ramon tried to push himself up, but that devil pulled out his machete, the tool that had hung at his waist during the whole trip. He raised it up and before we could react, he slashed down and separated Ramon's head from his body."

Manuelita bent over with hacking sobs. Estelle and I pushed back our chairs and went to her. We held her shoulders and patted her until she calmed. Then we simply sat quietly with her for several minutes while she emptied her eyes of tears.

*"What happened next? "*Estelle gently asked.

Manuelita took a deep breath. *"That crazy, evil man! As Ramon's head rolled away, he laughed. I grabbed Felipe's hand and we began to run back to the border. The evil one, he followed us. Thanks be to God, Felipe and I moved fast, and we were fortunate—a jeep with border patrol agents came rumbling up it a few yards ahead on the road and we ran to it. The agents did not seem to notice that we were running the wrong way, toward Mexico. I screamed at them to stop. They stopped and questioned us. I told them we had just come across.*

The coyote simply disappeared, and I was too scared to say anything about the horror we had just experienced. Felipe simply shuddered and would not speak. They put us in their jeep and took up to a place where Felipe was taken from me and I was sent here."

I wrapped my arms around her again. More tissues, more water. More tears. Then Estelle asked her, *"What happened next? What made you so afraid tonight?"*

Manuelita choked out the story of claiming asylum, separation from Felipe, being sent to Oja.

She told us another woman from her border crossing group, someone named Carmen, showed up in Oja today. When she thought no one could see, she shoved Manuelita down a flight of steps and told her it was a warning. *"Carmen demanded to know where Felipe was sent and told me that I needed to call him and tell him to be quiet. That I needed to be quiet. But I cannot find Felipe. Each time I was where he was sent, the officers just mumble at me. Only Lina knows we are here so I called her."*

After translating, Estelle said what I was also thinking, "We have to get her out of here as soon as possible and get Felipe out of Casa. That's where most of the separated children are sent from here."

I nodded. I told her I sure I could get Manuelita's case scheduled for the next day or so and have her released to her Aunt, but this Carmen is a threat right now."

Estelle smiled. "I have contacts with an abused women shelter. My sister Anita is a social worker. The authorities already suspect Manuelita to be an abused spouse. You explain this to the Aunt and the judge, and we can have Manuelita sent to the shelter tonight. And she will be shielded from the Coyote and his friends because those locations of those are not made part of public record."

Estelle explained our plan to Manuelita. I texted a few folks and a friendly judge granted the order we needed to extricate Manuelita from the facility where she was and send her to the shelter. We waited for two hours with Manuelita until the bilingual rep from the shelter came to get her.

I treated Estelle to breakfast at an all-night diner and then went into the office. From there, at a more decent hour, we called around to have a hearing for set for Manuelita to release her into Lina's care. We phone Casa to find Felipe and schedule a hearing for him.

"We did not take in any boys named Felipe in the past few days," the Director, Mrs. Bright, told me. She went on to explain that a picture would help since some of the children did not give their names.

"We don't have a photo," I admitted. "His Mom is at a Shelter for abused women. I will not see her again until her hearing, two days from now. I might be able to bring her over then."

Mrs. Bright said she hoped so.

Estelle's social worker sister met with Manuelita who gave us the bad news that when she and Felipe ran from the Coyote, she dropped her tiny suitcase containing the precious objects of her life—all photos, her rosary, a few clothes—onto the desert floor.

The Judge was not ready to release Manuelita to a relative. He ruled that she had to return to the shelter. Disappointing, but still, she was safe. Estelle had Manuelita describe the boy: "*Shaggy straight black hair, big black eyes, olive skin, small for his age, wearing loose jeans and a tan shirt. He had a small neckerchief, red.*"

*****

Estelle and I drove to Casa. Mrs. Bright brought in five boys who might be Felipe. None was.

"There is one other possibility," Mrs. Bright said. "Your Felipe may have been transferred to another center right away, before even stopping with us. That day fifteen children arrived at our door—some separated from parents and some unaccompanied minors. If Felipe could or would not answer our questions, he could not be classified and may have been sent to a center with a higher staff to child ratio without us ever recording him here."

The Director showed us the list of transfers from the two days we had targeted. Two were unnamed girls. There were three boys—Pedro, Ramon, and an unnamed boy. The unnamed boy or the boy named Ramon might be Felipe. All the last names were blank. The children had been sent to three different places.

Estelle went home to rest. I went to the office and poured coffee into my tired self to keep my eyes open as I got on the phone to all three centers. I had trouble convincing the center staff that I was the attorney for one of their detainees—especially since the child would not be able to identify me or my name. It was maddening that not even the government knew where all the young children were. I had no time to focus on that. We had to find the boy before the coyote could harm him.

A privately operated center in Minnesota looked like the most likely place. They had taken in the unnamed boy and both girls. I decided to head home and nap and head out to Minnesota after meeting one more time with Estelle and maybe her sister, Anita, the social worker who was making regular visits to Manuelita in the shelter. I texted Estelle.

After a refreshing nap and shower, I fixed myself an uninspired salad and watched some television. At eight o'clock, I began to worry. In six hours, Estelle had not returned my text. Not like her. I called. Estelle answered her mobile in a frantic voice.

"The shelter called me. My sister and Manuelita are missing."

"Where are you?"

"I'm at the shelter now. I have Anita's purse and phone. They told me to come since obviously security had been breached and they were going to have to move all of the women."

"Give me the address and I'll be right there. Police on the way?"

"Already here."

I threw on my clothes and drove over. Estelle explained she was to have met her sister at five at a diner. At six, the center had called her and told her Anita and Manuelita were missing and told her to come over.

Estelle helped translate for the police as they interviewed the shelter women, so she found out that a new woman, a blonde, had claimed she needed to go shopping for clothes and asked for Manuelita and Anita to go with her. When the three of them were not back by supper time, they checked Anita's office, found Anita's purse, but not her cell phone. "I went into the room later and looked around some more. In the trash can, I found a picture of Manuelita and a little boy."

I cursed loudly—in my grandmother's Italian /Neapolitan dialect (a language that offers many and varied cursing options). That coyote, whoever he was, must have connections in the court system. He had managed to discover the address of the battered woman's shelter in just a couple of hours. I figured if he was that good, he might also know that Felipe was not at Casa and was likely one of the transferred children.

"Did you give the cops the photo, Estelle?"

She smiled slyly. "I forgot.

"Make a copy of it. Give them the copy and palm the original. We need it."

*****

Estelle did as I asked.

While we were talking, two unmarked vans arrived to transfer the remaining women to another house, hopefully a more secure one. The police cleared Estelle to leave. She followed me in her car until we got to my house where we both had a glass of wine. I made pasta. Pasta helps me think. It calms me too. We propped the photo up against a bowl and studied it while we ate. Estelle pushed her rigatoni with peas and ricotta around on the plate. I finished mine and had an idea.

"Look at the picture again, Estelle. Look closely."

It was almost midnight, and we were both getting sleepy but at my words, Estelle perked up. "I see Manuelita and a boy, maybe six or seven or eight. He is so slight. It's hard to judge his age. I don't think they had regular meals even before they left for the States."

"Look closer, Estelle. Look at the boy's long hair. You knew it was Felipe, but if you didn't know it was Felipe, might you think that child was a girl?"

"*Dios Mio!*"

Estelle didn't have time to say anything else because her phone rang. "It's my sister!"

Estelle pressed accept and hit the speaker button. Her sister was crying. A harsh male voice shouted over the crying. "Tell us where the brat is, and we'll let your sister go."

"Let me talk to Anita."

We could hear Anita in the background: "He's going to kill us all, Estelle. Don't tell him anything he…" The sound of a hard smack and tears followed.

"I'm a man of my word. I'll kill them both unless you tell me where the boy is."

"Where is Manuelita? Let me hear her too."

The phone went dead. Estelle began to cry.

"Hold it together, Estelle. We've got to figure something out to save them and Felipe too.

I think Felipe was misidentified as a girl. I'll bet he's one of the two little girls who would not speak. They were sent to a center near Minneapolis. I am going to leave right now drive to LA and get a red-eye flight to Minneapolis. I'm not leaving from here because that coyote is too well connected. Who knows how many people he has corrupted? Let me take the picture with me so the boy will trust me."

"That's what they're planning to do too, I bet!"

"You're probably right. That's why I must move fast—in case they haven't quite figured it out yet. But one thing puzzles me. Why didn't he just kill Manuelita if he is worried about her being a witness to Ramon's murder?"

Estelle looked at me. Before she could speculate, I was throwing things into an overnight bag.

I began to wonder if drugs were involved in the coyote's people smuggling business. Were some of the people being used as mules?

For sure, Manuelita knew something important, something that she would not tell. Why was getting Felipe the key. I thought perhaps, the coyote would use the threat of killing Felipe to get Manuelita to cooperate. Or, maybe, Felipe had some important information or items, and the man would use the threat of killing his mom to get the boy to cooperate.

I finished packing my carry-on. Estelle burned rubber out of my drive to help find Manuelita and Anita. She had connections she knew she could trust.

The coyote was so confident he had not covered his tracks that well. Anita had managed to turn the phone on before being tied up. Before I boarded my flight, I got a text from Estelle that the SWAT team had rescued Manuelita and Anita.

*****

By now it was apparent that the coyote was likely working with others. Felipe might still be in danger, so I pressed on to LAX where I purchased a ticket on the first flight to Minneapolis.

It left at midnight, arrived at 4 AM. Non-stop. I knew that even if others figured out about the boy as I had, they had a twenty-nine-hour drive, give, or take a potty stop or two, so I would get there ahead of him. After all, the coyote probably didn't have credentials to fly. Unfortunately, I did not count on others in his nefarious group being citizens.

When I arrived, I made my way to the 24/7 Star Car Service stand. I'd used them on a work trip in pre-retirement times. The "Welcome Children Center" was about two hours away, north of the airport. Before setting out, I called and woke up my former law school study partner, still working in the Minneapolis DA's office. I told her I needed her help and why. She agreed, then added she would ask the local police from the little town where the Center was to meet me at the Center.

I grabbed a cup of coffee and a banana muffin at the terminal's Starbucks to eat on the drive. I was so busy with my preparations I didn't notice that the well-dressed blonde woman who got off the plane with me, was following me in the blue minivan that had picked her up.

When I arrived at the Center, it was only a little after seven in the morning but there was already activity. I could hear children shouting and laughing. I pounded on the door. The woman who opened the door, the Director, a short, stern, gray-haired woman sporting the grandmother from hell look on her face, was not happy to hear my story. She was even less pleased when a blonde woman came up behind me, also with a photo, claiming to be Manuelita's attorney. I had to admit, blondie looked more the part than I did at that moment. My face showed my lack of sleep and my graying black hair was frizzed to the max.

Before I could explain that little Felipe would not know either one of us, the Director told a staff member to bring Felipe. While we were waiting, she explained, "They had him labeled as a girl when he arrived. Good thing we have both a boy's and a girl's wing here. He didn't speak at all when he first came, but he is beginning to talk now. At least now we know his first name is Felipe."

In a minute, a tall, slim, smiling redhead appeared pushing Felipe ahead of her. Before I could say anything, the blonde stepped up. In fairly good, (to my ear), Spanish, began babbling to the boy.

"No, No!" I shouted. Felipe turned to me. "*Yo soy tuo abogado!*" At least I know that much Spanish. At that moment, my friend and a couple of local LEOs walked in. The blonde shrank back, trying to pull Felipe toward her. He struggled a bit. I reached out and pulled him to me.

I called Estelle. She was able to put Manuelita on the phone. I began to tear up with relief. Felipe, the little dear, all he could do was repeat, "Mama, Mama." Through the Director, who spoke Spanish, and Manuelita herself via phone, we convinced Felipe that the blonde worked with the coyote and that *I* was his true "abogado", lawyer.

While the blonde squirmed in her chair, the Director translated Felipe's story. "The coyote gave each migrant a small package. Mama had put hers in their little suitcase. I had shoved mine into my pocket. One night, when no one was watching me, I unwrapped the outer covering and opened the tiny, zipped pouch inside. It was full of clear sparkly stones," he told us.

Diamonds. The coyote's connections were branching out from drugs to gem smuggling.

"After they shot Papa and Mama and I ran and I was taken from her, I decided to hide the stones.

In the first place they put me there was a little garden and I buried them where there were sunflowers. I like sunflowers. I did not like the idea of being found with the stones. I was afraid someone would think I had stolen them."

He told us he had been afraid to talk, so it was not until he arrived in Minneapolis, the "cold place" as he called it, that anyone paid attention to the fact that he was a boy and not a girl. He said he wondered why they kept putting him in the bathroom line with the girls. By this time, he had no idea where his mother was and until her heard from her was not going to tell anyone about the stones.

Thanks to my judge friend, I was able to get Felipe released into my custody and we flew back to San Diego. A few legal maneuverings later, he was with his mother at Aunt Lina's house.

The authorities soon dug up the diamonds where Felipe had hidden them. However, since we can't prove where they came from or who was going to receive them. Now that the diamonds were no longer a factor, I was pretty confident they would be safe.

The blonde was happy to trade a reduced charge for revealing names of some of their sources in Border Patrol and in the judicial records office. Agents patrolling the area where Felipe and Manuelita had been found made a wide sweep of the area but could not find a body so no one would be charged with murder or even accessory to same. But she would not say anything about any murder business, drugs, or gems. She admitted only to "helping migrants come across."

I think both blondie and those she identified are more frightened of the drug/diamond people than of anything our legal system can bring down on them.

I don't think I'll be able to get the FBI interested in the kidnapping case of Anita and Manuelita, either. At some point I might try, but it doesn't matter in the long run. My real concern was and always will be the safety of Manuelita and Felipe and others like them. These two are now headed on the long path that hopefully leads to citizenship. Maybe helping two out of all those thousands doesn't seem like much, but it sure helps me. Plus, I think my Dad would be happy to know I was able to aid them and that I did it for his sake. Even though it was relatively easy for him to become a citizen in the 1930s by the time I was in college, in the late 1970s he counseled me to become a lawyer—not just to help unions and immigrants—"Everything is so complicated today, he told me before he died, every family should have at least one lawyer on hand." So, each morning when I go to the office, I extend my feeling of family to the folks whose folders rest on my desk." I work hard for them, as I would for any family member. As I get older, though, I do also send up a prayer or two the Judge of all Judges that I will be spared another midnight call.

Dead Man's Blues
Glen Bush

Johnny Soul was a guitar man a step and a half behind the great Robert Johnson and Leadbelly. His style of playing the six-string was as unique as his appearance. Depending on the time of day, he could've been of any race or creed. The sun made him light, the shadows made him dark, and the night made him the best damn guitar player in the city. Johnny was one of those jokers who glided through life ignoring all labels. Laughing and loving. He told me once, "I don't have time for nicknames and handles, I'm too busy playing the blues." An invisible man who made himself visible with his guitar. Tonight, though, the cops and EMT crew gave him his last soubriquet. *Corpse—DOA.*

When Lieutenant Sean Arlen got on the scene, he called me. Arlen knew Johnny and I went way back. Johnny knew a lot of people and counted few as enemies. Why kill him? He had nothing but his Fender guitar and sack of songs.

When I pulled up to the alley behind the *9th Street Lounge*, the EMTs were putting a body bag on the stretcher. It was four a.m.—that time lost between night and day when even the drunks and junkies crawl into their cribs.

I stopped the EMT guys from loading Johnny into the back of the meat wagon. I needed to take a look at him before the M.E. got to cutting on him. Pulling back the cover, I stared at his face, eased his eyelids back a moment, and turned his head from side to side. The .22 Short had entered his right temple and stayed in his head, no exit wound. The .22 and the powder burns told me it had the features of a professional hit. Probably a hollow point. Fragmenting in his brain. No casings on the ground so good chance the killer used an old shorty revolver.

"Thanks, boys. You can take him. I've seen enough."

I felt a tap on my left shoulder. "You okay, Quinn?"

"Yeah, L.T., I'm fine and dandy. I always look this way when a friend of mine gets his brain mangled by a hollow point."

"Sorry, Quinn."

"Any ideas about this yet?"

"Nope, not yet. Don't seem right to me, Sean. That hole in his temple looks like it was made by a .22 Short, a professional hit. But why? Johnny played music. Wrote songs. Didn't gamble or do drugs, smoked a joint now and then, but no drugs. Never bothered another man's woman. For a streetwise guitar man, he was fuckin' clean. Did ya find anything around here before I got here?"

"Not a lot. I called you as soon as I saw it was Johnny. Did you happen to look at his hands? Damn bloody. Looks like the killer tried to crush them with something heavy, maybe a brick or cinderblock, then decided to jump on them with both boots. Also, get this, his friggin' shoes were gone."

Now I'm really confused. A professional hitman blows Johnny away, neat and clean as a butcher with a cleaver, and then crushes both his hands and steals his fucking shoes. Don't make sense.

"Sean, I'm in on this one. I don't like soundin' like one of them movie P.I.s, but I got to find this son-of-a-bitch. Johnny was my bottom ace. I was there when he signed his first recording contract with Dirt Road Records and took the name Johnny Soul. No more John Washington. We celebrated over at *Mother's* with Pete and Mickey. That's before you moved to town. Yeah, Sean, I'm fuckin' in, one-hundred-percent."

"Got it, Quinn, but stay inside the lines or I'll have your license and gun." I'd heard that story before, but this time the look on the cop's face told me he wasn't fuckin' around, but then, I wasn't either. I gave him a short wave and a tip of the hat, and said in my best James Cagney impersonation, "See'ya around, copper."

*****

I knew Johnny was getting ready to re-sign with Dirt Road, and he'd told me Frankie Khan, the Syrian hood, wanted him signing with his company, American Rainbow Recording. Trouble is, Johnny never liked hoods, in any color or breed. So, I figured, why not, give it a shot. Khan might give me something. Besides, I'd met Khan when I'd worked a job with a merc years ago, he could be a tough bastard, but for some reason, we hit it off okay. Maybe that ground was still smooth. Khan worked out of *The Damascus*, his restaurant, in the Hills neighborhood. Before going there, though, I needed to do a little legwork and gather some background information from the police and the M.E.

At this time of morning things moved slow. Nobody was going to be too excited about doing the work-up on a dead bluesman. Besides, I was hungry, and I hate working when my stomach is yakking. I grabbed the morning edition of the *Post* and went to *Dolly's Diner* for the Farmer's Breakfast Special. The one-arm Vietnam vet with the 101st Airborne tatt kept my coffee fresh and hot. When eight o'clock rolled around, I swallowed the last drop of the coffee, paid my tab, and slipped a ten toward the vet and said, "Book it, Grunt," and headed to police headquarters and Lt. Sean Arlen.

Arlen hadn't gathered much from the alley or forensics. He said it looked like Johnny had been killed somewhere else and dragged to the alley. The bar where Johnny had been playing was at the other end of the alley. The M.E. told Arlen he wouldn't have anything on Johnny until late in the afternoon or the next morning. The morgue was being swamped with gangbangers, junkies, battered wives who didn't make it this last time, and the general run-of-mill DOAs. Johnny had to wait his turn. *The Damascus* would be open for lunch soon, so I headed east.

*****

It's a good restaurant. I like the lamb stew and black coffee. Khan had introduced me to Arak. Good liquor. Since I started laying off the booze, though, I hadn't had any, and I didn't plan on jumpin' off that wagon today. I spotted Khan at the bar reading a Syrian newspaper.

"Hello, Frankie. Long time, no see."

"Damn, if it isn't Liam Quinn, the shamus. Stop in for lunch?"

"Nope. Business. I hear you've been tryin' to get Johnny Soul to sign with American, and he hasn't been too excited about that. True?"

"Why you asking? You working as Soul's agent now?"

"Nah. Johnny's dead. Took a slug in the right temple. Looks like somethin' one of your boys might do. So, seein' that Johnny was a friend of mine, and that I know you, I thought I'd stop by before the cops got here and ask you what it is."

"Dead? And you'll thinking I did it? Why? Johnny's worth a lot of money to me. Fact is, he still is, hell, maybe even more now. Y'know, the music of a dead guitar man can bring in a lot of sympathy cash. I ever tell you I met

Hendrix's go-to-man once? He told me he was sorry Jimi was gone, but he sure as hell enjoyed his new house in Malibu." Khan's voice was flat, no emotion. He could've been reading his grocery list to me.

"How you gonna make money off a dead man under contract to another house?"

"Ha, ha, ha! Quinn, you gotta start watching *TMZ*. I bought Dirt Road Records last weekend. I got all their artists and all their songs in my pocket at American Rainbow. Johnny was my bitch one way or the other. So, you see, I didn't want him dead. I didn't even need to rough him up. All I needed him to do was keep playing his guitar and croonin' his tunes. Don't look so down, Quinn. I'm not your killer. I know I just made your work a little harder, but look at it this way, we're still friends, come on, have an Arak with me."

I could feel that old urge in my gut begging me to take Frankie up on the Arak. I shook my head and smiled. "No, thanks, Frankie, next time. So, you got any ideas about who could've whacked Johnny?"

"Nope. Not a clue. But if I find out, I'll call you…after I get my pound of flesh you can have yours."

"Thanks, Frankie." I gave the Syrian a wave and headed for the street. I like Frankie Khan. He's a hood, but he's a stand-up hood. If he says he's gonna whack ya, he will. If he says he ain't, he don't…well, he usually don't. I like that. Stand-up guy.

*****

Nothing changed with the police. Blackstrap molasses poured faster than the city police looking for clues in the death of a Black guitar player. I knew Arlen had his hands full, but I also knew the whys and wherefores of city politics. Some suburban college kid had gotten carjacked in the wrong neighborhood that afternoon. The mayor was upset. I could hear the mayor now, "Those people kill each other every day, nothing we can do about that, but we sure as hell can protect the good people of our metro area." The difference between Blackstrap molasses and sweet cow's milk, between a buck and C-note.

*****

The front door of the *9th Street Lounge* was draped in black cloth with an eight by ten photograph of Johnny sitting on his stool playing his six-string Fender. *R.I.P. Johnny Soul* was hand-written below the photo. I didn't stop to look at the picture. I'd been there when the geek took it. I didn't need to see any pictures of Johnny Soul, I needn't his killer in my hands.

Betty and Spook were sitting at the bar drinking Seven-Sevens and eating pork rinds with Louisiana hot sauce. They'd owned the *9ᵗʰ Street* for nearly thirty years. They were an odd couple, but a good couple. When Johnny was fifteen, they hired him to play the early Friday and Saturday night shifts and the Sunday afternoon, after-church shift. His Momma and Daddy used to sit front row, center, sipping their highballs. They'd bring him to work and carry him home. In those days, Johnny had two mommas and two daddies, and no one fucked with young Johnny Washington.

"Hello, Betty. Spook." I slid a barstool over next to the couple and watched the bartender pour me a double-rocks glass of black coffee.

"Hey, Quinn. How ya doin' boy? Ya doin' okay?" Spook still had glassy eyes and tear-stained cheeks. Betty looked about the same.

"Yeah, Pops, I'm fine."

"I'm tryin' to find who did Johnny. I've talked to L.T. and Khan, but nothin' there. You got any ideas?" The coffee was strong. Chicory. Shipped up from New Orleans. Looking over my glass of coffee, I could see Betty shaking her head. Spook, his big eyes staring at the ceiling fan, was doing the same. "Had he been havin' words with anybody around here? Money or women? Y'know the routine?"

"Nah, he ain't had no trouble with nobody," said Spook. "Some back-and-forth with that half-wit Jimmy Bones about some song, but that's natural for them boys to go at it about music."

Betty had a puzzled look, "It don't make sense, Liam. If the jew cop or the Syrians don't know what's what, where's that leave you? You believe them when they say they don't know? Just being a cop or a gangster don't make them Truth-speakers."

"Yeah, Betty, I got that. No doubt about Arlen. He called me right after he got to Johnny. As for Frankie Khan, I figured him for the gun but when he told me he'd already bought Dirt Road and Johnny's contract, why knock 'em off? There's no percentage. That don't mean he didn't do it, but it does mean I believe him for now. I'm lookin' around. Was Johnny workin' with any new guys? Maybe on some new routines or music?"

Spook thought for a minute, and then said, "Johnny's been hanging around that new girl, what's her name, Betty?"

"Lorene somethin' or another. Texas girl. I think San Antone."

"Yeah, Liam, Lorene from San Antone. Real looker. Curves that keep on curvin'. Reminds me of Betty back in the day."

Betty reached over and slapped Spook on the side of his head and yelled, "Fuck you, Spook! I still got my curves. More curves than you can handle, you gray-ass rooster."

"Willis, Lorene Willis from San Antone, Texas, that's her name."

"Knock it off, both of you! I'm here about Johnny, not about your old asses. Now, besides Lorene, anyone else? And where can I find Lorene?"

Betty picked up her phone and checked her contacts. "Here's her name, number, and address. She'll be working here tonight. Comes on at ten." I logged the info into my cell and waited for anything else they could tell me.

'Betty, what'dya think about that young guitar player that's been hangin' around here playin' with Johnny? Jimmy Bones. Johnny always calls him Half-Bone."

"Yeah, that Tennessee boy, country as a bale of summer hay, hell, he's been pestering Johnny to no end. He's even gettin' on my last nerve. Somethin' about a song Johnny wrote. He wants Johnny to let him record it."

"*Cocaine Blues*. That's the name of the song. I don't know what Johnny was gonna do with it. They played it in here the other night. Sounded pretty good. Had a little jazz side to it. Not the regular down-home blues. Johnny said he liked it, but he ain't rushin' it."

Betty thought for a moment and then said, "But remember, Spook, Johnny said he didn't think much of Jimmy. Didn't trust the kid. But that's just the way musicians talk about one another. Talkin' trash like a couple barnyard banty roosters."

"So, where can I find Jimmy?"

"I ain't got no information on him, but he usually shows up here carrying that shiny guitar around ten or so and joins in with Johnny. Stop back by. And if you miss Lorene, remember, she'll be here about that time, too. I put her waitressing since Molly had the baby."

I finished my coffee and tipped the bartender. I needed to find Lorene. Maybe she had a hint on this or that. When I got to her apartment, she wasn't there. There was mail in the mailbox. Looked like a couple of days' worth. I went back to my place to figure out what I could do. I needed to be at the 9th

Street by ten, so I had to get a little rest before I strolled in there.

I needed to figure out who and what were Lorene Willis and Jimmy Bones up to, if anything.

*****

There was no mistaking Jimmy Bones. In his country-ass mind, he was dressed like a big city bluesman. Black suit. Gold, shiny gold, shirt. White tie with an emerald stick pin. Black and white Italian shoes, pilgrim style. And a broad brim white Knox fedora with a wide gold hatband. He wore fake diamond rings on each pinkie. And to nail his bluesman persona, he sported his coke bottle slide on a leather string around his neck. I had the distinct feeling watching this wannabe saunter up to the bar that he was happier than a drunk sailor in a Bangkok whorehouse. Looks like Johnny turning up dead cracked the door for Mr. Bones. My question was, did Jimmy help Johnny find his demise?

While watching the bluesman, I saw a waitress walking by. As she crossed his path, he reached out and grabbed her, rough, like she was his bought-and-paid for property. He held her tight with his right arm while holding his guitar in his left. Kissing her hard and long, he was letting everybody in the bar know she was his. Jimmy, though, forgot one thing. As soon as he let her go and before he could let his slippery words be heard, the waitress slapped him, sending a loud *Wham* over the soft Brubeck tune coming from the jukebox.

"Damn, bitch!" he yelled while drawing his right hand back ready to return the slap. But before he could let go of it, Spook surprised everybody in the joint with a quick, smooth leap that landed him next to the youngster. Spook's large hands grabbed Jimmy's lapels and spun him around, sending him bouncing off the bar.

"Half-wit, you ever touch Lorene or any other woman like that again, and I'll damn well put my razor to good use. Ya understand?"

Wiping his face with his white handkerchief, Jimmy looked at the old man's large round eyes and nodded, finally saying, "Yeah, Spook, I understand ya, but do me a favor, don't call me outta my name. I was jest funnin' with Lorene. I didn't mean no harm. Right, Lorene, y'know I didn't mean nuthin'. I was jest helpin' ya to forget Johnny, that's it. Y'know, a favor."

"Lorene, go check them tables in the corner. And you, Jimmy, go up on stage and get ready for your set. Since Johnny's dead, you'll be standin' in for him until I get somebody to take his place."

"Take his place? What about me, Spook? I'm as good as Johnny Soul ever was. I should be the headliner."

"Jimmy, you're a punk. You may be a decent guitar player, but you ain't Johnny Soul. If ya work out, I'll make ya the headliner. If not, ya can play backup or move on to another club." Spook's words were direct, no-nonsense. He didn't yell or talk loud. I barely could make them out myself and I was sitting pretty damn close. One thing I knew for sure, Jimmy Bones was hungry, and he had a temper. He wanted to be the headliner playing his music, not someone else's music. I sipped my coffee and watched him go up on stage. I'd talk to him later, between sets. For now, though, I needed to talk to Lorene. I walked over to the waitress station and sat down and waited for her to come up with a drink order or there was a lull in the drinking. It didn't take long.

"Give me a scotch and water, light ice, Jack and Coke, two Miller High Lifes." Her Texas drawl seemed out of place in a jazz club this far North. While she fiddled with her money, I asked her about Johnny.

"Lorene, my name's Quinn, I was a friend of Johnny's. I'm looking into who killed him. I'm thinkin' ya might be able to help me.'"

"Yeah, I heard Johnny call yer name oncet or twice. But, hey, I don't know nuthin' about who killed Johnny. He was a swell guy. We had a lot of fun. But, like I said, I don't know nuthin' about nuthin'. And if I did, I ain't talkin'."

"Why not?"

Lorene looked at me like I was completely bat-shit and said, "Y'all crazy? I don't wanna end up in the alley like Johnny. He played his cards and lost. He shoulda jest played his guitar and sang his songs and not bothered anybody about nuthin' else. Life is short, Quinn, and he jest made it shorter for himself. I ain't like that. I plan on havin' grandkids and talkin' to cops or about who did what ain't the way to have'em."

"Sorry you feel that way. I was wishin' you could help me. Y'know, friend to friend."

"Wishin'? Y'know what my Momma said about wishin', *friend to friend*? Wish into one hand and shit in the other and tell me which one fills up first. Got it, Quinn?" She then turned to look at the four drinks sitting on her tray and said, "If y'all ever want to talk about sumthin' else besides who did Johnny in, I'm all ears. I hear yer a pretty good guy to know." With that Lorene from

Texas smiled and walked away with the drink tray above her head and a sway to her hips.

After my third glass of coffee, I switched to club soda and lemon. Only so much caffeine can run through my veins before I start hanging from the fans.

Jimmy Bones was a good guitar player. He made those six strings moan and coo. I couldn't help thinking about Johnny's early days, back before I went into the Army, when I was still boxing for chump change. Johnny made more tips in one night than I made fightin' six rounders. That's when I decided Uncle Sam had more to offer me than the glory of the square ring. Jimmy looked like he was in that same spot.

I didn't hear Spook walk up on me. He had a way of being quiet. "What'cha think, Quinn? Jimmy as good as Johnny?"

"Don't know if he's that good, but he's good, damn good."

"The only thing about Jimmy is he's a fuckin' half-wit. All he thinks about, all he knows is playing music and chasing those high-tail girls like that there Lorene chick. When ya talk to him, you'll see what I mean. He can't carry a conversation more than a couple of minutes. He starts lookin' around like he's lookin' for mosquitoes. I don't think he's retarded, but he damn sure ain't a rocket scientist. Maybe jest countrified. Bottom line, don't be surprised if he starts lookin' at cha like you're from Mars or somethin'."

"I hadn't heard that. He looks like any other musician. Ratty as bat-shit. By the way, what was that scuffle with Lorene about?"

"Same-o, same-o. Lorene was runnin' with Johnny and didn't act like she cared about Jimmy. Some rumors have her playing both sides of that bed. In any case, now that Johnny's dead, Jimmy's thinkin' he can pull her for himself. Thing is, Jimmy's jest a little too thuggish. Always actin' like cotton field Superfly around women when everybody knows he ain't half that."

Looking over at the stage and listening to Jimmy sing an old B.B. King tune, I could see what Spook meant. Jimmy looked like a man trapped between being a twelve-year-old boy and a fifty-year-old bluesman. Neither mind nor body knew exactly which way to turn.

"But y'know, that boy can play that guitar and he can write some damn fine lyrics. He can't read notes and such, but he's got the feel for the music. It's his gift. Talk to him. You'll see what I mean." With that Spook turned and walked back to his place at the bar next to Betty.

At the end of the first set, Jimmy came up to the bar to get a refill on his Hennessy and Coke. Standing there next to me, lighting his smoke, he stared at Lorene walking from table to table, taking orders and picking up empty glasses. He reminded me of a kid looking through the window of the neighborhood bakery, staring at the chocolate cupcakes, mouth drooling and eyes growing bigger by the minute. Jimmy Bones wanted a bite of that cupcake. I hated spoiling his fantasy, but I needed to ask him a couple three questions.

"So, Jimmy, my name's Quinn, I'm a P.I. I'm lookin' into Johnny Soul's murder. You mind talkin' to me a little bit?" Jimmy looked over the top of his shades at me, sipped his Hennessy, and then let his eyes float back to Lorene.

"I don't know nuthin' about nuthin', man. Y'all need to talk to somebody else. I jest play the blues and mind my own bizness. Understand, man?" His eyes never left Lorene. Since he didn't look like he was going to be very forthcoming with any information, I figured I'd might as well throw a few meat scraps in front of him and see if he'd jump for them.

"Thing is, Jimmy, I hear you and Johnny were at odds. You wanted to headline, and he wasn't in the mood for sharing the spotlight. You didn't like that, you figured with Johnny gone, you'd get that center stool fulltime and get Lorene there, too."

Jimmy set his drink on the bar and turned toward me. Suddenly, Lorene wasn't his number one concern. Taking a long drag off his cigarillo, he slowly blew smoke in my face, crossed his arms over his chest, and said, "Look, asshole, I don't know nuthin' about nuthin'. I told ya, and I ain't gonna keep tellin' ya. If ya keep fuckin' with me, mudderfucker, I'm gonna fuck'ya up so bad yer momma won't even know yer ass. Ya feel me, mudderfucker? Now, why don't'cha chop cotton somewheres else?" With that, he flicked the half-smoked cigarillo at me, sending it over my left shoulder and down the bar. He was a punk, an easy target, but I didn't need to go in that direction. I knew Jimmy had something to tell me, but I was going to have to find a better time, one more to my liking.

"Yeah, Jimmy, I feel ya. I'm just doin' my job."

Jimmy walked back up on stage, adjusted his fedora, caressed his guitar, and forgot all about me.

*****

Later that night, after the third set, the saxman, Petey Breedlove, came up to me and said he had a little sumthin-sumthin that may be of help. Turns out he'd heard Johnny and Jimmy arguing about a song Johnny had written. According to Petey, Johnny was holding off on the song, but Jimmy was begging for the song, said he needed the song real bad to kick-start his solo career.

"Yeah, Quinn, I heard Jimmy say that some guy name Khan said it would be good for his career if he got the song from Johnny. Seems like this guy Khan had been talkin' to both of them dudes, kind of playin' one against the other. But then when Johnny saw me standing near the door, he shut up and walked out of the club and into the alley."

"When was that?"

"Two nights before they found Johnny's body."

"Just for the hell'va of it, was Lorene around?"

"I didn't think about it, but yeah, she was, she walked out right after Johnny, 'ceptin' she stopped for a quick minute and looked back at Jimmy and shook her head like she couldn't believe what she'd jest heard. But I don't know what that was all about. Hope that helps ya, Quinn."

"It does. It gives me a few breadcrumbs to follow. Peace out, brother."

It was time I headed back to Frankie's place and see what he knew about the music argument.

*****

The Damascus was still open when I drove up. A small group of hardcore Syrian and Persian customers, smoking from two hookah pipes and sipping strong Arabic black coffee, were talking quietly. Frankie sat with his back to the wall, a bottle of Arak near his coffee cup. That wasn't my crowd, so I settled myself at the bar and ordered an American coffee. The Arabic brew would keep me up for the next week.

"What brings you back, Quinn?" Holding his glass of Arak, Frankie sat down next to me.

"Like always, Frankie, questions and more questions. You got a few minutes?"

"Sure, why not? I'm just killing time until the crew over there decides to head home."

"I'm hearin' you was tryin' to get Jimmy to record one of Johnny's songs, but Johnny wasn't liking that. Maybe you started pushing Jimmy a little hard, encouraging him to do whatever to get that song from Johnny. That sound about right?"

Frankie never flinched. His eyes stayed steady and square. Long poker games and longer conversations around the Khan dinner table had taught him how and when to use his dead man's stare.

"Quinn, I run a business. The recording business survives only as long as there are musicians who can turn out new material while keeping their core audience. Both Johnny and Jimmy are guitar players. They share some of the same audience. But Johnny was getting old. He couldn't relate to the youngsters coming up in the club scene. Jimmy's part of this newer crowd. He can play blues, jazz, and mix in a little hip hop now and then. The thing is, and I'm guessing you know this if you've talked to Jimmy, he's a couple bricks short of a full load. I was just trying to . . . *educate* him. You understand, right?" Then, standing up and walking around to the other side of the bar, he poured himself a cup of American coffee and leaned his forearms on the bar in front of me. "What more can I say? It's all about money." Lifting his cup up and motioning toward the crowd in the corner and then around the restaurant, he said, "Coffee, booze, food, music, women, it's all about the green and the black. Nobody goes into business to go broke."

"You mean, a man's got to do what a man's got to do?"

"Yeah, Quinn, just like John Wayne. I'm just another version of your American cowboy, the Syrian cowboy."

Standing up and sliding a ten-dollar bill on the bar next to my coffee cup, I looked at Frankie one last time and said, "I just hope you don't turn out to be Billy the Kid. I don't want to be Pat Garrett coming for you."

"Pat who?"

I ignored Frankie's ignorance and said, "See ya, later, cowboy."

*****

The next day, about noon, I decided to look up Lorene and see if I could get her to tell me a little more about what went down between Johnny and Jimmy. I knew from experience that cocktail waitresses and bartenders seldom get up before noon, so I felt safe knocking on her door at that time. She answered the door in her UT football jersey. I couldn't tell if she had anything else on under the jersey. There was enough leg and thigh to tell me exactly why Johnny and

Jimmy were blowing in her ear. Looking at me, and then turning around and walking toward the kitchen, she didn't bother to say anything, she just waved me in. If I didn't know better, I'd think she had been expecting me. Still without talking, she poured two cups of coffee. It smelled fresh. I had guessed right, she hadn't been up long.

"Cream and sugar?"

"Nah, black is cool. You, uh, expectin' me?"

"Sooner or later, I knew you'd be back with more questions. I don't know what I can tell ya, but I knew ya was comin'."

"Good coffee, thanks."

"Ummm. Y'hungry? I can fix'cha some eggs and bacon, grits and toast."

"No, thanks. I had breakfast a couple of hours ago, and I'm not hungry now. You…always answer the door like this and offer coffee and breakfast to the men knocking?"

"Is that why ya came by, to ask me that question? Because if it is, fuck you, leave." Her tone was straightforward, no bs. I liked her.

"Nope. Just the small stuff before I ask ya the real stuff."

"Drink yer coffee and get to askin'. I have things to do and places to go before I go to work today. I'm working happy hour, so I don't have time to lollygag."

When she sat down on the stool next to me and crossed her legs, she answered my first question. I kept my sigh inside me and decided to ask the real stuff.

"What d'ya know about Jimmy and Frankie Khan?"

"Not a lot. Jimmy kept tellin' me that Khan wanted him to do this song Johnny wrote. He said that song could make Jimmy a headliner. Thing is, Johnny wasn't hip to letting Jimmy do it. He reckoned the song would be his next hit, and he needed another hit, but he was waitin' for the right time. I don't know when 'cause the way I saw it, Johnny Soul was already half-way out the door. He needed to get his ass in gear. Y'knew Johnny, he hadn't had a hit in almost ten years. Some small stuff, but nuthin' big, he was afraid of fading away. Well, Khan was tellin' Jimmy to get the song any way he could and bring it to him and he'd set up a recording studio for him. Together they could push the song out on the market, and Khan's attorneys would take care of any legal blowback."

"You think Jimmy killed Johnny? Sounds like he had the best reason, but I'm still wondering, was that it, *one song*? Seems like the best reason I've found so far, but a weak one."

"Hey! Quinn, I'm here," Lorene pointed to her face, "not here!" pointing to her thighs.

A little embarrassed, but not enough to blush, I smiled and looked at her brown eyes and said, "Yeah, they're nice, too. Sorry. Well, did he shoot Johnny?"

"Jimmy's a weird cat. He keeps tryin' to remake himself. He wants to be like all those old-time bluesmen, y'know, Leadbelly, Robert Johnson, Mississippi Whoever. Shooting Johnny could help make that rep for him and give him the song Khan wants. But Jimmy's a little scared. He really don't like trouble. He likes makin' trouble, but he wants to be gone before the stink of it gets all over him. Like he told me one time that Khan invited him and a couple of other guys over to his place to watch old gangster movies. He said Khan loved them old black and white flicks. Whenever one of the gangsters shot somebody, Khan would analyze it. Tell Jimmy if the shooting was a good shoot or not. Y'know, if it would really work in real life. Jimmy said Khan told him the best gun to use for a hit was either a .22 or a .38. Said, Khan had a whole damn theory about whackin' folks, y'know, like Khan had personal experience. He even laid two pistols on the coffee table in front of Jimmy, a .22 and .38, and told him to take both of 'em and try'em out, just for fun. Weird guy, Khan."

It was then that I started putting the pieces together. Khan was playing a fucked-up game with Jimmy Bones. I was starting to lose my respect for the gangster. I expect hoods to do gangster shit. But fuckin' with a guy who ain't playin' with a full deck, that ain't right. Shoot him. Beat the fuck outta'em. But don't fuck with what little bit of a brain he's got. God dealt Jimmy a raw deal. Another reason I don't put a lot of stock in God or his Master Plan. And now Frankie comes along and starts playin' puppet master. Lorene told me a couple more things about the relationship between Johnny and Jimmy, things that added up to where I was going. It was then I figured I'd ask the obvious question, "You makin' it with Jimmy, too?"

"Ya mean am I screwin' him?" Stopping for a second, she looked around, lit a cigarette, and then back at me. "Once in a while when Johnny ain't around and I'm bored. Jimmy's a fun cat and he's got a fuckin' pipe."

I had figured as much but wanted her to confirm it. I knew Johnny wouldn't go ape-shit over her screwing Jimmy, but he wouldn't want people at the bar to know she was two-timin' him. I told her thanks for the coffee and information.

"That's all? You ain't gonna thank me for anything else?" The smile on her face could've made a pimp blush.

I looked at her thighs again as she stood up, and said, "Yeah, and thanks for that, too."

"Come back sometime. Maybe you can do more than look."

I nodded and tried to smile, but all I could do was focus on the door and think about finding Jimmy Bones.

*****

On the way across town, I called Spook to get Jimmy's address. It was close to the bar, so I had time to stop at the Precinct and talk to Arlen. Maybe he had turned up something that I could use. Arlen was a cop who didn't mind trading a little information. Lorene's lowdown could be a little chip for me. By itself, it wasn't worth much. Any detective would have come to that spot along the way, but it would show good faith on my part.

"Naw, Quinn, all we have is Johnny and Jimmy were competitors for the headliner spot at Spook's club. Word is they were both banging that Lorene chick. Nobody was surprised about that. She was known to be about as free as one of them Texas tumbleweeds. One thing, though, Quinn, the night Johnny got killed, he had gotten into a fight with a drunk customer. Johnny kicked his ass. On the way out, the guy yelled he'd get even. Some white guy, twenty-something, big guy, close cut hair, military style. No surveillance footage so I've got a couple uniforms checking the other bars in the neighborhood. It's a long shot, but a shot. What you got?"

I gave Arlen what Lorene gave me and we called it even. After shaking hands, I left and headed toward Jimmy's place.

*****

It was just after six p.m. when Jimmy opened the door. He left the chain on the door thinking that that would stop whoever wanted to get in. I could tell from his glassy eyes and sweaty forehead his day wasn't going as he had hoped when he had poured his morning coffee.

"What's wrong, Jimmy?"

"N-n-n-nuthin," he stuttered.

"Right, asshole," and I kicked in his door, breaking the cheap door chain. There, on the white carpet in front of the coffee table, lay Lorene Willis. She had come a long way from San Antonio just to be shot and killed in a guitar man's apartment. A .22 revolver lay on the coffee table next to the turtle shaped green ashtray, filled with cigarette butts and the remnants of more than a few joints. Lorene's blood had begun to seep into the carpet. Looked like she'd been dead for over an hour, maybe more. I could feel Jimmy standing next to me, his breathing quick but quiet.

"What the fuck, Jimmy? Why?" Looking at Jimmy, I could see he was high and scared. A high, scared, half-wit guitar player with a gun. The stuff that makes the blues the blues.

"I didn't want to, Quinn, but she said she was gonna tell the police about Johnny. I couldn't let her do that. That would've ruined my chances to headline at the club. I couldn't let her do that, y'know what I mean, right, Quinn, y'know what I mean, right?"

I spotted the glass and bottle of cheap scotch on the end table. I told Jimmy to sit and pour himself a drink. Steady himself and tell me what happened. He opened up like a seven-year-old spilling his guts to his momma.

"Lorene came over a few hours ago for some afternoon delight. She liked that. When we was finished, we started talking about me headlinin' at Spook's place. Then, like I don't know what, she got all pissed off and started saying stupid shit, callin' me a murderer and shit. Damn! I told her to shut the fuck up. I told her Khan killed Johnny, not me. But that's when she opened the desk drawer over there and pulled out the .22. She said she found the gun when she was lookin' for a book of matches. I fuckin' snapped, Quinn. I didn't mean to do it, but I grabbed the gun and shot her… twice in the heart." Stopping for a moment, he looked at me like he just got hit by a falling brick, "Quinn, ya think the police will believe me if I said she kilt herself, y'know, suicide?"

I shook my head, "no."

"What about if I tell'em that she had the gun and tried to kill me when she was high and it went off in the fight, what about that, Quinn, what about that?"

Again, I shook my head "no."

"Jimmy, what happened with Johnny? Why'dya shoot Johnny?"

A calmness came over the young guitar man. Almost like he was going into a trance or some Zen thing, and then he spilled it, his confession.

"Mr. Khan gave me the.22 and the .38. He said Johnny was stoppin' me from bein' a headliner. He was stoppin' me from gettin' a good recording contract with American. He said if somebody didn't do somethin' about Johnny, all I could ever hope for was a low-wage contract with Dirt Road."

"Did Khan tell you to kill Johnny?"

"Naw, Mr. Khan jest said somethin' had to be done to make things right for me. He didn't tell me to kill nobody. I loved Johnny. He was like a father to me. I knew Johnny would understand so that night after work when we was smokin' a joint in the alley, I told him what Khan said, but when I told him, he said he didn't care what Khan said. Said Mr. Khan was a gangster. That's when I remembered the .22 in my pocket. I felt it hard in my hand. While feeling it, I remembered the old gangster movie over at Mr. Khan's when the gangster put the .22 next to the punk's head and pulled the trigger. I knew that's what I had to do. So, I did it. I put the barrel next to Johnny's temple and pulled the trigger. Quinn, I loved Johnny. I didn't want to hurt'em. But he wouldn't listen to me. I needed that song. I needed it to be somebody. I don't wanna be jest another guitar player playin' the blues for peanuts and drinks. I jest wanted a little meat to go along with my potatoes and cornbread. What's gonna happen to me, Quinn?"

"You're goin' to prison for a long time, probably the rest of your life, Jimmy. I'll call Detective Arlen." Then I remembered Johnny's bloody hands and missing shoes. "Say, Jimmy, what happened to Johnny's hands and shoes?"

"I don't know nuthin' about his shoes. After I dragged Johnny down the alley so I could put his body behind the pizza place, y'know them I-talyans don't like us folks. Maybe the cops would think one of them killed Johnny. Anyways, when Johnny was layin' there, the streetlight was shining on his body, and I could see his hands. Them same hands that wrote the song I needed and played the guitar like I wanted and I got so damn mad I picked up a brick and started smashin' Johnny's hands. He wasn't never gonna play any blues again! That's it, that's the whole story, Mr. Quinn."

I didn't hate Jimmy. I felt sorry for him. I hated the man who turned Jimmy Bones into a killer.

I told Jimmy to pour himself another drink while I covered Lorene's body and put the .38 in my waistband. I left the .22 on the coffee table. It was the murder weapon. Then I called Arlen.

*****

As the officers escorted the handcuffed Jimmy Bones out of his apartment, Arlen asked me if I thought Frankie Khan had anything to do with this. We both knew Jimmy was too dumb to plan this out on his own. If there was ever a puppet, he was walking out that door right now. I knew arresting Frankie wouldn't do any good. He had an army of lawyers. His top mouthpiece was Morris Kalbach, the number one criminal attorney in the country. Jimmy would tell the court that Khan never told him to kill either Johnny or Lorene. Frankie Khan was smooth, smooth as baby shit. So, I lied, "No, Sean, I don't think Frankie had anything to do with this."

"Me neither." Arlen returned my lie. We were even.

Just as I was walking out the door, Arlen hollered at me, "We found Johnny's shoes."

"Where?"

"On a wino sleeping it off about a block from the club. He admitted to snaggin' the shoes off Johnny after he saw Jimmy leave. We let him keep the shoes."

"Good. Somebody got something out of this."

*****

The Damascus was closing when I got there. Frankie was at the bar with his coffee and Arak. The bartender had already left. I had waited to make sure of that.

"What's up, Quinn? Kinda late for you to be out on these mean streets, isn't it?"

"Thought I'd stop in for that drink of Arak you offered me. I'm celebrating. Cops caught Johnny's killer. Turns out Jimmy Bones killed Johnny over some song Johnny wrote. Then he killed Lorene Willis, a waitress him and Johnny had been bangin'. Looks like you're in the clear."

Pouring two shots of Arak, Frankie said, "What I tell ya, Quinn, I'm a clean guy, a businessman just trying to make a dollar."

192

The licorice liquor went down smooth, coating my tongue and throat, bringing back memories of those black licorice sticks from my old neighborhood.

"Salud."

"Salud."

"Why'dya do it, Frankie? Why'dya set up Jimmy like that? You could've made a ton of money off both Johnny and Jimmy, ya didn't have to get Jimmy to kill Johnny. Y'know Johnny Soul and me go way back, longer than you been around. But you just had to have that extra money quick, you couldn't wait. Is that it?"

Frankie sipped his coffee and stared back at me and finally said, "Quinn, you don't understand. Business is business. Those guitar players weren't going anywhere without a little help from me. And the way they were acting, they were both more trouble than I needed. So, what if I gave Jimmy a couple of suggestions. And as far as Johnny being your friend, get over it. You'll find another friend. There's a phone book over there with a shitload of possible friends."

"You're right, Frankie, I'll get over it, and this will help me." I pulled out the .38 and fired one clean shot into Frankie Khan's right temple.

The night air was good, clean, I could smell a hint of rain coming.

*****

"Ladies and gentlemen, my name is Petey Breedlove, and this is the Breedlove Quartet. We want to begin tonight with a tribute to two dear friends who sadly have left this stage far too soon, two great guitar players and bluesmen, Johnny Soul and Jimmy Bones. Before he died, Johnny wrote this song for him and Jimmy to perform. I've taken the liberty to change the name of it to *Dead Man's Blues*. Singing it tonight will be yours truly. We hope you enjoy our rendition of it."

Sitting at the bar with Betty and Spook, sipping my coffee, I leaned back and listened to the sax man sing Johnny's tune, imagining a young Johnny Washington, all smiles and hope.

A Slice on Secaucus Street
DL Shirey

Detective Armbruster is impatient. She crosses her arms across her chest, the death-grip clutch of unmanicured hands on opposite elbows as she bear hugs herself. When she summons me to the precinct station there's usually a stiff nod and a crisp $20 bill of appreciation. But not today, at least not yet. I'm the last chance to find a lead on a perp she knows is a scumbag.

Beyond the pane of glass in front of us, five men of various hues and sizes shuffle into the line-up room.

I'm Det. Armbruster's snitch, her paid informant. She's calls me in because of my ability to recognize faces. With a single glance, I know—know—if I've seen a person before. Some describe my talent with a fancy name like Hyperthymetic Identification or Photographic Facial Memory. I just call it Backvision. Those other terms imply immediacy, while what happens to me is a slow flashback of recognition. It's like a picture developing in a grindingly slow photo lab, where my memory needs to soak in different trays of chemicals before the portrait ghosts into existence. I'm talking days or weeks. When it finally renders, my recall is super sharp; I can describe where I saw the person, what they were doing, who they were with and when it happened.

"Number three, hoodie off." Armbruster releases the talk button and reclenches her arms.

The man in the middle acts like Armbruster's request is a monumental imposition; he takes one hand from his hoodie pocket and yanks his head free. Everything above the sweatshirt is shaved shiny-smooth, not a trace of hair on his scalp or face.

"That's the guy," she says to me. I can hear the chafe of desperation in her voice.

What's frustrating the good detective is that she doesn't know how long it's going to take me to remember. I've helped her break cases before; not that I've witnessed the exact crime Armbruster was investigating, but that my memory provides additional clues about the suspect involved. For her the clock is ticking. My Backvision, on the other hand, takes its own sweet time.

My memories usually involve the part of town I work in— The Scuzz. In my business, I deal with every kind of deviant and lowlife imaginable, watching them do disgusting, often criminal activities. The Scuzz are those three blocks on Secaucus Street, between 12th and 15th, with its vast collection of bars, strip clubs, porn shops and gambling venues. There's also one liquor store, one convenience store, a free clinic and the pizza joint I own. I'm there every night, doling out slices or delivering whole pies to the hookers, johns, pimps, perverts, addicts, grifters, beggars and rookie cops who get stuck on Scuzz patrol.

I used to hire college kids to run deliveries, but the tips suck and the streets are dicey, so they never stay more than a week or two. With Joaquin baking pies, it's easier to do everything else myself. Funny, I've lived and worked in the neighborhood 28 years; long enough to be instantly recognizable, yet invisible at the same time. Perfect for what I do for Det. Armbruster.

"Okay, Pizza, this one give you a tickle?" Ever since she made detective, she uses the nickname they call me in The Scuzz. It's all business between her and me now.

She calls me in a few times a month so I can do my thing. A line-up serves two purposes: it lets the bad guys know that Armbruster is watching them, but it also gives me the chance to eyeball a key suspect. Number Three is here for me, to see if his face literally tickles my fancy. It's how Backvision feels when it starts: like the tickle in the back of my throat when I'm about to cough, except it prickles my midbrain, about an inch behind my left eye.

"Nope," I say.

Armbruster's arms unlock and her chest returns to its normal carriage beneath the clean, off-white blouse and rumpled navy pantsuit. She hooks her shaggy, walnut-brown hair behind both ears and readjusts her glasses. The specs are as square as she is, with no brand name etched on the black, plastic frames. In the thirty-five years Armbruster has lived, fashion has not been part of her make up. Neither has makeup.

Her pale green eyes darken a bit and she pokes the talk button. "That's all."

A uniformed cop ushers out the quintet. The man in the middle returns the hood to its place and flashes a golden smile. The harsh light glints off the grill beneath his lips. Armbruster watches until the line-up room is empty, then places her hand on a stack of file folders on the table next to us.

She has more work for me to do.

"Tatanni, Angela." She reads the name on the moderately thick folder atop the pile. The files come in various bulks, the ones with the most paper are lassoed by a daisy chain of rubber bands linked together with paper clips. Armbruster unbridles the folder, wrapping the elastic around her wrist. It looks like a bracelet made by an uncoordinated kindergartener.

"You know this enchanting lass?" She plucks out a mug shot; a female Caucasian so white that one shade lighter would have made her translucent. The eyes scowl as if possessed by wicked magic: irises the color of tap water, which make the pinpoint pupils seem extra black and the surrounding bloodshot the reddest red. The hair is hacked short, unkempt and clumped like used cotton balls pasted haphazardly to her skull.

I tell Armbruster that I've seen "Tats" Tatanni a hundred times, usually on the backstreets, shooting junk behind a dumpster or hunched over a driver in a parked car to earn another fix. Even in those shadowy recesses, her skin and hair attract any available light to be almost phosphorescent. She is always visible, even in the dark.

Armbruster waits, wanting more. She thumbs the edge of the rap sheet, an incessant, papery flick that won't stop until I give her something. I've explained the limitations of my Backvisions too many times to count, but she won't move on to the next folder until I say it again.

"Tats is a white shadow, a ghost on the periphery," I say. "She's usually around The Scuzz somewhere. Because she looks the way she looks, she always registers. She's so unique there's nothing unique about seeing her. It's the unfamiliar faces, the one-offs that spark my memory, not the jerk-offs I see every night."

"What does she do? Where does she go?"

"Why is Tats on your dance card?" I ask.

The detective doesn't answer, repeating her previous two questions instead.

"Like I've said before, The Scuzz has a front and a back, sidewalks where the hustle goes down and alleyways where no one in their right mind wants to be. You been back there. You can't see the blacktop for all the broken furniture, cardboard boxes, busted glass and trash. Bodies lay there until they wake up or the coroner comes to bag them. Tats is always around, on her knees to scrounge a tossed cigarette or doing some freak that no other street worker would touch."

"And you're back there because…"

"The pizza place only has a counter on Secaucus, the one door is in the back." I'm bored repeating this over and over, but Armbruster listens as if she's never heard the story before. "When I make deliveries, I take shortcuts. I know which basements connect to another, the roofs where the stairwell doors are unlocked, what windows to duck through to take a fire escape back down when I ain't carrying pies. Why do you ask me this same goddamn question?"

Armbruster doesn't smile, doesn't blink. She raises one eyebrow glacially slow. "Because sometimes you tell me things you never did before. Just now, taking the fire escapes down, that's new information. You never know when a couple of words will break a case."

Then she says, "Have you ever seen her with this man?"

The next folder is unnamed and unencumbered by rubber bands. No mug shot or rap sheet, only a grainy still from the liquor store's security camera. A broad-shouldered gentleman in a Panama hat, the wide brim hiding most of his face. The only revelation is a gap-toothed smile and razor-thin mustache shadowing his upper lip.

There's that unscratchable itch behind my eye: I've seen that jaw before.

Along with a tickle, my Backvision brings an accompanying impression or emotional twinge. Ninety-nine times it's always the same—a nagging angst, like the answer is right there on the tip of my tongue. This mystery man, though, is one in a hundred. Unadulterated dread oozes from that spot in my brain and crawls like cold molasses down the inside of my skin leaving gooseflesh in its wake. I glance up to Armbruster, if for no other reason than I can't stand looking at that chin any longer.

"Well? Have you seen him?" she asks.

"Maybe," I lie, wondering if my poker face is holding, "If his eyes were there, I'd know for sure." What *I am* sure about is that all the other faces in that stack of folders won't mean a thing to me. I didn't know until now that Backvision had an express lane, but the gap-tooth man in the Panama hat just became a priority. A rush job. The only problem is, there's no rushing my memory. I don't know if I can find a way to speed up development, but if I don't try, something very bad is going happen. If it hasn't happened already.

*****

From Secaucus Street, above the sidewalk order window, the sign reads Pizza Kitch. Big letters cut from plywood, weather-worn and faded to pink. The EN is missing. Bolt holes in the stucco are physical reminders where they used to be, and I can still see the big red letters if I let myself imagine it. But it's never a good idea for me to drift away, except to sleep.

I didn't do well in school because I daydreamed too much. The most trivial things would set me off and I'd lose myself for countless minutes, wide-eyed and catatonic. Home was no different. Pop would slap me on the back of the head if he caught me staring into space. 'You're in the way,' he'd say, or 'Chores won't finish themselves.' Mom would just shake her head knowingly, until that dreamy glaze repainted her face and she'd go back to her washing or ironing.

Pop started Pizza Kitchen, but because he thought I was a slacker, he rarely let me work there. He always had a summer job lined up for me somewhere else in the neighborhood and would threaten me with reform school if he heard that I'd been lazy. Mom tried to defend him, explaining that Pop wanted more for me than slinging pies on Secaucus. The business barely paid the bills, she'd say, and it wasn't a good life. With my grades, college wasn't an option, so that left the Army. Or would have had Mom not died. She ran the stoplight on 14th and was gone long before they could pry her out.

Her mind was elsewhere, and no one can convince me otherwise. It's why I refuse to own a car. Daydreaming and driving don't mix.

Pop died slowly thereafter. It was like he instantly became an old man, feeble and listless. With Mom gone he needed my help to keep food on the table, even if it was mostly leftover pizza. From then on, Pop didn't quibble or criticize my work; I don't even think he saw the decline on Secaucus Street when we'd walk from the house to Pizza Kitchen and back. The lunch trade ended about the time when The Scuzz got its nickname. Pop didn't want to work nights, so he went to live with his brother in Hoboken. He never came back and I've been here ever since.

After Pop left, the pizza went downhill. Not that the people who eat here consult Yelp to find the best local cuisine; they walk by and stop to cram down slices, chasing them with off-brand soda. I do what's needed to cut corners, and the limp, greasy triangles still get eaten. I can stay in business if I don't use too much real cheese, and it's become a waste of time to make sauce from scratch when I can get big vats of the stuff wholesale. Fat Wok, what everyone calls Joaquin, still tosses fresh dough. It's cheaper that way, besides the fact that my joint has no room for a freezer full of pre-mades. As far as the menu goes, it's two choices: plain cheese or the special, which is plain cheese sprinkled with whatever's laying around. Today it's fresh bell pepper that Fat Wok lifted from the greengrocer on the way to work, and petrified discs that used to be Canadian bacon.

"Gimme a cheese." I can tell without turning around it's Dee for Delores. The first time I met the hooker, with her stick legs and mini skirt, she asked me to call her Dee, Dee for Delores. It's been that way ever since.

"One for three or two for five?" My standard deal for regulars is to knock a buck off the second slice. When she gives me the peace sign I pull two from under the heat lamp and onto separate squares of wax paper. I throw in a napkin. "Enjoy."

The guy behind her I do not know, just another stiff in a trench coat. He inquires about the special and I tell him. He takes one and I take four dollars. Another bill for a soda makes five.

"You got Parmesan?" he asks.

"No."

"Pepper flakes?"

"No."

"An extra napkin?"

"Here."

"Got any of those wet wipe things in a little pouch?"

"No. Use the grease to go jerk off. Get outa here."

He holds his hands up like he is being robbed at gunpoint, "Okay, okay," he says, grabs the slice and can and leaves.

"The nerve of some people," I say to Fat Wok.

He winks at me, peeking past the edge of an enormous plastic cup as he gulps down water. It's always hot in here, so it must be hell for a man his size. Wok never says much, expect to ask me to refill the pizza fixings. He rarely moves beyond the miniscule space between work table, sink and pizza oven. He looks like an off-duty Sumo dressed in short shorts, flip flops and sweat-soaked wife beater, rivulets streaming from every fold of skin.

I turn back to the customerless window and fix a stare out at nothing in particular. That little tickle behind my eye starts again compliments of that last customer, the man in the trench coat. Like I said, don't know him, never seen him before, but there was something in the way he held up his hands, palms toward me like he wanted to play patty cake.

That pose sets my mind in motion, sparking a memory. Except, instead of trench-coat guy, it's the guy from my Backvision. The man in the Panama hat.

Dread seeps in like a sepia tint on an antique photograph. I've seen him before, I just can't tell where, yet. He's in that same pose: five fingers on either side of his head, gapped teeth not showing this time. His mouth is shaped like an O and the razor-thin mustache surrounds it like brackets. The brim of his hat is raised, but no eyes have developed yet. Everything else is varying shades of murk, a semi-dark oval where the face will go, and total black behind it. In the foreground there's a glowing orb of fuzzy illumination. It's like an eclipse in reverse, a spherical object over-brightening its portion of the image in my head. I get the feeling this scene takes place in an alleyway, perhaps, and there's an associated smell that I can't quite remember. Then I get a dull prodding at my rib cage, which totally confuses me because it doesn't fit into my Backvision. Another jab pulls me back to reality.

Fat Wok has the long-handled pizza paddle in his hands. He has seen me in this trance-like state countless times, knows my senses are otherwise occupied and I would not hear the ringing phone without a physical nudge. I grab the wall-mounted landline.

"Pizza Kitchen, whatcha need?" I grab the pad by the phone and scribble out a ticket. "Can I have a name for the order?"

*****

I slide the walk-up window closed and hang the sign that says BACK IN 5. It's not that I don't trust Fat Wok with the register, he simply won't budge from his station. Forget about serving customers, I've never seen him leave to use the toilet. Two pies steam on the side counter. I box them up and head out the back door to D'Angelo's. He's got a card game across the alley and up one flight. I don't know if it's penny-ante or high-rolling because I don't go in, just knock and leave the boxes on top of a heaping garbage can.

I keep thinking about my Backvision, but it's too soon to tell Armbruster about it. There's nothing to give her to go on—no hard ID, that it maybe took place in an alley, some kind of smell. She'd give me the look that says 'don't waste my time.'

I'm all the way down stairs when I hear 'Pizza,' not an acknowledgement of my delivery but someone calling my name. D'Angelo fills his doorway, backlit by smoke and amber lights. As I retrace my steps, the smell of cigarettes—and a whiff of something that tickles with familiarity—mingles with the scent of pizza and garbage.

"Got a surprise visit the other morning, a friend of yours asking questions." He talks in a flat, Jersey monotone, but emphasizes words by poking an accusing finger in the air between us. The black-dyed hair conceals his true age as does the bad facelift: stretches where wrinkles once were, eyebrows higher than they used to be. "It was Armtwister going door to door. You and her is pals, what's up?"

I never liked Armbruster's nickname. And we are friends, or used to be, anyway. We grew up together, only she was seven years ahead of me. Believe it or not, she's the one who took my cherry, along with the promise to never tell my older sister, her then best friend. Sis left town but Armbruster stayed, if you don't count those 22 weeks when she went upstate for police academy. I never really got over her, being my first time and all, but she was done with me by the morning after. Strictly business between us now: the $20s she tosses me help pay the bills. The only other thing Armbruster and I have in common, we get the same food gift from my sister at Christmas.

"Don't know what she was doing here," I answer, "Seems like you were the last to see her, what did she say?"

"Liar." D'Angelo pokes twice in the brief silence. "I saw you leave the police station this afternoon. Who else do you hang with at the precinct? Who else would let you fuck them?"

"That was a long time ago, one time, and you know it. Went there 'cause I had a couple extra pies, that's all; dropped them off for the boys. The next time shit goes down in The Scuzz, I might need a favor."

"They prefer cash in that regard. Besides, your pizza's not that good, may your father rest in peace." He makes the sign of the cross and continues, "No offense," D'Angelo says, "But I only bring in food so players don't leave. That and you let me run a tab."

"Which is pushing up against $75."

D'Angelo pulls out a wad of cash and peels off a Benjamin. "An extra five for your trouble and twenty in credit. Now, let's get back to Armtwister's visit."

Oh great, I think to myself, more ridicule about me and Armbruster. For that I've only myself to blame. Our one-night stand became common knowledge around the neighborhood when I got sloppy drunk at Murph's and sobbed my story to Murph himself. Of my many barroom regrets, it's the one I relive most often. And I might have, this minute, gone off to daydream-land had I not been standing at D'Angelo's door.

A man with a full-moon face nudges D'Angelo aside.

"Gimme dat, I'm hungry." The big lug shoulders into the doorway, reaching past D'Angelo for the pizza boxes. He's an Asian gentleman, Hitler mustache, teeth gripping an ornate, silver cigarette holder. On the end is a smoke with a black wrapper and funny odor.

"Excuse you," D'Angelo says, hip-checking the interloper as he pulls the boxes into the room. Asian Hitler growls, his bared teeth flick the cigarette holder up to a 45° angle. The smell hits me again.

"What's she investigating?" D'Angelo asks me.

"What?" I have to concentrate hard on his words, the smell of that cigarette begins to resurrect the Backvision.

"Armtwister. She never said it straight out, but…" D'Angelo turns to see if Asian Hitler is within earshot, "I got the distinct impression it was the Ubimanyu brothers she was nosing around about. Or their store, at least." D'Angelo winks an eye, but his skin-tight forehead never moves. "She talk about the Ubimanyus? You cuddle after sex, right?"

I throw up my arms and bellow, "We did it one time. Ten years ago. Let it go, D'Angelo." I turn and stomp down the stairs, barking obscenities.

I'm sure my dramatic outburst didn't phase D'Angelo; in fact, because of my tantrum, he is probably 100-percent sure that Armbruster and I are romantically involved. No, my theatrical rage was the only thing I could think of to cover my panic. In my mind, the Backvision is growing clearer. I have to get down the stairs before it elbows out all my other senses.

The tickle becomes insistent. I've got to find a place to hide before it overwhelms me. I stumble into Skinflix. Mikey who has his head buried in the sports section of a newspaper. He flaps down one corner, recognizes me and returns to his reading.

"Need a room. For a few minutes," I stammer.

"Never seen you in here before. First time for everything," Mikey says, not looking up this time. "Any stall, except number three. Preview discs on the rack to your left."

"What, what do I owe you?" My mouth is having trouble forming words.

"If you like what you see, five bucks off your DVD purchase. Or ten bucks for ten minutes." His monotone cadence doesn't vary, even when he turned the page of his newspaper.

"No movie, umm, just the room," I say.

Mikey has seen it all before. He shrugs. "For you it's on the house. Knock yourself out."

The lurid photos and raunchy titles blur as I stagger toward the viewing booths. They look like public bathroom stalls: four narrow rectangles, divided by metal walls that start about a foot above the dirty, tile floors. The doors hinge outward, all open except the one stenciled #3, its half-circle of red proclaiming it OCCUPIED. I pull the door to #1 shut. Instead of a toilet there is a wall-mounted TV, an older model with one slot for DVDs and one for VHS tapes. I collapse into a cheap, plastic chair, which takes up most of the floor space inside the stall.

I can barely see the blank, black TV set in front of me, it's shape becoming an afterimage to my Backvision: It was two nights ago, and I was returning from delivering a pie, coming down the fire escape. I was in the alley behind the convenience store, climbing off the ladder when I saw her.

Tats was on her knees, hip deep in trash, harvesting butts from an old coffee can. She picked them out, one by one, giving each a sniff. 'Jesus Christ,' she said, 'who'd smoke these shits.' I could smell it too, stronger now that I was reliving the scene: the sickeningly sweet, smoky scent of clove cigarettes. The place reeked of it. 'Fucking Indonesians,' Tats said, standing up. Her white skin and hair glowed from the light coming from the open door of the convenience store. Then a shadow darkened the doorway. 'Hey Mister, got any real smokes?' Tats asked the man who had reached the exit. At first he ignored the request, but did a double take at the talking ghost and stopped to face her. He pushed up the brim of his Panama hat and a cruel smile revealed the gap in his teeth. He flashed his palms on both sides of his face and said 'boo.' His eyes were as round as his mouth.

And something else; something about his hands were odd. It felt important, a valuable clue Armbruster would need. I strain to make the answer come, but the replay skitters and stops. It's like a movie projector in my head that clatters to a halt, freezing the picture. I know there will be more to the scene, but I cannot control a Backvision. For now it will go no further.

I don't know how much time had passed. Mikey hasn't moved, but is now reading the Metro section. Pizza Kitchen is closed when I return.

I unlock the door and keep the lights off. The streetlamps and neon out on Secaucus give me enough to see that Fat Wok's station is spotless, but the floor is unswept and there's trash everywhere. All of that can be done when I come back in the morning. The cash register's till is missing, but I find where Wok had stashed it, under a stack of unfolded pizza boxes. I pocket the bills and lock the back door on my way out.

For The Scuzz, midnight isn't late, though Armbruster would probably be home now. I walk past my house, up another ten blocks and right on 47th. It is a nice night for a walk and the neighborhoods are more manicured on this side of town, where the streets weave their way uphill. Armbruster's Volvo is in the driveway of her neat bungalow, one light on, in the kitchen. I see her shadow on the blinds. She's still up.

I find her number in my phone but hesitate. This is where it always gets weird. A call to her at night, even if it's police business, always makes me think twice. I know that she knows I'm still nuts about her, as does everyone in the neighborhood thanks to my sloppy barroom lament. And she knows that I know nothing will ever happen. Still, my finger hovers over the phone just above the call button, its color green as grass.

Suddenly, I'm imagining myself back in high school, left field in my baseball uniform. There's a crack of a bat and I see the ball arcing over my head. I backpedal as fast as I can, thinking I can catch it, then feel the ground change beneath my feet. Grass under one foot, the dirt of the warning track under the other. I jump anyway, knowing that any second I am going to slam hard into an unyielding wall. But I've still got a chance to make the catch.

That's what it feels like when I phone Armbruster at night; like I'm one step away from the warning track. And there's a possibility, however remote, she'll let me call her KellyAnne again.

I press the green button and she answers. "You up?" I say.

There's a pause, like she's double-checking the caller info on her phone. "Yeah. Are you okay?" As much as I wanted her words to mean 'how are you feeling tonight,' I could tell by her inflection she meant 'is there anything wrong.'

"Pizza?" Armbruster says, "You there?"

"Yeah. It's about that photo from the liquor store. That gap-toothed guy in the Panama hat, I've seen him before. Tats has seen him before, too."

"Hold that thought," she replies. "I want to hear all about it, but I just got called out on a 10-54, possible dead body. Can I meet you at Pizza Kitchen, say in an hour?"

*****

Almost exactly an hour later, I'm in the alley behind Ubimanyu's convenience store. Armbruster is a block down, where the alley empties out onto 15th Street. The 10-54 is in The Scuzz and the crime scene looks like Christmas with all the twinkling cop car lights and garlands of yellow caution tape wrapping the place. An officer lifts the tape so Armbruster doesn't have to duck. She has a few words with the uniform, and when she's through, I walk to meet her.

I tell Armbruster all about Tats and Panama Hat, "The smell of cloves, the butts on the ground. Yeah, I'm sure it was here behind Ubimanyu's."

"I want to hear Angela's side of it—Tats, I mean. Got someone looking for her right now," Armbruster says, "Wait here a minute." She enters the store through the back door.

The inside light illuminates the trash in the alley. I kick at the rubbish revealing a coffee can heaped with black cigarette butts. Then a shadow fills the adjacent doorway and I shudder. It's like the Backvision is rerunning again in real time, except the shadow isn't Panama Hat, but Ponco Ubimanyu, one of the owners of the store. Armbruster follows him out.

"Don't like to lock the front door," Ponco says, "S'posed to be open 24/7, so every minute I'm back here's costing me money."

"It won't take long," Armbruster declares, "Unless you want me to call up Catur, get him in here to talk instead."

Armbruster knew which button to push. Catur and Ponco are identical, 35-year-old twins of Indonesian decent, skinny as skeletons. Their first names, literally translated, mean 'fourth born' and 'fifth born.' Since none of their other siblings have immigrated, birth order gives Catur dominance in family matters. Everyone in the neighborhood knows that Catur would be furious if Ponco couldn't handle this little problem himself.

"It's fine," he replies.

Armbruster glances up the alley, still distracted, the flashing lights reflecting off her glasses. Her gaze returns to Ponco, "You sell a lot of clove cigarettes? What is it your people call them, Kreteks?"

"Yeah, I smoke them too. Little Jakarta restaurant is one block over. Cooks and waiters and customers come in and buy. My older sister ships Kreteks to us. Not against the law is it?"

Armbruster shakes her head 'no,' then produces that picture, the man in the Panama hat. "Does he smoke Kreteks?"

Ponco takes a close look. "No. He don't buy much, not at night, at least. I've sold him toothpaste and shave cream. One time a can opener before that."

"He must live near here," Armbruster muses, "You were pretty quick to recognize him for not coming in here much."

"He got this ring. A gold ring he taps on the counter while he waits. Both times he was in, tapping like a nervous habit or something," says Ponco. "Stuff like that drives me crazy."

"Which hand?" Armbruster asks.

"What?"

"The ring, right or left?"

"Left."

"Married?"

"Not a wedding band. Big, ostentatious thing on his number one finger." He demonstrates by pointing his index finger skyward.

Ostentatious. Ponco loves learning advanced English words and using them in conversation. Armbruster is still listening to him, but her attention is drawn to a pair of people walking toward us. One is a uniformed officer backlit by flashing lights from the police scene, the other's skin and hair glows snowy white. Armbruster signals the officer to stop a few paces away, then pockets the photo. She says to Ponco, "Anything else?"

He squints his eyes shut, as if thinking. They pop open again. "Couple times he used the store for a shortcut, you know, get from the sidewalk to the alley without going around the block. Pizza does it too." Ponco is talking to me now, "Drives me crazy when you do that. Indecorous is what it is. A decent person would buy something."

"If it bothers you so much, why don't you lock the back door?" I say, offended. I don't even know what indecorous means.

"Catur wants both doors open. Says breeze keeps the store from getting too hot." Ponco waits. "Is that it?" His head does a couple swivels between me and Armbruster.

"Yeah, you can open up your store again," she says. When he leaves Armbruster turns to me, "Pizza, I need you to go inside so I can talk to Angela. But stay close. When I say so, walk out into the alley and do that thing you told me about."

"What thing?"

"Pretend you're the man in the Panama hat. Come out and say 'boo.'"

I step inside the back door of the convenience store. The narrow hallway has two other doors. One is marked TOILET, the other leans against the wall, off its hinges, next to the closet it once enclosed. The ceiling is tall and the bare bulb lighting the hallway is high overhead. I lean against the wall, right under that bulb so I don't cast a shadow toward the back door. It's close enough to overhear.

"Is this the one you're looking for?" Male voice, must be the officer.

"Why, you find a lot of women who fit this description?" Armbruster is sarcastic, then she's serious, "Before you go, any update on the body?"

"Still in the dumpster. The trash covering the victim has been removed."

"And that trash?" asks Armbruster.

"As requested, ma'am, photographed in place and bagged for further analysis. The victim hasn't been moved, but the Medical Examiner hasn't arrived yet.

"Winslow's taking photos, what does he think?"

"Says the body is well past rigor," the officer replies, "Best guess is that it's been in there at least 48 hours.

"Did you see it? The body. After the trash was removed."

"Yes ma'am."

"Anything, uh, missing?" It sounds as if Armbruster doesn't want to put words in the officer's mouth.

"No ma'am. A finger was snapped back this time, though. Out of joint but still attached."

"That's all, officer. Thank you." In the space of a breath Armbruster's voice lost it's official edge, becoming gentle, "You okay, Angela?"

"People don't call me that no more."

"Okay. Tats." Armbruster speaks like she would to a child. "I just want to know if you're all right."

"Nah." Tats has a soft, whispery voice. "I just gotta go."

"To the bathroom?"

"Nah. Just go. Someplace else."

"You can go in a minute, but all these police, they aren't after you," Armbruster says. "Maybe you can help us find the man who did it."

Tats didn't ask 'did what?' And the way she gives non-answers to Armbruster's questions about the dumpster and the victim, it seems like Tats saw what went down. Armbruster keeps pressing, trying to elicit any scrap of information, but Tats closes up and starts answering with one and two syllables. Armbruster eases up a little, changes the subject to clove cigarettes and what Tats was doing here two nights ago. Armbruster paints the picture, reminding Tats that she was here picking up butts when a man walked out.

My cue. I take two paces out the door and do my best to recreate the Backvision. Tats recoils in horror. Her reaction is more violent than being startled by me jumping out and saying 'boo.' Tats is genuinely frightened.

Armbruster grabs one of my wrists and says to me, "Don't move." Then she turns to Tats. "You remember this, don't you? The man who was here two night ago?"

Tats nods, peeking out slowly from behind protective forearms.

"You've seen him before, haven't you?"

Another nod, arms falling away.

"You know where he lives?"

"Nah. Some guys you don't follow," Tats says. "This dude, best to stay clear, you know?"

"Yeah, I know." Armbruster tightens her grip on my wrist. "Okay, Angela—Tats—think hard. Is there anything that stands out to you. From the other night."

"Like what?" Tats is staring at the ground, not at Armbruster. Not at me.

"Look at him, try to remember," Armbruster says, "Were there any tattoos, scars, jewelry, something about his hands."

Armbruster is still squeezing my wrist. Tighter. And when Tats finally locks her colorless eyes on mine, a switch flips in my brain. There wasn't even a tickle. Suddenly, I was reliving the Backvision, but this time from Panama Hat's point of view. I don't know how, maybe because I was standing exactly where he stood, but if Armbruster hadn't had hold of my wrist, I would have fallen down. Nothing like this has ever happened before, yet there I was, inside his skin: I could feel his hands on either side of his head and I could see him looking at Tats.

Armbruster squeezes my wrist again, snapping me back to reality. She says to Tats, practically begging, "He's right here. In front of you. He pushes up his hat and says 'boo.' What do you see?"

"Rings," Tats replies, "Not on the hand you're holding, the left hand. He has two rings."

Armbruster releases my wrist, but I'm frozen in place. When Tats said 'two rings' my brain jumped back to seeing everything through Panama Hat's eyes: how he lowered his hands and extended his left arm, pointing at Tats. There's a big gold ring on his index finger and another—fatter, gaudier, diamond encrusted—jammed on his thumb. He looked at Tats and laughed. Then he raised his arm, pointing again; this time behind Tats, at a man climbing down the ladder from the fire escape.

Me.

And in that instant, memory and reality overlap. I blink away my out-of-body perspective and snap back into real time. I stand here, dazed, for only a moment, until everything tilts sideways and inky blackness floods in from all sides.

*****

Tap tap tap.

Tap tap tap. The sound is far away at first, but draws me closer with its insistent, annoying regularity. I'm not exactly sure where I am, but I'm lying down, flat on my back. It's dark. But it should be dark because my eyes are closed, yet I can tell the lights are on above me. I know if I open my eyes the brightness will hurt. Don't want bright right now, just to lay here.

Tap tap tap. I can't quite identify it. Water dripping from a faucet? No, more metallic. Then I remember Ponco's story about the gap-toothed man in the Panama hat tapping his ring on the counter. My eyes jolt open and the overheads blind me. I mask my eyes with my arm and know immediately where I am— on the floor of the convenience store.

"He's coming around." A voice I don't recognize.

A hand on my shoulder. Another pulls my arm away from my face. My eyelids slam together to keep out the light, and everything that's happened, past and present, begins to reassemble.

"Joey, you're all right." She says it like a statement of fact, but there's concern in her voice.

Nothing could have kept me from opening my eyes in this moment. Armbruster's face is poised above me, shading the harsh glow of fluorescents. She called me Joey. Not Pizza, not Joe.

"Just take it easy for a minute," she says.

I'm in Ubimanyu's store, back by the tall glass doors stacked with dairy and soda and beer. The tapping sound is coming from the display case, part of the labored whirr from the refrigeration unit. Tap tap tap.

All the puzzle pieces snap into place and I raise my head. "He's stealing peoples' rings, isn't he?"

"Easy," says Armbruster, "You fainted. Scared Tats bad enough that she ran off. Just lay there and rest."

I want to, but my mind starts doing jumping jacks. "The body in the dumpster, broken finger, the man in the Panama hat stole his ring, didn't he?"

Armbruster looks up to see if anyone is close by, "Yeah," she whispers, "The sixth, that we know of. The rings are those big, expensive ones that show off the bling. Always men. They aren't necessarily killed, not if the victims give up the rings willingly. A couple, though, got their fingers cut off. Perp is good with a knife."

Seems to me that's an awful lot of trouble to go through for a ring. "They must be valuable then."

"Suppose so," says Armbruster, "He hasn't hocked one yet. We even leaned on the guys who fence jewelry and got a big, fat zero. Not that they'd give up any names."

"Then he keeps them. Collects them maybe."

"We just don't know." She moves gracefully from her knees to a crouch, tugging me up with her. "Just lean up against the cooler. Let's see if you're okay."

She called me Joey.

"I'm okay," I say.

"I've got to get back to my 10-54, unless you want me to stay."

Yes, please. And hold my hand for as long as you want. "I'll be all right."

"You sure?"

I am. Relieved that the Backvision is complete and hopeful it will help Armbruster, I give her a nod. She pauses a moment, then stands and leaves. Half a tick later Ponco hovers over me.

"You gonna buy something, or what?" he says.

⁎⁎⁎⁎⁎

Fat Wok is moving to music only he can hear. A hip-shaking jig to the beat of whatever is playing on his headphones. The old floorboards tremble when he spins and stomps, catching the airborne pizza dough on the back of his hairy wrists. I have to laugh.

Tap tap tap.

The sound makes me do my own dance. I whirl around to the order window, almost tripping over the boxy Styrofoam tub of iced soft drinks. I half expect to see a crazy, gap-toothed smile, its owner shaking his ring-laden fist, brandishing a knife. No, it's Armbruster knocking on the smudged glass and I push the slider aside.

"Wanted to make sure you were okay after last night," she says.

"Sure," I lie. It's hell on one's nervous system to have the man accused of amputating fingers—and maybe murder—know that I was there in the alley after his most recent felony. "Just another night in pizza town."

"This is Officer Lanz," Armbruster thumbs a fist toward a stocky, young Latina in the blue uniform. "We're putting on an extra beat cop. She and Muskowitz will be around if you need them, but feel free to call me if you see anything out of the ordinary."

"You pretty much described everything that goes on around here," I say.

"You know what I mean." Armbruster leans in closer and lowers her voice, "I've got to stake out Goldie's pawnshop tonight. Can you run a couple slices over before you close?"

"Ginger Ale to go with it?"

"Please. And if Lanz wants anything now, it's on me." Armbruster slides me $20 and walks away. I've learned over the years that it's no good to offer her a freebie or make change for the bill she hands me. "Want anything, officer?"

Lanz steps forward and raises up on her tiptoes, eyeballing the interior. She wrinkles her nose and with a curt 'no thanks,' walks off in the same direction as Armbruster. With the uniform gone, the sidewalk crowds up a little more. Up steps Dee for Delores.

"Is the special anything special?" She grins at her own witticism.

"Meat lovers," I announce, then whisper so only Dee can hear, "Mystery meat. I'd pass if I was you."

"Okay, thanks. One cheese and a soda. Anything diet'll do." She tosses up a $5 bill. "Keep it."

I fetch her slice and rummage under the floating ice and find a can of diet root beer. There's only a few cold sodas left, so I'll need to drop in another dozen to get me through the night. I hand the root beer to Dee and tell the guy behind her, a man in a black do-rag, to give me a minute.

I bend down, shoveling cans into the ice bath, when that funny feeling starts: the man at the order window seems very familiar. The tickle starts and compounds quickly until it feels like a giant bug buzzing around the center of my brain. I barely made eye contact with Do-Rag, but I'm sure I've seen him before. An urge grips me, to stay down on my hands and knees, just crawl away instead of facing the man.

"Come on, let's go." His voice has a nasally whine to it. Then I hear a resounding smack that could only be Do-Rag's hand slapping the counter, loud enough that Fat Wok hears it.

Wok says, "Easy, my man. We be with you in a sec."

The squirming sensation in the middle of my skull has me confused. What happened last night in the alley had me convinced that the scene with Panama Hat was fully revealed, that my Backvision about him was complete. But there is something awfully familiar about Do-Rag. Maybe the tickle is telling me about a whole new face.

"Ain't got all night." His nasal impatience is punctuated by flesh striking the counter again.

My backbone finds a way to straighten. Do-Rag's mug fills the order window in full sneer, gold glints where his teeth should be. As soon as I recognize him, the tickle subsides and the descent into Backvision evaporates. It's the man from yesterday's line up. He has no hoodie tonight, but he's still clean-shaven below the rim of his skullcap.

He cocks his head and says, "Hey, don't I know you?"

"I'm here all night, every night. Probably seen me around."

"That must be it. What pizzas you got?"

"Plain cheese and the special," I say, "Meat lovers."

"That's it, huh. Then I'll take a whole cheese to go."

I glance back at the near-empty platters under heat lamps and to Fat Wok waiting by the oven. "It'll be a bout ten minutes for that pie."

"Then gimme a slice of meat while I wait."

I quote a price and turn toward my pizza maker. I shout his name and make a circle in the air to indicate a whole pie. "Cheese to go," I say, loud enough for Fat Wok to hear over his music. Behind me, a hand smacks the counter once again.

I turn to see that Do-Rag has slapped down two twenties, his palm still resting on the bills. There's a big gold ring on one finger, mindlessly tapping while he waits. Handing over his slice, I pluck away the bills and make change at the register. As I return, Do-Rag has pulled the golden grill from his mouth, clutching it in one hand. The other—the one with the ring on it—guides the limp, meaty triangle into his mouth. He tears off the bite with familiar gapped teeth.

It's him. The man in the Panama hat has changed his look.

As calmly as I can, I lay his change on the counter. Then I think about Armbruster and grab the pad by the telephone.

I try to hold my voice steady, praying to God that the man doesn't recognize that I was in the alley with him and Tats. "Can I have a name for the order?"

"What the fuck you need— it's Dewey, okay? Dewey. Just hurry the hell up."

The name he gave me is probably a fake, but maybe it's an alias Armbruster can use. I turn my back to the man and head over to the stack of unfolded pizza boxes. Glancing sideways, I make sure he isn't watching me. I pull out my phone, peck out a text to Armbruster and tap the send button. I stare hard at the screen, willing an immediate answer.

In my periphery, Fat Wok shovels out the steaming pie and slides it on the counter next to me. The motion startles me, then fear jumps into my throat when Dewey pulls himself up through the window. His arm is hooked around the counter like he's about to climb inside.

"Box it, man. I gotsta go."

I turn my back, hoping he won't see the phone, giving Armbruster a few more seconds to answer. Dewey growls something nonsensical and I imagine him clawing his way over the counter, teeth bared, bits of the half-chewed pizza slice falling from his mouth. In a panic, I fling my phone aside and make a show of boxing his pizza, hinging up the folds of flat cardboard, tucking in the flaps.

"I know you're hungry," Fat Wok calls, "But it ain't that good."

Dewey dismounts at my approach, standing outside the window with his arms outstretched. He grabs the box and sprints down the street. I stick my head out the window and see him duck inside Ubimanyu's, three doors down.

In that instant I know Dewey is taking a shortcut. I've got about 15 seconds before he exits the store into the alley. I want to be back there to see where he goes, tail him for Armbruster. I slide the counter window shut and hang the sign.

"Back in five," I say to Fat Wok.

I'm almost to the back door when I hear the ping of a text message. My phone is nowhere in sight, so I search in and around the counter and stack of flattened pizza boxes. Nothing.

The phone pings again. It has fallen behind the counter, next to the short wall that defines Wok's pizza-making station. I can see the lit screen and I try to cram my arm into the gap, but it's just out of reach.

"You okay?" Wok says.

Ping. I know it's Armbruster, but if I don't get to the alley now, Dewey will be gone. I abandon the phone and rush out the back door.

Dewey lopes out of the convenience store, turns back and shouts, "Fuck you. I ain't buying shit." Then turns and runs in my direction.

"Miscreant!" Ponco emerges, shaking his fist. "Reprobate! Stay out of my store. Don't ever come back."

I step out into the center of the alley and Dewey slows to a standstill. He drops the pizza box and flashes his gap-toothed smile. He takes a slow, deep breath, shoulders growing wide. The man is three-inches taller and a half-foot broader than me.

"Wouldna come back, but I had to see if you'd recognize me." His eyes narrow. "Guess I was right."

At that moment I knew the Backvision was gone, the perp was fully revealed. But by the way he was scowling at me, I was starting to doubt whether I would live to help Armbruster again.

"All this for a couple of rings?" I said, hoping to buy more time. I could see Ponco walking up closer.

"A couple." Dewey smirks and hooks his thumb around a thick gold necklace. One by one, a dozen rings pop out from under his tight t-shirt, clattering musically. "These are good luck charms, man, trophies. Each one makes me stronger, smarter. They speak to me."

I had to ask, "And what do they tell you?"

"They told me to change my looks, for one thing," he says, daring me not to believe him. "For another, to come check you out. They was right. The more of them I got, the more they tell me truth."

Ponco is not quiet in his approach. Dewey releases the necklace and reaches around to his back pocket. He pulls out a fistful of shiny chrome. I laugh, because it looks like a harmonica.

"What you giggling at?" Dewey flips the metal piece, laying it flat on his palm.

"Balisong!" Ponco warns.

I don't know the word, but the definition becomes clear when Dewey transforms the object like an evil magician: the thing dances in his hand, sprouting steel wings and emits a menacing, metallic purr before the handle snaps in place, revealing the blade.

I don't move. It was as silent as a city can get until a siren pierced the night.

Dewey looks up as if the approaching sound has visible substance. He grabs his necklace again, holding a handful of rings protectively, almost like he's listening to their counsel. His head snaps toward Pizza Kitchen's back door. Fat Wok is there, pizza paddle at the ready, crouched for a fight. Headlights and the siren's wail fill the alley in back of me. Dewey turns back toward Ponco, ready to charge, but Officer Lanz materializes from behind, gun drawn, shouting a warning. The only other possible exit for Dewey is that doorway up to D'Angelo's place, but the players from the card game have already gathered there, come down to rubberneck. In back of me, the car skids to a halt, siren winding down.

In the bright headlights, Dewey unclutches his jewelry. Shards of sparkles glint off the diamonds that sway against his t-shirt. Behind me, a car door opens.

"Walk back to me, Joey. Slowly," Armbruster says over the sound of her cocking pistol, "Stay where you are, Dewey. You got no place to go."

But he did. Dewey grabs my shoulder, spins me around and puts the knife to my throat. Bug-eyed with fear, my first reaction is to try and cover my eyes from the bright lights of the car. Dewey pulls me hard against him. I can feel the chunky knuckles on his necklace press against the vertebrae at the base my neck.

Dewey presses the flat of the blade tighter against my skin, nudges it upwards. "The only time you move is when I move. Or when I say so. Got it?"

I want to nod in reply, but I don't. I grunt an affirmation and stay frozen in place, my forearm still shielding my eyes from the headlights

"Hey, asshole."

Dewey turns me toward the voice. It's Mikey from Skinflix.

"Why don't you let the man go," he says. "I know you think you still have a chance, but you don't. You're outnumbered."

Fat Wok grips his pizza paddle like a baseball bat. "Last thing you want is to hurt my boss. If you do, the rest of us will make sure you don't leave standing up. If that's okay with you, Detective."

"Fine by me," Armbruster says. "So it's up to you, Dewey; a ride to the station with me, or I'll leave you to The Scuzz. Your choice."

Dewey wrestles me again toward the overbright headlights, blade still at my throat. I peek over my forearm at a figure emerging from the light, glowing bright as an angel. So white, in fact, I'm surprised she even casts a shadow.

"Boo yourself, motherfucker," Tats whispers and holds out her hand. "Two choices, you give me the knife or you give me Pizza. One or the other."

"Yeah, okay," Dewey snarls, "Here's your slice."

A slit of pain stings my throat. At the same time I reach behind my neck and make a fist around as many rings as I can grab. As Dewey pushes me at Tats, I feel the catch and release of the necklace, moments before my knees slam onto pavement. I hear a symphony of dissonant chimes as the rings follow me to the ground. Dewey emits an anguished howl and I sense him behind me, scrabbling frantically, attempting to retrieve his trophies. But as I slump forward, all I see is Tats trying to catch me, the soft glow of her cotton-ball hair, the tendrils of dark liquid staining the white skin of her face and hands. She gently lays me down.

Tats screams with rage and leaps over me. There's the noisy scuffle of people closing in from all sides, then a gunshot; the sounds are muted and dreamlike, like I'm slipping into a Backvision, but I know I'm not. Then Armbruster's voice snaps me back. She yells Lanz's name, tells her to holster her weapon, there are too many citizens about, call an ambulance, do it now.

"Hurry up," Armbruster shouts over the tumult, as my friends pummel Dewey.

With help I roll over onto my back. "It's okay, Joey. You're all right, just stay with me."

Armbruster's face floats into focus. I can't tell if she's smiling or gritting her teeth. She strokes hair up off my forehead, wipes something off my throat and holds her hand firmly against my neck. My lips move as I try to tell her how nice and warm her hand feels. She leans in to listen, almost like we're about to kiss. I close my eyes, like they do in movies.

And I'm in my baseball uniform again, peddling backwards. One foot hits the warning track and I jump. She's there in the stands watching me and I'll be the hero of the game if I can only catch the ball. I brace myself, knowing I'm one moment away from slamming into the wall. I reach up as far as my arm can go and feel the ball land firmly in the pocket of my glove.

"For you, KellyAnne," I say, but I have no idea if it was out loud.

The Usual Unusual Suspects

Peter Ullian's post-apocalypse, post-pandemic, near future neo-Western, *The Last Electric House*, is published by *Swamp Angel Press*. He is the author of short stories that have appeared in *Cemetery Dance Magazine, Hardboiled Magazine, Frontier Tales Magazine*, and the DAW Books anthology *Star Colonies*. He was the 2019-2020 Poet Laureate of Beacon, New York. His poetry has been published in anthologies and periodicals and nominated for the Rhysling Award and the Pushcart Prize. His poetry chapbook, *Secret Histories and Exobiologies,* is published by *The Poet's Haven*, and his full-length poetry collection, *The Fevered Dream Crimes of Pulp-Fiction Poets and Other Love Stories: New and Collected Poems*, is published by *Lion Autumn Music Publishing*. His works for the stage have been performed off-Broadway, regionally, and internationally, and published by *Broadway Play Publishing, Smith & Kraus*, and *No Passport Press*. His stories *The Ballad of Beeve Wellington* and *Dreaming of Pesach with the Last Bandito* both won the Reader's Choice Award for Best Story in the issues of *Frontier Tales Magazine* in which they were published (April and October 2021). Both stories will appear in the forthcoming anthologies *The Best of Frontier Tales Volumes 11 & 12. Dreaming of Pesach with the Last Bandito* is the first story in Peter's forthcoming historical fiction series inspired by real-life 19th century Jewish lawman of Wild West Los Angeles Emil Harris. His books available for sale can be found at: https://tinyurl.com/PeterUllian.

S.E Bailey's stories have appeared in the American magazines *Thuglit, Switchblade* and *Mystery Tribune* as well as the *Noirville* anthology from *Fahrenheit Press*. He's currently working on a historical crime fiction novel when he isn't toiling at the day job.

N. M. Cedeño writes mystery short stories and novels that vary from traditional to romantic suspense and from paranormal to science fiction. She is a member of Sisters in Crime and its Heart of Texas Chapter, where she has served as a chapter vice president and president. She is a member of the Short Mystery Fiction Society. Her short story entitled *A Reasonable Expectation of Privacy* tied for third place for Best Short Story in the 2013 Analog Reader's

Poll. Ms. Cedeño is the author of a paranormal mystery series called *Bad Vibes Removal Services* and she blogs with several other Heart of Texas mystery writers at InkStainedWretches. For more information please visit nmcedeno.com.

Edward St. Boniface lives and works in London UK and writes across various genres including crime and science fiction and fantasy and contemporary literary fiction. He's always interested in exploring an unusual angle to a story, and is keen to build up a readership. In addition to work freely available on his WATTPAD account he has also self-published several novels and surreal humour pieces available on KINDLE. He believes literature like all the arts should start from being Fun, and hopes you enjoyed his story. https://www.amazon.co.uk/Edward-St.-Boniface/e/B00JBCZMDS

Jan Glaz is a reporter and writer for *Village View Publications Inc.*, located in downtown Chicago, IL. In 2018, she was named, along with *Village View Publications Inc.*, as the winner of the Best of Chicago Writers Award. In addition, she has published a host of five star bestselling fiction and non-fiction books.

Eleanor Luke lives in Spain with her husband, two teenagers and a small menagerie. She writes flash fiction, short stories and has a novel in the pipeline. She has been short-listed in the *Poetry on the Lake* short story contest 2020 (as Lucinda Carney) and her work has appeared in various publications including *The Dribble Drabble Review*, *FlashFlood* and *The Birdseed*. When not writing, Eleanor can be found eavesdropping on other people's conversations or trying not to fall off her bike. You can find her on Twitter at @Eleanor_Luke24

Momodou Bah is an avid writer of all things fiction and non-fiction. When he isn't typing away on a university essay due the next day, he is sitting alone at his writing desk, ignoring all calls from friends inviting him out to socialise, and typing away on a new idea late into the night.

Eve Fisher has been writing since elementary school, and her mystery stories have appeared regularly in *Alfred Hitchcock Mystery Magazine* and other publications. She's part of the mystery writers' blog, *SleuthSayers*, at www.sleuthsayers.org (every 2nd Thursday!), and a fan in Shanghai is translating her work into Chinese. She's been volunteering at the local penitentiary with the Lifers' Group for over a decade, which gives her interesting acquaintances. A jack of all trades, she also writes historical articles, fantasy and science fiction. She lives in South Dakota with her husband and 5,000 books.

John M. Floyd's work has appeared in more than 350 different publications, including *AHMM, EQMM, Strand Magazine, The Saturday Evening Post*, three editions of *Best American Mystery Stories*, and *Best Mystery Stories of the Year 2021*. A former Air Force captain and IBM systems engineer, John is also an Edgar finalist, a 2021 Shamus Award winner, a four-time Derringer Award winner, a three-time Pushcart Prize nominee, and the author of seven collections of short mystery fiction. In 2018 he was the recipient of the Edward D. Hoch Memorial Golden Derringer Award for lifetime achievement.

Joan Leotta plays with words on page and stage. Her poems, articles, essays, and short stories have appeared or are forthcoming in *Yellow Mama, Drunk Monkeys, anti-heroin chic, Haunted Waters Press, Verse Visual, Verse Virtual, Crimeucopia, Bould Anthology*, and others. She has been a Tupelo Press 30/30 author, and a Gilbert Chappell Fellow. She is a 2021 Pushcart nominee, received Best of MicroFiction in 2021 from Haunted Waters. She was a 2020 nominee for the Western Peace Prize. Her chapbook, *Languid Lusciousness with Lemon*, is out from *Finishing Line Press*. Her other chapbooks are available online: *Nature's Gifts* Stanzaic Stylings, and *Dancing Under the Moon* and *Morning by Morning*, both from *Origami Press*. As a performer, she tells folk and personal tales featuring food, family, nature, and strong women.

Glen Bush is a retired teacher who now lives in the Lake of the Ozarks, Missouri, USA. Since retiring, he has been writing crime noir short stories and urban fiction. While teaching, he published over thirty academic literary articles and book reviews. In addition to *Dead Man's Blues*, Bush has recently published other crime stories and is working on a new novel as well as continuing to write his stories of Liam Quinn, Private Investigator.

DL Shirey lives in Portland, Oregon under skies the color of bruises. Occasionally he lightens up, but his dark fiction can be found in _Confingo_, _Zetetic_, _Liquid Imagination_ and in anthologies from _Truth Serum Press_ and _Literary Hatchet_. Short of listing them all, visit www.dlshirey.com and @dlshirey on Twitter.

16 stories ranging from the 14th to the 21st Century, all from women authors whose forte is crime.

Featuring *Karen Skinner, Hilary Davidson, Pauline Gostling, Linda Kerr, Kate Miller, Tiffany Lindfield, Lena Ng, Ginny Swart, Sandrine Bergèss, Michelle Ann King, Amanda Steel, Kelly Lewis, Paulene Turner, Claire Leng, Madeleine McDonald and Joan Hall Hovey.*

Paperback Edition ISBN:
9781909498198
eBook Edition ISBN:
9781909498204

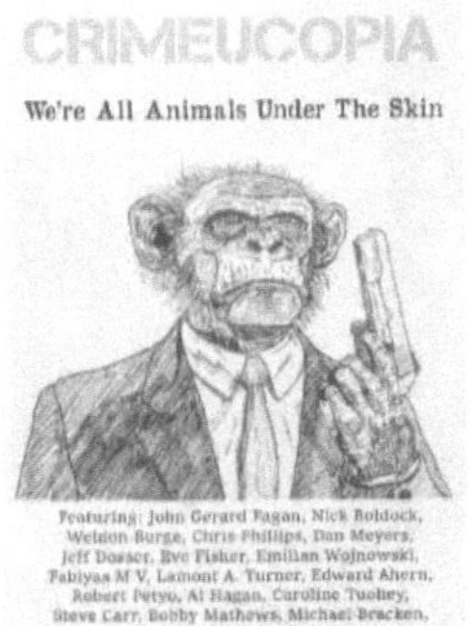

18 authors take time to look under the skin of the people who sometimes inhabit their heads, and put what they find down on paper.

Featuring John Gerard Fagan, Nick Boldock, Weldon Burge, Chris Phillips, Dan Meyers, Jeff Dosser, Eve Fisher, Emilian Wojnowski, Fabiyas M V, Lamont A. Turner, Edward Ahern, Robert Petyo, Al Hagan, Caroline Tuohey, Steve Carr, Bobby Mathews, Michael Bracken, and June Lorraine Roberts.

Paperback Edition ISBN:
9781909498235
eBook Edition ISBN:
9781909498228

17 writers take us on Cosy journeys - some more traditional, while others are very much up to date.

Eve Fisher, Alexander Frew, Tom Johnstone,
John M.Floyd, Andrew Humphrey, Joan Leotta,
Gary Thomson, Eamonn Murphey,
Matias Travieso-Diaz, Madeline McEwen,
Lyn Fraser, Ella Moon, Gina L. Grandi,
Louise Taylor, Judy Penz Sheluk,
Joan Hall Hovey and Judy Upton.

Paperback Edition ISBN: 9781909498242
eBook Edition ISBN: 9781909498259

CRIMEUCOPIA

As In Funny Ha-Ha

Or Just Peculiar

***Putting the Outré back into
OMG are***

*Jesse Hilson, Gabriel Stevenson,
Maddi Davidson, Brandon Barrows,
Robb T. White, Regina Clarke,
Martin Zeigler, K. G. Anderson,
Andrew Hook, Ed Nobody,
Jody Smith, Michael Grimala,
W. T. Paterson, James Blakey,
Emilian Wojnowski,
Andrew Darlington,
Lawrence Allan, Ricky Sprague,
Bethany Maines, John M. Floyd and
Julie Richards*

**Paperback Edition ISBN:
9781909498266
eBook Edition ISBN:
9781909498273**

The five writers here have very respectable track records in the Western genre, and are old hands when it comes to telling compelling stories.

So join
John M. Floyd
Alexander Frew
Jim Doherty
Bruce Harris
and
Brandon Barrows

and let them take you back to a time of six-guns an' whiskey, an' wild, wild fiction.

Paperback Edition ISBN:
9781909498266
eBook Edition ISBN:
9781909498273

Oh Baby, Baby, How Was I Supposed To Know…

Is Love ever perfect? Or is it an obsession that remains rather than just a passing phase? And who's to say that Revenge isn't, in fact, a dish best served hot from the flames of passion?

Fifteen writers tell us about affairs of the heart – some with humour, some with a darker intent, and others that are never quite exactly what they seem. Is it all about manipulation? Can there be more than one agenda? And does Love really conquer all, even when it's supposedly blind? Or maybe Love is just an old Devil, looking for mischief?

Steve Sneyd, Ange Morrissey, James Roth, Michael Wiley, Gustavo Bondoni, Matthew Wilson, Peter W. J. Hayes, Wil A. Emerson, Brandon Barrows, Bern Sy Moss, Michael Anthony Dioguardi, Russell Richardson, Robert Petyo, Sam Westcott, Bryn Fortey and *Vicky LaPerso* – all of whom take us on roller coaster rides through a fictional Tunnel of Love.

Paperback Edition ISBN: 9781909498303
eBook Edition ISBN: 9781909498310

It Was 3:15 in the A.M…

Investigators and investigations are the mainstay of most Crime fiction sub-genres. Everything from the original *Golden Age* of country houses and the amateur sleuth, through to the high tech ultra-modern 21st Century – a place where the cyber investigators sometimes appear to be baffled by old-fashioned motivations of power and greed, and human foibles such as love and revenge.

So is there any real difference between the Private and the Public Sector investigators? Not much, if writers are to be believed, and the two can often be found straddling both sides of the 'what's legal procedure?' fence.

Of the twelve authors contained within, eleven are voices new to the world of Crimeucopia - and although the theme is *Investigators*, the material ranges from Cosy, through to not too Hardboiled - and most are touched with a vein of humour, be it light or dark. Rather like a box of chocolates…

Featuring: Mike Job, Jill Hand, Joe Giordano, Michael Thomét, Michele Bazan Reed, Paul R. Paradise, M. C. Tuggle, Edward Lodi, Lynn Hesse, Kelly Zimmer, John M. Floyd and Shannon Lawrence.

Paperback Edition ISBN: 9781909498327
eBook Edition ISBN: 9781909498334

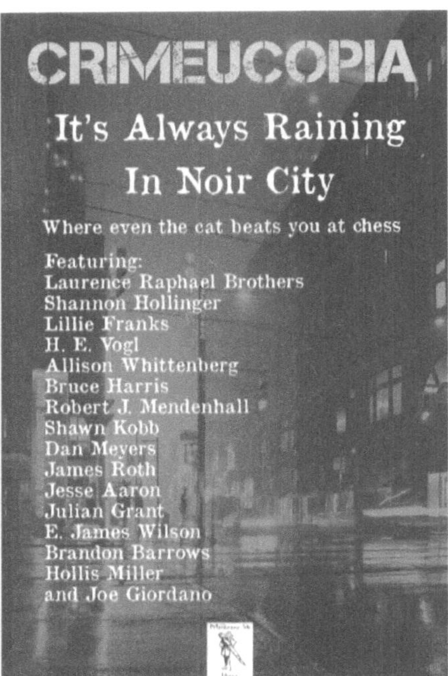

Is the Noir Crime sub-genre always dark and downbeat? Is there a time when Bad has a change of conscience, flips sides and takes on the Good role?

Noir is almost always a dish served up raw and bloody - Fiction bleu if you will. So maybe this is a chance to see if Noir can be served sunny side up - with the aid of these fifteen short order authors:

Laurence Raphael Brothers, Shannon Hollinger, Lillie Franks, H. E. Vogl, Allison Whittenberg, Bruce Harris, Robert J. Mendenhall, Shawn Kobb, Dan Meyers, James Roth, Jesse Aaron, Julian Grant, E. James Wilson, Brandon Barrows, Hollis Miller and Joe Giordano

All fifteen give us dark tales from the stormy side of life - which is probably why it's always raining in Noir City....

Paperback Edition ISBN: 9781909498341

eBook Edition ISBN: 9781909498358

Small town, big city, watercooler or the back of that 1950s beat-up Chevy Bel Air with the leather back seat that your parents told you never to get familiar with. It doesn't matter where you hear it, gossip is 100% pure ear addiction – and knowledge is, after all, power when all's said and done.

So why don't you settle down, get yourself comfy, and pour yourself a drink – long and tall, or just short and nasty, the choice is yours – and let these 16 story tellers:

Penny Hurrell, Teresa Trent,
Wendy Harrison, Maroula Blades,
Tom Sheehan, Jan Christensen,
Bryn Fortey, Michele Bazan Reed,
Carol Willis, Madeleine McDonald,
Adam Meyer, Nikki Knight,
Regina Clarke, J. W. Wood,
Deb Merino and Alison McDonald

spin their tales as only they know how.

**Paperback Edition ISBN:
9781909498365
eBook Edition ISBN:
9781909498372**

www.ingramcontent.com/pod-product-compliance
Lightning Source LLC
Chambersburg PA
CBHW030144200726
48285CB00006BA/2090